WORLD WEAVER

World Weaver

DANIEL WALKER

Prologue

A quiet stillness inhabits the forest of Kairon. The morning sun crests above the horizon, bathing the world in warm light. Tiny creeping creatures skitter silently through the brush, their movements scarcely disturbing the grass and brambles around them. Tree branches, their leaves spiky and stippled with golden hues, tremble softly in the gentle breeze. Perched high upon the tallest tree, a nesting bird awakens. It shakes sleep off its wings and departs from its roost, brushing a few dying leaves off their resting place and sending them spiraling slowly to the ground. They come to a delicate halt at the base of the thick, knotted tree, atop a mound of fresh brown earth.

Like the reflex twitch of a grazing beast, the mound of soil jerks at the touch of the golden leaves. The leaves scatter in the air, caught on another gust of wind, and drift to a stop again on a trail of purple cobblestones.

An unseen force continues to animate the earthy mound. It shifts and reforms, seeming to draw clumps of dirt and grass from the ground under and around it as it grows in height and takes on a more distinct shape. The top of the pile morphs into a thick-set head, with pointed ears, a long, horned snout, and a rectangular mandible. The head rises, bolstered by living earth underneath it, which reshapes into broad shoulders set atop a muscular back. The soil further arranges itself into the form of angular limbs, which end in cloven hooves.

The creature, finally, takes on full form. The size of an ox, with the features of a boar, its appearance is fearsome and imposing. A small rodent scavenging nearby squeaks and scampers away. The massive earthen creature raises itself onto powerful hind legs, switching to an erect, bipedal posture. Patches of grass like green tufts of fur accentuate its features— its back, its torso, the crown of its head— and loose crumbles of dirt cascade from its body. The beast lumbers forward, away from the shadow of the great tree, to bask in the light of the rising sun.

In the air above the beast's steepled ears, a purple column of smoke formulates and then curls toward the ground a few feet across from it. As it touches the grass, a flash of light glows brightly within the smoke, before subsiding and giving way to a second creature. This feathered biped, a flightless bird the color of ash, stands at the same height as the boar. Their eyes meet: muddy brown to beady black.

The bird breaks the silence, speaking in a voice that seems to emanate from deep within.

"Solivara," it says, inclining its head almost imperceptibly. "He is coming."

The boar, Solivara, shifts its weight backward, seeming to almost shrink in size upon the words of its companion.

"How now, Opius," it retorts. "Surely you don't mean—?"

"I do, and I am certain." The intonation of Opius's pronouncement is final. "It is beginning."

Solivara begins to pace anxiously, trampling grass and stones under heavy footfalls. Disturbed by the noise, a few birds nesting nearby take flight into the cloudless sky.

"Calm yourself." Opius affixes Solivara with a judgmental eye. "This is unbecoming of you."

"Where is the Guardian of the Center?" Solivara frets. A thick globule of mud drops from the hide of its trembling form and makes a wet sound on the grass. "What are we to do?"

"I was, myself, unable to make contact." Opius transfers its gaze from Solivara to the ground. "Nevertheless, we must trust that it will attend presently."

On cue, the atmosphere seems to shimmer and distort. Bending and fracturing into impossible geometry, a translucent crystalline structure hangs in the air between them. Polyhedrons and tesseracts split out of it, becoming solid as Opius and Solivara observe. A warm light begins to shimmer and intensify as the shapes take on a distorted, almost humanoid, form. A head, limbs, and a face, built intricately out of a whirring mechanism of light, come into focus. At last, the Temporal Guardian of the Center reveals itself to them. Solivara relaxes its tense posture, returning to full size and finally standing still. Opius remains equally immobile, only following the motion of the clockwork creature with its piercing gaze.

"There you are! Opius says he is coming. What is to be done?" Solivara asks, its hoof scraping the ground as it speaks.

"The foretold one arrives." The Guardian of the Center folds its arms and shifts its glance from Solivara to Opius. "Him, and the others."

"So, the moment approaches." A gust of wind blows, ruffling Opius's feathers as it interjects. "The Third Era stands upon the threshold, and we shall witness its first tremors. We must consider what will be."

May 27, 2014

We are seated across from each other. The principal's assistant eyes me up and down. She is a squat, frumpy-looking black woman who is considerably shorter than me, though it is hard to tell by how much because she has been sitting down since before I entered the room. The woman's manner epitomizes middle management. I briefly avoid her withering stare and glance around at the clutter on her desk. Assorted pencils and pens are scattered on top of two overflowing file folders. There are half-finished worksheets and stapled packets of scratch paper. It all looks like work.

"I'm sure you already know why we're having this meeting," she says. I do.

A public school year is 180 days long. That's a perfectly sufficient amount of time to familiarize the administrative apparatus of a middle school with the needs of its problem children.

"Yes, I've received the emails already. And read them."

For this meeting today, there is the matter of the question of what to do in the years to come. Tacked up on the pastel blue painted wall there is a poster that asks, "is your child college and career ready?" My eyesight drifts over towards it and she matches my gaze, then looks back at me. She brushes the pens and pencils off the file folder on top and places a cupped hand on the cover.

"Mister Morrissey, we need to talk about your son."

June 6, 2014

English class, for Lance the final period of the final day of the school year.

Just like any other day, some of the students talk while others concentrate on the assignment, scribbling a few sentences about what they plan to do with their summer break.

But there are also teachers, and most of them know the routine.

Just like the students, but perhaps moreso, they are silently counting down the minutes until they can leave, free to have a summer full of wine tasting and day trips to the Smithsonian and laying around in the front yard so that they can humblebrag to their friends in August about how much sun they got whenever their new tan lines come up in conversation.

Lance, who is wearing an orange t-shirt that says "LFMMS" in black lettering, has his attention diverted from the busy work on his desk which no teacher in her right mind would bother grading, instead chatting up Cora and Anastasia about his summer plans.

"—beach house my uncle is renting for the summer but we'll only be there for like a week or two," Cora is saying. She has an earnest round face framed by chestnut hair.

"And 'm hoping I can see One Direction live in concert!" Anastasia says excitedly. Anastasia, a notorious boy band fanatic, is slightly chubby with a pinched face and a small strand of hair wrapped up in a nylon weave, haute couture in the early 2010s adolescent scene.

"You really think you can get tickets?" Lance asks.

"They're doing three tours this summer, so hell yeah!"

"If you go, *please* post pics!" Cora raises her fists up to her collarbone level then shakes them with anticipation. Her face red with embarrassment from the potential social backlash from this act of physical expressiveness, she quickly drops her hands and makes an awkward stifling motion like she doesn't know what to do with them.

"My parents don't let me use Twitter or anything like that but I can totally text them to you!"

"Uh yes puh-leeze!"

The two proceed to exchange phone numbers while Lance pretends not to listen, fixing his gaze on the classroom walls which have recently been stripped of decorations and trimmings. In reality, he has just committed both numbers to memory, for possible use at a later time should he ever need them.

"How about you, Lance?"

"Huh?"

"Whatcha doin this summer?"

"Oh, my dad is the senior vice CEO of Adventure Land Parks. I get behind the scenes access so I'll be testing out a bunch of cool new rides all summer without having to wait in any lines!"

"No way!"

Lake Forest Mountain Middle School, so named for its equidistant proximity to three eponymous landmarks, is the newest in the district and currently in its fourth year of operation. The first year, the student body population numbered a bit less than half of its current figure, as the school was primarily being used to contain spillover from other middle schools in the district, and some of the money had yet to be appropriated, and there was the matter of further redistricting that had to be taken care of, and so on the final day of that school year, all of the students were dismissed at the same time from the cafetorium, a plan which was logistically simple and executed without a hitch. However, the following year, year two, with over 80% of the current population and a (now significant) short-staffing problem, this same proposal of dismissing the whole student body at once led to a tremendous stampede, in which one student tripped and sprained her wrist, poor unfortunate Jimmy Smith was knocked over by a group of eighth-graders and trampled, and the traffic jam in the parking lot took two hours to resolve. On the third year, with the additional oversight of an administrative assistant for both the principal and vice principal, as well as a carefully orchestrated plan dreamt up by the Parent-Teacher Association, final day dismissal was handled by dismissing students only one grade at a time, so that there was only one-third the traffic throughput exiting the cafetorium door and leaving the parking lot. It went swimmingly.

Which is why Lance now finds himself sitting, "criss-cross applesauce", on the cold linoleum cafetorium floor surrounded by peers of direct alphabetical proximity.

The principal addresses the seated crowd, a bulky man with a red face and receding hairline, who was a high school football coach for several years but never achieved his fantasy of carving a genuine professional talent out of even one of the many teenage blank slates he coached before eventually becoming too old, and frankly too fat, to carry on the profession. When he got dressed this morning, he squeezed into a brown polyester suit with a sizable tomato sauce stain on the midriff that he failed to notice. Having just received a memo from the vice principal's assistant that bus number 52 is running late, he now stalls for time by admonishing the children not to let this summer go to waste as an opportunity to retain and build upon the knowledge they learned in their classes this year.

What did Lance learn this year?

There are about a million different works of fiction written on the subject of middle school, primarily consumed by middle schoolers, which make the grades 6-8 experience out to be a roller coaster of life-changing moments happening one after the other; Lance made a conscious vow at the beginning of the year that come what may, he would find the inner fortitude to weather whatever storm might come. But then the storm never came. In actuality, sixth grade proved to be little more than a check in a box on the path of life. Actually, one unfortunate fact did prove to be true, which is that middle schoolers are almost universally total assholes, especially to each other.

Cora and Anastasia are seated a few rows apart. Lance reasons that even now, driven by insecure envy despite the facade these girls put up when talking face-to-face, they are likely each badmouthing the other to their friends in a proto-Machiavellian fashion, Anastasia smearing Cora for her ostensibly snobby rich family, and Cora smearing Anastasia for her boy-band obsession, so that the talk of the town for the rest of the summer any time they came up in conversation would begin and end with "Bougie Cora" and "Obsessed Anastasia". Lance views himself as a social pariah among his peers for his refusal to get involved in middle school drama, but the truth is he's just not that popular.

With the bussing delay finally resolved, the principal ceases his awkwardly improvised bloviating and dismisses the sixth graders. Lance rockets out of his seated position and flips his backpack off the floor in front of him and onto his back in one fluid motion, then proceeds to gallivant out of the cafetorium without a care in the world. He has survived the school year. The long nightmare is over. Now for a pleasant ten weeks of kicking back and doing absolutely nothing, if he can manage to keep out of trouble at home.

June 30, 2014

At this point, the luster has worn well off of the idea of summer vacation. Lance has so far poured over a hundred hours into his favorite video games and watched his favorite movie five times already.

His dad took him on a day trip to the aquarium, and aquariums always make him so tired, with all the walking around and the dim lighting. Plus they happened to go amid major renovations so half the exhibits were closed. Plus when they visited the touch tank with the stingrays and Lance told the aquarium worker that he is a marine expert and she started quizzing him, an embarrassed single mother's toddler puked in the tank while she was distracted and the staff had to close that exhibit too. So the aquarium experience that day was very underwhelming and they stayed at home every day after that.

He has spent the better part of the morning today driving his father crazy by walking laps around the main floor of the house and proclaiming "I'm bored!" in an outdoor voice while his father attempts in vain to focus on his work at the computer.

"For Christ's sake, kid, go do what my generation did when we were young and find something to do outside!"

"I already tried that!"

"Remember what I told you about the truth, Lance?"

"Ugh, fine! You suck, daddy! Bye!"

With a huff and a theatrically calculated front door slam, Lance embarks on the beginning of his quest to find something — anything at all — to do with himself out in the heat.

There is a hill that slopes downward alongside his house which leads away from the road and towards a large ditch situated at the mouth of a forest. When it rains all the water in the area runs down toward this ditch and fills it, so that it becomes a creek. And on days when it has not rained for a while, the creek dries up and the ditch is a dry gulch.

When Lance was younger and he and the other kids on the block were more inclined to spend their summer days outside, this grassy trough became a central figure in their imaginative play, a river to cross when it was wet and a ditch that they could be outlaws and dump each other's "bodies" into when it was not. Plus a million other things.

Looking upon it now, Lance is struck by how much smaller and more pathetic the ditch now looks. Everything seems so much bigger when you are small.

He approaches the crevasse and lowers himself into it. At its widest, the width of it barely exceeds his current height, and at its deepest part where he now stands the top of it barely comes up to his waist level. There is a pittance of water at the bottom, but not even enough to seep into his shoes and dampen his socks. It is all so underwhelming.

Lance scans the horizon. When he was eight, he and Joaquin Anderson from down the street "built" a "bridge" stretching across the width of the ditch, which was really three two-by-four planks lined up next to each other. They were very proud of themselves for their achievement at the time, which had added a whole new dimension of play to the neighborhood's favorite hangout spot. Looking at it now, Lance is half-surprised to see that the planks remain exactly where they had been placed, untouched except by the subtle signs of the passage of time. The sight awakens a feeling of nostalgia, which is then overturned by confused intrigue as Lance peers into the entrance to the forest and sees something entirely new.

Some twenty or thirty feet into the forest, a conical fort built immaculately of branches stands arranged around a tree. Lance reasons as he approaches it, transfixed, that it must have been put up by other kids probably from around the area, except that the craftsmanship is impeccable; it must have taken forever to gather the 50 or so large and nearly uniform branches which form the fort's walls and interlock them like that, so that the structure is freestanding.

As he approaches the gaping maw of the fort entrance, Lance sees that the interior is about a head shorter than he is, so he ducks to a crouch and gets inside. Allowing his vision a few seconds to adjust, he sees nothing inside but leaves and dirt. The perfect blank canvas for perhaps the ultimate hangout spot. Already, Lance is running ideas through his head of the optimal ways to trick the joint out. If successful, this'll perhaps even attract the attention of the other neighborhood kids and he'll be able to rekindle friendships that had faltered for years while he became too... *whatever it was* for people apparently to handle.

Lance, bent at the knees, does a 360-degree turn at the center of this fort, taking in the sheer potential of it all for just a single precious moment. He drops to his knees to crawl back out the doorway... and then keeps dropping, as the ground beneath him gives way and he tumbles, over and over, into an all-encompassing blackness.

July 22, 1998

Marissa wipes the sweat off her brow and sticks the pitchfork in the ground, resting against the side of the barn. Time to catch her breath.

The cows were milked today, which meant they had to be brought in from the pasture and kept in their stalls. 30 cows leave a lot of manure over the course of eight hours, and even with Tobias's help the work of cleaning it all out is grueling and unpleasant, and usually takes the better part of an hour.

The manure will be rotated to fertilize the corn crop, but first Marissa needs to take a break. She can feel her pulse race in her chest, and the throbbing of her temples is a reminder to slow down and drink some water, lest she overwork herself and encounter another episode of heatstroke.

No one ever tells her anything, which is frustrating because at nineteen she *is* a legal adult and the family farm belongs as much to her as it does to her parents. Between the furtive glances shared by Mom and Dad at the dinner table, the breadcrumbs of information Tobias is able to discover and report, and the time her father spends looking increasingly busy with bills while holed up in his office day in and day out, she can tell the financial situation of the farm is bad. In fact, it has obviously been getting steadily worse for at least three summers now.

People always seem to assume she doesn't understand things just because she can't hear, which is no fair. Or perhaps her parents fear that telling her about the situation will somehow make it "real", as though it weren't already.

Tobias appears, walking down the aisle of the barn like a groom meeting his bride. It's the first time she's seen him all day. His t-shirt already has a ring of sweat around the crewcut neck, which envelops his collarbone and the surrounding area.

< Missed you, > he signs. < Work sucked today. >

Marissa runs and grabs him in an embrace, taking in a precious moment to feel his body press against hers and experience his scent. Then she backs up, so she can see what he says next.

< You look absolutely lovely today, beautiful. The cow shit really brings out the sparkle in your eyes. >

< Shut up Tobias, you dork. > Her laugh is received by Tobias's ears as a wild and untamed sound, the most beautiful thing he has ever heard.

< I wanted to tell you, your dad finally told me last night about the true state of things for your farm. >

Now, THIS is news.

< Well, how bad is it really? >

A frown creeps across his face. He spreads his hands apart, fingers in the shapes of Ks.

< Worse. Worse than we thought. >

July 21, 1998

"I tell ya Toby, this country is going to hell in a handbasket." Marissa's father, Robert, who most people know as Rob, puts the paperwork in his hand down on the dining room table and rubs his hand frustratedly across his dirty blond hairline. Behind the thumbprint-coated lenses of his reading glasses, gray-blue eyes peer out, bloodshot from lack of sleep. The weary man continues.

"I look around and I can't even recognize the country I grew up in anymore. Everything's being turned upside down. Look, no, you can take a seat, it's fine. Go ahead, pull that chair up right there and set down. Do you remember the riots in LA some years back? Some thug was high out of his mind on PCP, drivin' down the highway like a crazy person, coulda killed a bunch of people, gets stopped by the police, resists arrest so they gotta smack some sense into him, it all gets put on TV and next thing you know all the blacks are tellin' each other the whole city is racist, they start burnin' and lootin' buildings and this goes on for weeks and weeks. Sixty-plus deaths, millions in property damage, and the damn mayor is egging it all on. You're nodding. Yeah, you're familiar with it, I figured as much since I know you were living roundabout there at the time. Well okay, it was the next town over, but that was a significant thing, right? But that just goes to show — in my opinion it's downright emblematic — it just shows the direction this country is headed in. Because a couple years after that we had another thug-turned-hero, O.J. Simpson. And you remember him, right? Killed his wife in cold blood and everyone knew it too, except that the media and his lawyers argued that he was only being accused because he's black. And he got away with it! The moral standards of this country are going straight down the tube. Damn president's a pervert, it turns out, and he was lying about it the whole time. Now they're talking about impeaching him because he was sleeping with an intern and lied about it under oath. You know what gets me about that? His wife! She must've known all along, never said anything about it, clearly didn't much care, probably put up with the betrayal because of all his political connections. I tell ya, I don't know what's going on with this country anymore. You're wondering what all this is about, right?"

A pause. Tobias raises an eyebrow expectantly and Rob continues.

"Toby, you should know my daughter absolutely thinks the world of you. You're a good guy. You're a hard-worker, you're responsible and you respect your elders, you've got the fear of God in your heart and Lord knows you've been a tremendous help around this farm. But the thing is — look, you're 21, right? Do you want some whiskey? I can pour you a glass. No, it's my pleasure. I'll get it for you. Just wait a second.

"Okay, here you go. Whiskey on the rocks. Drink it up. I wanna talk to you about the farm, the way things are going. Farming's already hard work, sure, and the summers already get hot around here, but it's honest, decent work, and it's important. Thing is, though, it's been getting harder and harder each year. A few years ago those pencil pushers in D.C. passed a big ol' trade agreement that pretty much doubled America's competition in the corn industry. Mexicans? They grow so much corn you wouldn't believe it. It's like they're up to their ears in the stuff. Now corn prices in America are down this year, big time, which isn't even supposed to happen at all. Government hasn't trusted the prices of most agricultural products in America to the market since the Depression, and since they bleed us dry with the taxes and the red tape, they give the whole sector subsidies to make up the difference. Now you know and I know that most of that money is not going to people like us, it's going to go to the corporate farmers and the multimillionaires and people like that, but the idea is that a rising tide lifts all boats, right? Except that with all this foreign competition, this farm is selling less every single year and making less per unit even in spite of the subsidies which are only being raised higher. You get it now, Toby? Family farms built this country, and now they're on their way out!"

Tobias, at this point having finished his whiskey, gazes into the melting ice cubes in his glass. He chews on the information that he has just been given.

"What do you intend to do about it, then, sir?"

A forlorn, pensive look crosses Rob's face as he removes his reading glasses and folds them up, placing them on the table.

"Toby, I just want to tell you again that you are a great young man. You've made a big sacrifice spending what at this point must be at least twenty or thirty hours a week helping out at this farm, in between all the schooling you're doing for being an insurance attorney or whatever it is exactly you're studying to be. Frankly I can't fathom how you do it. I want... Look, I want to relieve you of this burden, and in the process get this farm back on track. Starting in a week I'm going to be employing a team of five farmhands to split the burden of labor, maybe try to expand the crop acreage a little bit, and certainly get the job done faster. These men have agreed to work for me for cheap, but, well here's the thing."

"You don't want me to get in the way." *Get to the point!* Tobias wants to yell, but he stifles the thought.

"I don't want to imply you were ever *in* the way, Toby, that's not what I'm trying to say. But yes, while they're working here it would probably be for the best if you were not. These guys are going to be working demanding hours, and I'm trying to systematize operations the best way I can, with the crop rotation schedules and all that. I really, really wish there could be another way, Toby. I really do."

"I understand."

Tobias's thoughts drift to Marissa, and the weight of what he is being told crashes down upon him. How will he explain to the love of his life that they will have to say goodbye to each other, maybe forever? In private moments the two of them had discussed the possibilities of a future together. In fact, Tobias had thought about proposing at the end of the summer. Now? All of these things seem so foolish, the dreams of a child who believes in fairytale endings.

July 23, 1998

Marissa watches as her father goes into his equipment shed and comes out carrying a several gallons large container of liquid with a hose spiraling out of the top. He sets it down in front of her.

< Round-up, > he signs crudely, by drawing a horizontal circle in the air and then pointing upward. < Kills everything it touches. We use for weeds. Make it more fast. >

< I understand, > Marissa signs.

She lost her hearing in a head trauma incident when she was six, giving her father 13 years to learn ASL up to this point, and while he has a decent grasp of the fundamentals, he is unable to fully harness the grace and nuance of it. He tries of course, because he loves her, but he is a large and somewhat clumsy man and his deafness communication is primitive at best.

Marissa is sure this Roundup is another aspect of the big sweeping changes dad is unleashing upon the barn, having at this point been fully filled in by Tobias after last night. Before tomorrow morning, she will also have met the new farmhands, as they are set to arrive later tonight. But before that can happen...

< Hey, dad, Tobias will be here soon. >

Her dad looks at her for a moment, and Marissa can practically see steam coming out of his ears as the gears inside his brain turn and he processes what she just said. He makes an O shape with his mouth and nods, which is enough tacit permission for her to go to the edge of the property where it meets the road and wait for Tobias to pull up in his car.

From this part of the farm, the path back to the edge of the road is about a quarter of a mile long and lies alongside part of the perimeter of the corn field. By this point in the day, the sun has begun to go down and the distorted orange and pink light of sunset streams through the corn to light the path. The walk takes about seven minutes at her current pace, as Marissa periodically takes a moment to visually inspect each rock and tree, scanning areas of interest and observing the birds and the squirrels as they scurry about. The path along the edge of the corn field is a nice secluded stroll in the evening, even though a small pump house sits about 100 yards away. It is hard to get lost in the corn fields around here, as there are plenty of access points to the property and trails that are scattered throughout, if you know your way around.

The sun continues to sink in the sky as the dirt trail opens up onto the gravel road. Marissa has met Tobias at this time and place before on many occasions but tonight might very well be the last.

Headlights shine through the conifers around the bend. Then the rest of Tobias's old red station wagon appears, growing larger as it gets closer and the rest of the world disappears from Marissa's focus as her heart flutters in her chest and she stares transfixed at what will be her ticket out of here for the next couple of hours. The light coming from Tobias's headlights shines down on her like a spotlight revealing the mud and occasional splotches of cow pie accrued on her coveralls from today's work. Finally Tobias's stubble-laden face comes into view as he pulls up in front of her. His window is down, and he makes an exaggeratedly seductive smirk complete with an eyebrow wiggle, motioning around to the passenger side of the vehicle with his pointer finger, an invitation for Marissa to get in the car. She obliges, and the journey to Waffle House begins.

It is very difficult to hold a complex conversation in ASL with someone who is attempting to safely drive on a winding rural road at night. Conversation between Tobias and Marissa in the car is limited tonight, so Marissa occupies her mind by organizing her thoughts and planning out what she will say once they reach their destination, while also gazing out at the miles of farmland and forest zipping behind them and feeling the vibrations in her body from the music being played by Tobias's car stereo. The night air is cool, blowing in through the half-open window, a welcome respite from the heat of the day.

The sun has fully set by the time Tobias pulls up to the nearly empty Waffle House, and since it is a new moon the only light illuminating the parking lot is the warm fluorescent yellow of the restaurant sign.

< How do you feel about switching offices to Wisteria in a few days? > Marissa queries once the two of them enter and sit down.

< I don't know, > Tobias answers. < I'm trying to find the silver lining in everything wherever I can. Maybe this job won't be as bad as I first thought. >

"Wisteria" refers to Wisteria Drive, the road upon which Tobias's new office will be situated, about a half mile away from the previous one. He has been spending the past couple of summers working in various insurance consulting jobs around town. These experiences have been slow-going and soul-crushingly bureaucratic, with mountains of busy work greeting him every time he comes through an office door.

Corporate middle managers and secretaries love to dump legal-jargon infested documents on college kids, whose zealous naivete and earnest desperation to get a foothold in the job market make them the perfect candidates for all the jobs no one else feels like doing. Tobias's final week at his current location has seen him so far staring at more paperwork than ever, as his present supervisor is absolutely determined not to see him off until the company has a head start on most of the documents for the *rest of the current millennium*, some of which may be rendered obsolete as time passes.

< That Y2K guy is still milking you for your time? > Marissa asks, vigorously emphasizing the sign for "milking" with a sly smirk.

< You know how that crazy man is. He wants me to do everything twice, just in case of SHTF. >

Marissa shakes her head in sympathetic disapproval. A waitress approaches the table to take their order, and Tobias orders for himself (eggs, sunny-side up) as well as on Marissa's (scrambled) behalf.

< What about the farm? > Tobias asks, after the waitress leaves. < Have you heard any more about those big changes your dad talked about? >

< Later tonight, I'm meeting the workers. I think they might be foreign nationals. Or something like that. >

< That will be interesting. Are they big guys? >

Marissa nods.

< Well, try to be careful. >

< Of course, > Marissa says. < One other thing. New equipment will be coming in, plus dad wants us to start using Roundup on the weeds. >

< Doesn't that stuff kill the environment? > Tobias asks.

< Like dad says, it kills everything it touches. Still, all the big farms use it. >

< How do you feel about that? >

Marissa closes her eyes. Truthfully, she doesn't feel good about any of it. She has an ominous sense that circumstances are pushing her parents, her dad especially, into making bad choices without thinking twice about it. And she is *so* tired of corn. Seeing it, smelling it, tasting it all the time. It even shows up in her dreams, sometimes, where she'll have dreams that the corn is alive and trying to smother her. Sometimes the corn drives her absolutely crazy.

As if reading her thoughts, Tobias asks,

< Do you ever think about leaving the farm behind like your sister did? >

< You know I do, > Marissa answers. < But they need me at the farm, now more than ever. At least for now, until things get better. > *It wouldn't be right to abandon my family when they need me the most*, she thinks.

< You have so many gifts that are wasted on corn. You know, you could be a top student at UNL if you just applied. >

< I can't afford to go to college. >

< Marissa, you can't afford *not* to go to college if you ever hope to do anything else with your life besides toil away in a corn field. >

Marissa closes her eyes and forcefully exhales through her nose for a long moment.

< Can we drop the subject? I already know this, but there is nothing I can do about it. >

< You know I love you, Marissa. >

< Yes, I know. >

Tobias clears his throat. The waitress appears with their food and glasses of water, and he takes a big gulp out of his glass.

"How are we tonight, dears?" The rosy-cheeked waitress asks. "Great," Tobias responds disingenuously. "We're doing just great."

The waitress leaves and Tobias follows her path with his eyesight for a moment until she disappears back into the kitchen, then he returns his gaze to Marissa.

< So what can we do about this? > he asks.

< I say we leave town and never look back. Just get in the car and drive. >

< That would be nice. >

Tobias considers for a moment the long and winding road ahead of the both of them. This is not the first time they've entertained a similar notion, but now it seems more intangible than ever. Even if he were welcome to continue helping on the farm, the work his new supervisor will have him do at Wisteria will undoubtedly be yet more involved, more time-consuming, more intellectually taxing. And corn farming is certainly not in his future either. He has a life to plan for. One that, much as it breaks both of their hearts, might not involve Marissa. He may end up marching down the aisle to some mystery girl some day, some *other* he has either not met yet or has never considered, and they might move to some place lucrative like Delaware or Colorado, and his days spent in this rural corn town in the middle of nowhere in Nebraska will gradually fade away till they are nothing more than a burning memory.

After Tobias pays for the food and the two of them leave hand in hand, they share one last passionate kiss in the parking lot before packing back into the old station wagon and heading down the country road.

He drops off Marissa at the edge of the farm property with one last < I love you > that she reciprocates as she turns to meet these new foreign workers hired by her dad who have just pulled up in a van.

Then he takes off, leaving the farm behind.

Note from the desk of USAID Agent Garrett Johnson

My first meeting with Zambian populist leader Joseph Mulenga went horribly. He had just finished talking to someone from China's Baidu Corporation about technology in schools. When he heard I was American, he wasted no time letting me know there was nothing my country could offer that interested him or his people. In plain text, this is what he said:

"You must understand that when we look at the United States, we see a ship without a captain. We have no confidence in your country because your country has no confidence in itself. We see you white Americans holding ceremonies where you beg and plead black man's forgiveness for the trespasses of your ancestors. We see you white Americans defiling sacred churches with political slogans about the sexualities and the races, as if such things have a place in the house of God. On your television, you run messages paid for by junk food companies, telling people it's good to be fat. Your culture is self-obsessed and self-hating, so your people are obsessed with hating themselves."

I asked him what was so attractive about letting the Chinese invest in Africa.

"The white man came to Africa long ago and left it in ruins. Now the white man is busy ruining his own countries. Chinese come here and they are down to business, they are serious. They say, 'What can we do for you? And in exchange, what can you do for us?' They build schools, they build hospitals, they build all kinds of infrastructure."

But what about knowing that China will leave the African people in debt as soon as their investments are made?

"Debt? This is simple capitalism. There is no big investment without debt. We look at America and see, however, that this is what you are doing to your own people. You are putting your own people in debt, in exchange for the use of schools, hospitals, infrastructure, and you call yourself a fully developed country. And you are also in debt with the rest of the world. We may be in debt for a while, but we are smart. We know Zambians have nowhere to go but up from here. We look toward the future, and we see China eventually in decline. We look at America and we see an even steeper trajectory. All we have to do is outlast our lenders."

After a quick farewell, we went our separate ways. Later, a memo written by a colleague circulated into my office, making reference to a "Zambian space program" from the 1960s. Buried beneath charts and graphs about GDP, foreign capital investment, and future projections, this reference interested me the most. I made a note of it that evening.

Elsewhere

It is remarkable how our memories are able to distort and stretch time. Mere moments can be stretched out in one's mind, if the event is significant enough, to fill out what feels like hours and hours. Whole years of one's life can be compressed to the size of fleeting glimpses. When Lance fell through the ground inside of that fort behind his house, he fell for an eternity and then forgot about it instantly.

The first few seconds of his fall were dominated by confusion as it took him a moment to process the abrupt shift from solid ground to absolute nothingness. After he realized he was surrounded by an entirely blank void, unable to see anything beyond his toes in any direction up, down, or sideways, he began to hypothesize he had blacked out and was having some sort of bizarre dream, possibly induced by too much heat exposure. He began to vigorously shake and slap himself to wake up from the dream, all to no fitful avail. After the first couple minutes it began to dawn on him that this could not be a dream after all, and he began to panic over why this was really happening to him and how much it might hurt when he finally landed. Out here this long and still no ground in sight. But still, he had to be falling *toward* something, right? That was how gravity worked, he knew it from school.

After more than half an hour had passed, Lance began to sob uncontrollably, and he did so for quite some time, lamenting this apparently inescapable twist of circumstance. As the minutes turned to hours, Lance became numb to the sensation of falling completely and began to replay the highlights of the first twelve years of his life over in his mind. As the hours turned to days, and Lance found himself neither hungry nor tired, he began to wonder if he was possibly in hell. He could no longer discern the passage of time in any meaningful way and had run out of things to occupy his mind with other than this singular thought, that he was damned forever. He raged against God, against the world, and against himself. There was nothing he could do about this rage but let it all out, and he did so for sixty hours straight. Afterwards he cried once more, then never again.

As the days turned to years, Lance lost all sense of himself as his personal identity was destroyed. He had a faint sense that his life previous to falling into the void was no more than a fading dream, and that the existence of anything outside of himself and this endless, formless blackness through which he descended was an impossibility. Gradually all thought became impossible and Lance's identity became a vague and meaningless abstraction.

He was drifting deeper and deeper into
solitary
apathy, his mind dissolving as he moved further from all consciousness.

And then he
knew nothing
and he could think of nothing
or he was
filled with
a deep, burning hatred
of everything that was
ever would be
and of nothing
at all.

One Eternity Later

All of a sudden, Lance finds himself soaking wet with the taste of dirt and pond scum in his mouth. He is lying face-down in shallow water. Pushing himself up to a seated position and taking some time to wipe the grime off his fingers and eyes, he looks around to see that he now sits at the edge of a large pond, or possibly a small lake, in a completely unfamiliar setting.

"Whatchu doin' down there, young one?" A squeaky male voice calls from behind him.

"I don't, uh-" Lance begins to reply, but finds himself unable to answer the question. *How did I get here?* He was just in his backyard, right? Or...

A flicker of uncertainty crosses his mind, but he shakes it off. No, he was definitely in his backyard just a moment ago. Peeking around that tree fort someone had built there.

"Well, I'm not sure exactly."

"What's your name, son?"

Lance turns around to look at the voice's source. Up on a hill behind him, it is a short man looking down at him from atop a horse. No, not a horse. Something else, something unfamiliar. It is more like a giant lizard, all scaly and stocky with short, thick legs like tree trunks holding it up. Like a giant tortoise if it had a tough hide instead of a shell on its back and stood at the height of a human adult. In fact, looking back up at the rider more closely, it's clear that he too is something bizarre and unfamiliar. Not even a human at all, in fact. The dude looked like an elf, all pointy-eared with an upturned button nose, dressed in odd clothing and sporting a long, braided white beard. He also had blue skin.

"My name?" Lance asks, overwhelmed by everything that has just happened to him over the past ten or fifteen seconds.

"Yes, son, your name. You got one, right?"

"Uh, Lance. Lance, uh, Morr..." He trails off, feeling queasy all of a sudden like he's about to pass out.

"Lansamor, did you say? Did you just say your name is Lansamor?"

"Uh, sure, that's me."

"THE Lansamor? As in, like the chosen one, Lansamor, the one foretold to rescue this land and return it to the light? I must say you do seem a little bit shorter than we had expected, but it IS you, is it not?"

"Definitely," Lance says, fairly sure at this point that as long as he keeps answering in the affirmative he might be able to get on this strange man's good side. Head throbbing, he decides to test the good graces of this daft rider.

"Hey look, I don't really feel so great right now. Any chance you might know of someplace I could go and get a good rest?"

"Oh, why, certainly! Climb on the back of my Gorrpaa and I will take you into the village! They will give you a hero's welcome, I am sure of it!"

Inferring immediately that this reptilian creature upon which the blue elf sits must be a "Gorrpaa", Lance stretches out all his muscles and stands up. The mucky water comes up to his ankles. Then he summons a reservoir of courage and energy to pull himself up the hill, and hop on the mount with help from the rider.

"So what do I call you, then?" Lance asks.

"You may call me Gilead, Lansamor. That's the name. Now please, put your hands on my shoulders, my liege. Help you keep your balance."

As Gilead clicks his heels to make his Gorrpaa begin trotting along the ground, which is covered in purple cobblestones, Lance reflects on his current circumstances. Sure it's strange, and he can't really explain what's going on, and he'll have to figure out how to get back home at some point, but really being revered as some kind of "chosen one" doesn't seem like such a bad rap, so he figures that he'll let it play out for a while.

What's the worst that could happen?

September 30, 2013

This kid Lance is absolutely impossible, Brenda Lewis, math teacher at LFMMS, thinks to herself while examining a new streak of gray in her dark brown hair. She has just come out of teaching a particularly rough class period with Lance, which made forty minutes feel like two hours and seems to have resurrected a shooting pain in her hips that she hasn't felt since shortly after giving birth to her daughter. Hell, it could be arthritis.

This is her twelfth year now of teaching middle school children, and even though barely a month has gone by in this school year Brenda can already tell that Lance Morrissey's name is one that will stick with her in infamy.

He frequently calls other kids names, talks back in the middle of lessons, already on more than one occasion during a test has gotten out of his seat to write swear words on the chalkboard, crawls around under the desks when the mood strikes him, and more.

What's worse than all that is the lying.

Of course, Lance lies about typical things, like claiming that he's looking for the homework that he actually neglected to do, playing for time to quickly fill it out under the guise of rifling through his binder. Or asking for permission to go to the bathroom, then abusing that permission to avoid returning to class. Some of his lies are stranger than that. Brenda used to keep five staplers in the drawer of her desk until Lance went and nicked them all, then proceeded to deny culpability until another student spotted them in his open backpack in another class two periods later.

All of these things took place during the first four weeks of school.

Many of Lance's lies concern his personal life. In conversations with other students, and even in conversations with her and other teachers, he will concoct elaborate worlds of fiction describing all sorts of fantastical and impossible things going on at home and other places outside of school. It almost seems to Brenda that he is compensating for some insecurity about his family dynamic, which is why when she had her first (of what would turn out to be many throughout the rest of the school year) meeting with his father, she was expecting one of two possible things to be true. Either the elder Morrissey would be abusive or neglectful in some way, or there might be some truth to Lance's tall tales and he might be a true-to-life eccentric.

What she was not expecting was for him to be a perfectly reasonable, level-headed man.

"Thank you for calling me in today, Mrs. Lewis," he had said upon entering the conference room that day, wearing a polo shirt bearing the logo of his place of employment. "What can I do for you?" He was eminently polite.

Mr. Morrissey proceeded to listen very patiently as Brenda rattled off a list of a number of Lance's disciplinary infractions. His concerned expression demonstrated a grave sobriety regarding the matter, which she recognized and appreciated. Many behaviorally challenged kids have parents who either deny or disbelieve the existence of a problem in the first place, thus being enablers for bad behavior. Mr. Morrissey had next explained that many of the issues Brenda identified were ongoing issues which he was aware of and had been working for a while on trying to address with his son.

"As a parent, I am incredibly disappointed that his maturity seems to be stunted," he had said. "I just don't think he realizes that a lot of the leniency you get as an elementary schooler disappears once you reach middle school, and certainly it is all long gone, you know, by the time you reach the real world."

"My thoughts exactly," Brenda had agreed.

"Frankly, he seems to have almost an infantile lack of responsibility. I was never like this in my youth. I had my own problems, of course, but I always took responsibility. Of course, the key difference is I had both my parents at home. It's a lot harder for me as —" (and here his voice started to break for half of a second but he'd quickly restored his composure) "— as a single father, to be dealing with all this."

Though she can't remember every word that was spoken between the two of them at this meeting, Brenda remembers exactly how she felt and how the mood in the room seemed to shift after this revelation. Lance had always talked as if his mother was still in the picture. Another compensation.

She began to study the lines on Mr. Morrissey's face closely in the awkward silence that ensued, recognizing the broken countenance of a man who carries a searing loss with him everywhere he goes. Grief etches itself permanently into some people's skin, leaving behind a stain like tattoo ink. *I've just poured salt on an open wound,* she had realized. *I'm so sorry.*

Brenda had tried to console him by relating that she understood, that of course it was difficult, that she didn't know the boy's mother was out of the picture, that this would of course lead to attachment issues and honesty issues and all sorts of things during early development that would make the already difficult experience of raising a child during adolescence that much harder.

She tried to tenderly breach the question of what had happened to the boy's mother and Mr. Morrissey deflected, explaining that he did not like to talk about it. She told him that she understood and respected his privacy, and figured that this was a good time to wrap up the conversation by proposing that Mr. Morrissey should consider seeking an official diagnosis and treatment routine for Lance, including getting him tested for ADD, BPD, ASD, APD, bipolar OCD, and possibly even sociopathy. Then having him meet regularly with a specialist and report progress throughout Lance's duration at LFMMS to the school guidance counselor and administrative apparatus. Mr. Morrissey seemed to graciously agree, and the meeting ended on a hopeful note that the world might soon see a new and improved Lance Morrissey.

Just how long that might take, Brenda thinks to herself wryly, *is another matter entirely.*

Nine Months Later

The purple cobblestone road upon which Gilead and Lance travel stretches on into the forest, whose trees are thick and knotted and covered in magnificent golden leaves that seem to carry their own luminescence. A fine blue mist begins to cover the horizon as they embark down the amaranthine path, filling the trail with a refreshing chill.

"It's so beautiful," Lance says, taking it all in. Gilead nods.

"In the springtime, when the liliput birds are nesting, they fill the trees with their song," he says. "They tell the beautiful story of the people of this land."

"They tell a story? The birds do?"

"Yes. It is not a story of words. A story of feeling. Of feeling alive, of being fully present in the world around you, feeling completely every emotion. Sometimes one will come and land on the blade of my sword as it rests in front of me on my Gorrpaa."

"Why does it do that?"

He smiles. "Because I feel their meaning."

The mist parts somewhat as the trail begins to incline upwards, up the side of a gigantic hill. Gilead ducks his head forward as the Gorrpaa shifts its weight under them, and Lance reciprocates the action.

"Does it ever get tired?" Lance asks, pointing at the Gorrpaa's head to indicate exactly what he is referring to.

"No, my liege. The Gorrpaa is immunized against fatigue and practically all dangers," Gilead replies. *Dangers.* The word calls to mind something Gilead said earlier.

"What was that you said about 'rescuing the land'? Does that thing that everybody needs to be rescued from count as one of those 'dangers'?"

"All will be revealed in time," Gilead responds. Silence falls for a moment, and for the rest of the trip Gilead ignores all of Lance's further questioning, pretending as if he cannot hear him.

Finally the trail emerges at the mouth of a great hidden city. There are branching offshoots leading to mills, trading stands, wells, stables, and many tall towers. These towers are seemingly built in the style of homes from the middle ages, with lumber frames filled in by plaster forming the walls on some, and brick on others, and thatch roofs on all. Except that they stretch up into the sky, the shortest being (by Lance's estimate) a minimum of twelve stories tall, and the tallest stretching far out of sight.

The streets are alive with the hustle-bustle of foot traffic and many other Gorrpaas, some directly mounted, some pulling wagons. The people are colorful and diverse, with many sharing Gilead's pastel-hued elfish appearance while there are some that look like gigantic anthropomorphized birds of prey, wings tucked at their sides.

A third group of people is almost exclusively pedestrian, stout and green and pig-nosed, waddling about on webbed feet from place to place or standing in street corners having conversation.

Lance's mind brims with half-formed questions. *Why are they here? Where is here? Who are they? When did they arrive? What are they doing?* The sensory overload is incredible.

The Gorrpaa comes to a gradual halt in front of a set of crisscrossed bars sticking out of the ground alongside one of the side paths. Gilead slides off and lands on the ground, then motions for Lance to do the same. Lance's dismount is not quite so smooth, as the button on the back of his shorts gets stuck for a moment, wrenching him sideways as he comes down, so that he hits the ground with the side of his body. Expecting a rough landing, Lance is instead surprised to find his fall cushioned significantly, the ground soft and spongy.

"So where are we now?" Lance asks after getting back on his feet. They are standing in front of the entry gate of a walled manor. Gilead has his back to him, tying the Gorrpaa's lead rope to the bars. He looks over his shoulder to answer.

"This, my lord Lansamor, is the great hall of heroes."

The wall stretching around the perimeter of the manor is impressive in its own right, being made of rolled and welded stone covered in creeping orange vines, extending in either direction from the gigantic wrought-iron gate in front of them. The manor itself is even more impressive, and its design is very radically different from every other building in the city. Imposing and splendorous, with Greco-Roman style pillars and giant stained glass windows, flanked by a limestone-paved courtyard bridged by stone arches which leads from the gates to the front door, this building gives off a powerful aura.

As they approach, a towering brown-feathered hawk swoops down from the sky and lands on the other side of the gate, adjusting its posture so that it stands erect like a human would. Upon Lance's closer inspection, its wings end in what seem to be opposable digits, and he is shocked when it suddenly begins to speak in the bright, ebullient voice of a human female.

"Well, Gilead, what's the word?" she asks cheerfully.

"The word is 'savior,'" says Gilead triumphantly, making a showy gesture to Lance. The bird-woman's pupils dilate within her ochre-colored eyes.

"Oh my goodness!" She exclaims, ruffling her feathered wings. "Come on in! We have to introduce him to the others!"

The gate swings open with a creak. Side-by-side Gilead and Lance enter through and step out into the courtyard. With the bird woman leading, they cross under the arches and approach the front door, out of which three as-yet-unknown figures step gingerly to greet them.

The first of these is another elf like Gilead, albeit taller and lankier, with golden skin rather than blue, and a head of coiffed ginger hair with equally ginger mutton chops on the sides of his face.

"Is it really him?" the golden elf asks in a raspy voice, scanning Lance with his eyes from head to toe and back again. He looks excited, but leery, hanging back a few feet closer to the door.

"Oh my stars, it is! As the prophecy foretold!" the second one says in an excitable trill. This greeter appears to be cut from the same cloth as the pedestrian class in the city, green and scaly, with a pig-like snout and a waddle in her gait that resembles the sort a toddler might affect upon having crapped in its pants. She seems elderly, carrying the aura of an eccentric but doting grandmother, a universally comforting presence even in such a situation as this. Upon seeing Lance, she rushes up to him and pinches his cheek with her webbed fingers.

"There he is!" she exclaims to the others. "It's been so long since we've seen his face. We thought he'd lost us forever. You poor, poor boy! I was beginning to think that there was no hope for you, but I was wrong. I see I shouldn't have doubted."

Alarm bells are ringing in Lance's head upon hearing this.

"You've— you've seen my face before?" He is thunderstruck. *How could that even be possible?*

"Of course we have!" the bird woman interjects. "You didn't think the prophetic texts would be written without pictures, did ya?" Her comment is punctuated by a moment of hearty laughter shared by all except for Lance. She speaks with a gaelic accent that Lance had failed to notice before, which Lance makes a mental note to add to the growing list of things that do not make sense around him at this point in time.

"Oh, and your mother is surely over the moon!" Adds the old green lady. "She hasn't forgotten about you, dear. It's been so long!"

"My mother?" Lance asks. He is breathless. At once his heart begins to pound, his jaw clenches, and he balls his hands into fists. It has been years since he last heard anything about her. Seeing this, the golden elf moves in quickly yet calmly to interject, pulling the old woman gently by the arm so that she stands behind him.

"Please forgive my friend," he says. "She is long in the tooth and prone to getting confused. Nevertheless, *we* are how you say over the moon to see *you*. Please, enter the manor with us, we have much to discuss with you."

"What about him?" Lance asks, pointing to the third member of the group, who had just entered the courtyard. "What's his deal?"

This final member of the troupe looks, by all appearances, like a normal white dude (of the distinctly human variety) in his late forties, with a portly build, a receding dark brown hairline, a mustache of similar color, black-rimmed reading glasses, and a pristine red cardigan. This one is the strangest of them all simply for how normal he looks in the midst of everything, and yet he has not said anything so far nor done much at all other than to cast a vacant stare out into the world in front of him.

"All will be revealed in time," says the golden elf, as he pushes his way into the front door, beckoning the others to follow. "Come along!"

Lance's mind reels with anxiety, fear, and questions galore. Nothing that is presently happening should be remotely possible. Half an hour ago, he is pretty sure, he was just walking around without a care in the world in his perfectly normal backyard. Now, he finds himself smoldering in his emotions in the midst of some strange new world with unidentifiable creatures flaunting exotic, alien biology and living exotic, alien lifestyles, yet somehow all able to communicate with him perfectly. Why is it that in fantasy stories all the goblins and ogres speak English? Why is it that in sci-fi all the aliens can talk to humans, even when they are not remotely humanoid?

The alternative, of course, is that this is some elaborate hoax, that there is no such thing as a bird person or an elf or a Gorrpaa or a liliput bird and this is all one big phony sham being pulled on him. People in costumes, fog machines, one big hokey script being passed around for laughs.

His thoughts keep running laps around the comment about his mother. Could that have been an especially targeted attack meant to get a rise out of him or test his reaction? Who would want to be so deliberately cruel? Sure, there are people who don't like Lance all that much, but how could anyone go through all the trouble of organizing such an elaborate trick? No, it's just not possible either.

And he is surely awake. There can be no mistake about that. Not only the sights and sounds of this environment are richly real, but the smell of the air and the taste of it on Lance's tongue. It is palpable, it is definitive, as if he could open his mouth now and the taste would be there before his eyes, in the air around him. In other words, it must be real. He can't escape the feeling that he was almost expecting this; all this time he has been in a daze. He's having trouble coming to grips with what's happening, not to mention why. Nevertheless, he follows the rest of the group into the foyer of the manor.

Predictably enough, the inside of this "hall of heroes" is as impressive as the outside. From the very first step, a visitor is greeted by an unimpeachable sense of grandeur. The walls are dazzlingly ornate, emerald green with blazing golden spirals and pinwheels spelling out some sort of code. Throughout the room there are suits of armor tailored to the biology of the creatures of this place, each bearing shields with what appears to be a different family crest. On one wall there is a gigantic brick fireplace; the wall opposite it contains a stunningly beautiful tapestry, and the other two walls are lined with bookcases and interrupted in the middle by archways leading off to other rooms. In front of the fireplace are a cluster of high-backed sofas gathered around a table, atop which sits a gigantic map rendered on parchment.

Lance's attention lingers on the tapestry, which depicts a luminescent being with twelve eyes and five hands, of which one is holding a dagger, one is holding a torch, one is clenched into a fist, and the other two palms are flatly extended. It is rendered in blindingly indescribable color, and the whole thing seems to pulse and distort the more Lance fixates upon it.

"What the fuck is that?" he exclaims, breaking away from the procession to try to get a closer look. Gilead seizes him roughly by the shoulders with a surprising strength and redirects him over to the group of couches, where the rest of the group now sits.

The feeling in Lance's temples right now is reminiscent of what the eighth graders at LFMMS say being high feels like. He's overheard them describe it in hushed tones in the halls, conversations about their wild Saturday nights where dude they got totally baked.

"I can tell you're feeling, let's say, a little overwhelmed right now, and that's perfectly understandable," the bird woman who now sits next to Lance says kindly, gingerly placing the tip of her wing upon the top of his kneecap. "Perhaps it's time for a formal introduction."

"My name is Zhanniti, of House Dvora. This," she says, pointing to the golden elf, "is Skanot of House Carfassus. You have of course already become acquainted with Gilead, also of House Carfassus. Skanot and I are Guardians, but Gilead is not. He is, however, a trusted friend."

"And for one of us, an ex-lover," interjects the elderly green woman.

"Cor, and no bad blood between us though, eh Binnie?" Gilead says, chuckling.

"No bad blood, only happy memories, Gil!" she replies earnestly. "We may have been a hot mess, but we were a *hot* mess! Oh, the times we had together back in our prime!" Turning to Lance, she adds, "I'm Binnmerva by the way. House Malyumpkin, positively cheesed to meet you!"

"Well I guess it's nice to meet you all. But, uh, who's he then?" Lance asks, pointing to the balding man in the red cardigan.

"OH!" Exclaims Skanot. "That's Todd."

Todd smiles at Lance, revealing rows of canine incisors that instantly disfigure his otherwise normal-looking human face. Lance waves a cautious hello and Todd barks at him.

"Explain this one to me," Lance says. "Um, first of all... how are any of you real?" He laughs nervously. "I mean, you're clearly real. I am *not* crazy, right? So... how, exactly?"

Zhanniti, the bird woman, answers.

"We have always been real. We have always existed, just as long as everything else has existed. Our people, I mean. This land. The thing is, we're cut off from the rest of creation. That's where you come in, the prophecy!" She points her wing at the ceiling.

The ceiling of the hall of heroes is adorned, like some fantasy Sistine Chapel, with a depiction of an armored warrior leading a throng of mythical creatures out of a pit, with a giant beast looming over them. The beast has the body of a ferocious predator, with seven heads and ten horns, and each horn is adorned in glittering golden crowns, and on each head are written words that Lance finds himself unable to read because his eyesight goes fuzzy at the sight of them. *How does it do that?* He wonders.

He looks at the armored warrior. It's his dad. No. He does a double take. It's him. It's Lance, definitely. What an odd mistake to make. Wait. It's *Lance*.

"That's me!" he says excitedly, pointing up at the depiction of himself. "So there really is a prophecy, then. Because, how could you possibly have put that up there in the time since I got here?"

"We will never lie to you," says Skanot.

"And that beast in the background, behind all the people, coming out of the pit... that's the beast that lives here, that I have to find and fight, right?" Lance asks eagerly, finally feeling like he's putting the pieces together for the first time.

Skanot nods.

"The beast does live here, in the pit," he says. "And the power to save us rests in you."

"We will guide you, our prince," says Binnmerva. "You'll learn this power through us."

Behind them, Gilead paces around the room, murmuring to himself. Lance notices him, and the two make eye contact. Gilead ceases his movement and clears his throat.

"Well now, I must be off!" he says. "Gotta get back and feed them hogs!"

"Adieu, my sweet!" Binnmerva calls with a wink. "Keep in touch!"

Gilead whistles, bites his lip, and departs. Skanot's eyeline follows him out the door, then he turns his head to stare at Lance again. Lance can practically feel his intense glare burning on his skin. A shudder runs down his body.

"And now it's time for you to leave too, sir Lansamor," says Skanot matter-of-factly.

"Is it?" Lance asks defiantly.

"An exercise in trust," explains Zhanniti in a soothing tone. "We will know that you are ready to begin your trials when you return to us voluntarily. Today, there is nothing else to show you. Binnmerva, please introduce our esteemed messiah to the clockwork guardian."

Binnmerva grabs Lance's wrist and pulls him to his feet.

"Upsie-daisy!" she says cheerfully. "Let's get you home!"

She toddles out of the room, bringing Lance with her, while the others remain where they are. Down one elegant corridor they go, then down another, darker one into a room from which a faint plasmatic glow emanates.

The clockwork guardian is a strange creature. The same general shape as Skanot and Gilead, sure, but its body appears to be almost made of light, formed in concentric circles that spell out the general idea of a corporeal form. They each rotate around each other independently, creating a similarly indescribable pulsating effect to the one displayed by the tapestry Lance saw earlier.

"Great guardian of the temporal Center! I beseech you!" Binnmerva announces as they approach. "Grant this boy safe passage to his home!"

The clockwork elf nods, and its entire body seems to refract. It brings its arms up and spreads them widely apart, and great silky threads of sunset-colored light extend to connect its fingertips. Lance begins to feel a buzzing inside his temple and his vision becomes saturated and monochrome. He squeezes his eyes shut and the world around him falls away.

Lance reopens his eyes to find himself standing right outside that fort in his backyard. A wave of relief washes over him. Finally, normalcy. The world as it should be. He runs back into the house, slamming the door behind him. Then he approaches his dad, who is still type-type-typing on the computer.

"Hello daddy," he says. "I'm back!"

"Wow, you were outside for a whole hour!" Mr. Morrissey says, looking at his watch incredulously. "That has *got* to be a record. And you're all covered in mud. What exactly did you do out there?"

All his life, Lance's dad has told him to always tell the truth, even if it could get him in trouble. He has always said if you lie the consequences will always be worse than if you simply confess. Lance's mom lived by this philosophy, and look where she is today. So much for that.

At this moment, Lance decides to lie.

"I just... you know, played outside," he says. "Like a kid from your generation would do. Did you get any work done for your stupid adult job?"

"I actually did," says his father proudly. "A solid hour of hard work and peace and quiet, I tell ya that's just what I needed and it came at the perfect time."

"You know what daddy?" Lance asks.

"What, Lance?"

"You should quit that job and tell your boss to kiss your ass, I think," says Lance thoughtfully.

Mr. Morrissey chuckles.

"Gotta say, I've thought about it! But hey, I've gotta pay the bills, don't I? When you're old and boring like me some day, you'll understand. And remember what I said about watching your language."

Lance laughs, and for the rest of the afternoon he leaves his dad alone to his work, which allows him to finish it all early for the day.

In the evening they sit together on the couch and watch a movie. Mr. Morrissey goes to bed that night feeling hopeful for the first time in a long time about his son. *The new and improved Lance Morrissey,* he thinks to himself as he rests his head on the pillow and smiles.

October 10, 2033

The direct executive supervisor of Agent Garrett Johnson (whose office memo we read earlier) is a woman by the name of Kritika Agrawal. She is the only daughter of millionaire parents who made their fortune by getting into the cannabis business early on, using generational wealth as startup capital, themselves the children of Hindu Brahmins who left India soon after the caste system was legally abolished.

Highly ambitious, she had her sights set on a seat inside the esteemed halls of America's federal government since she was very young. In fact, she can remember the day that this ambition first began very vividly. It would have been about twenty years ago now, when she was still in grade school, and her family took a trip to D.C. for a special guided tour of the Capitol building. Standing under the giant dome of the rotunda, she had felt the weight of all the cumulative history behind the country her family had inherited, and instantly developed a hunger to mark herself within that history. It would be her way of proving a point.

Stubbornly, self-consciously, she wanted to be able to say that the actions of Kritika Agrawal made the world a better place.

Today, director Agrawal is strutting down Constitution Avenue, her stilettoed heels clicking loudly on the pavement as she saunters past starry-eyed foreign tourists and drowsy uniformed members of the Capitol police force. She has just exited a lunchtime meeting with a representative from EUCOMM's humanitarian delegation and is now returning to USAID headquarters to handle a considerably more unpleasant piece of business: the deteriorating situation in Southern Africa, punctuated by her underling Garrett Johnson's recent failure to clinch what, by rights, ought to have been a very straightforward diplomatic agreement with Zambia's foreign commerce minister.

As if to pour salt into a festering wound, the cell phone in Kritika Agrawal's breast pocket begins to vibrate insistently. She halts her stride and collects herself to answer it.

"Hello?"

On the other end of the call comes an effete voice which Kritika recognizes as belonging to the Deputy Secretary of State.

"Mizz Agraval, how *are* we today?" he asks, briefly affecting an ethnic accent to pronounce her surname.

"We're doing well. Yeah. Definitely doing well." She forces a smile that she hopes will make her voice sound ingenuous.

"Just wanted to put a bug in your ear about something, if that's alright." The DSS's voice sounds casual, almost lazy. Director Agrawal can see him in her mind's eye lounging on his desk and clipping his toenails as he addresses her.

"Sure, what do you want to talk about?" She glances around and decides this is probably a good cue to resume her commute back to work, sensing a multitaskable conversation about to commence.

"We've decided to pivot on our multilateral China strategy and extend our focus toward a greater emphasis on underserved areas of the global community. I just wanted to make sure we're on the same page about some things."

"Yeah, absolutely," Kritika Agrawal says. "Go for it."

"This fiscal year, the president really wants to focus on outreach to the Global South. Can we touch base on where things are at with that right now?"

As she steps off the curb and crosses the street, Director Agrawal's heel catches an unseen pockmark in the pavement. She almost loses her balance, but quickly manages to regain composure before answering the Deputy Secretary's question.

"Oh, yes, sorry," she replies hastily. "What would you like to talk about? We've made great progress on the Indo-Pakistani front in recent months, and my office just authorized an aid package to Latin America which should help us normalize relations with Colombia."

"That's all great," her conversational partner replies flatly, "but POTUS particularly wants us to focus on Africa. As I'm sure you know, getting the SADC involved in our energy initiative will be critical going forward."

As diplomatic tensions between the world's leading superpowers escalated throughout the third decade of the twenty-first century, beginning with that infamous pandemic, circumstances aligned to put Kritika in a critical position to shape America's engagement strategy toward the Global South. In this role, a doctrine of world politics took root in her mind: that PRC China had abandoned its founding Marxist ideals and was regressing into imperialistic aggression, not unlike the European empires of the nineteenth and twentieth centuries. This, if not taken seriously, could become an existential threat to the values of multiculturalism and egalitarianism, not only in America but across the world. Injustice, tyranny, patriarchy, and so forth would be left unchecked to dominate the world through the vehicle of a PRC global hegemony. Only America, enlightened by the struggles and contributions of its constituent minority groups, could serve as an effective military and economic counterweight in an existential battle for world domination.

The veracity of such a theory is, of course, debatable, as are the axiomatic assumptions underpinning it. Nevertheless, by the end of the 2020s, it had become the prevailing worldview of the liberal wing of the United States government and a popular consensus among reading members of the public. This is due in no small part to the early career work of Kritika Agrawal.

After she spends a few minutes groveling, her counterpart in the State Department excuses himself to engage in other business and terminates their call. Just as well, as Kritika Agrawal is descending an escalator into one of the district's most insulated underground metro stations, where cell signals rarely deign to penetrate. The metro station smells slightly rank today, with a damp stench riding the stale air that hits her as she descends into it. Director Agrawal pretends not to notice, banishing her disgust to another part of her mind. In truth, she enjoys riding public transportation. It makes her feel gloriously humble.

She lives in a small apartment just a few miles away from the building where she works, and despite the high cost of D.C. real estate, she could probably afford to live in some place even bigger. However, she refuses to do this, partly because she spends so little time at home, and partly out of a fear of backlash from her friends in progressive circles should they ever find out she comes from a family of wealth.

Kritika's hobbies outside of work include posting pictures of her cat and plants to social media, walking aimlessly around the exhibit rooms of the National Museum of Women in the Arts and staring fixated at the walls while mentally entertaining political power fantasies, and shopping online.

It has been nearly 24 hours since USAID Agent Garrett Johnson had his meeting with Joseph Mulenga. She read the note he had written about it twice already, which had been sent as an attachment to her inbox. *In a few moments,* she thinks, sitting at her desk and sucking on the last bit of a rapidly disintegrating piece of hard candy, *he will be here in this office. And he had better be ready for the deep shit he's about to find himself in if he can't turn this deal around.* America may be wearing thin its credibility on the world stage by this point in history, but a foreign dignitary straight-up refusing to meet with an American diplomat is rare, and never a good sign. Clearly, Agent Johnson had fucked something up. And if he didn't fix it, the fallout would land squarely in her lap.

Just now: a triple-knuckle tap at the door.

"Come in please," says Kritika Agrawal.

Pallid and chubby, Garrett Johnson timidly enters the room with a bit of an awkward shuffle.

"Sit down," she directs curtly, nodding her head in the direction of the chair in front of the desk as if to suggest that he cannot see it. Johnson complies.

"Describe to me," she says in an even tone, "Mister Mulenga's response to our proposal for a carbon-neutral Lusaka-based embassy for the recognition of American-African diversity and friendship."

"Oh, it's all in the attachment in the email I sent you." Johnson's face shines brightly.

"Tell me, what did he say about the revenues this project would generate for his country? Or the jobs that would be created in the construction and operation of the embassy?" Kritika asks.

"Well, uh, I didn't quite get... that... far, exactly," he says stupidly. Kritika clasps her hands together in front of her and flashes a pithy toothless smile.

"Do you have any idea why that might be?" she asks.

"Well, no, not —"

"Let me rephrase that. Do you — *as a white man* — have any idea why that might be?"

"I promise you," Agent Johnson says earnestly, "I have done all of the sensitivity training. I'm working very hard to decolonize my mindset, I promise!"

Kritika sighs.

"Look," she says politely. "The fault is on me. Forget about your mindset for a minute. Consider the *optics* of a white man barging into Africa and demanding that his country start putting developments all over the place."

"Well — I didn't — there was no *barging* really —" the agent stutters.

"It's fine, you can't help it. I just picked the wrong person for the job, that's all. I wasn't thinking. You have my most sincere apology. And for the record, I am going to set up an online meeting with him today, and we will see as a *person of color* if I can get any farther than you could, ok?"

"And, um, if you don't?"

The question hangs in the air.

"Then we'll figure out what to do from there," Kritika answers with a tone of finality. "That's all for now, good-bye. You will probably receive your replacement assignment tomorrow."

With a wave of her hand, Garrett Johnson is dismissed. He tilts his head forward deferentially, collects his coat, and leaves.

August 1, 1998

The sun beats down from overhead. It is a cloudless, humid day. The sort of day where the air shimmers when you look at it and you're not sure if the shimmer is actually real or if it's some feverish hallucination induced by exposure to temperatures hot enough to start to maybe melt your brain a little bit.

It has been a week since Marissa has last seen or spoken to Tobias, but the sheer volume and intensity of the farm work has mostly kept her mind off of it. During this time she has gotten acquainted with her family's new coolie labor force: five bulky hispanic guys of varying heights with buzz cuts and enough substantial muscle mass for the base of their skulls to be fused together with their deltoids by enlarged sternocleidomastoids and trapezium. In order from shortest to tallest, their names are Jorge, Tomás, Enrique, Juan, and Don Pablo. All of them except for Jorge knew each other back in Mexico and are a part of the same family line, apparently. Extended cousins or something.

The workers wake up at the crack of dawn like Marissa does, and in the mornings they go out with her to detassel the corn. Then, they proceed with taking care of the AM cow routine (bringing them in from the pastures, giving them feed, hay, water etc). After that's done everyone splits up to do his or her own thing.

Marissa and her mom have lately been working on repainting the entire fence around the pasture, while her dad and the workers either continue with the cows (milking, bathing, and so on) or help clear the forest land that will be used in the future for additional crops, or perform chores around the barn like repair the siding and maintain the equipment. Every couple of days or so everybody goes out in the field together to spray or pull out the weeds, tackling it systematically as a group.

Marissa can't help but find herself on guard around the workers. Something about these guys makes her feel leery and uncomfortable. She has never communicated with any of them directly, since they barely speak any English and none of them know a lick of ASL. Her mom, who is fluent in all three languages, has been acting as the main interpreter in most of the interactions Marissa or her dad have with the workers.

Language gap aside, their presence is made even more alienating by the cold, distant attitude they cop around Marissa whenever she is nearby. On many occasions she has caught their eye and waved hello only to be met with a blank stare that borders on being overtly aggressive. Sometimes she will walk in on them when they are in the middle of a conversation, and they will turn to look at her all at once then abruptly stop talking until she leaves, even though they know there's no possibility she could overhear whatever it is they're saying.

At night the laborers get intoxicated and bicker with each other, and sometimes the bickering turns physical. Every once in a while they all gang up on Jorge and shove him around because he's smaller than them and they seem to enjoy making him squirm. Marissa finds their behavior odd enough when sober, but she senses that when drunk they are probably capable of truly diabolical things. For this reason, her dad, who they know as Señor Rob, always keeps a close eye on them whenever they touch liquor. She knows they will never do more than engage in a little bit of tomfoolery under the watchful vigilance of Señor Rob, but she dreads to think what should ever happen if they do get really inebriated when he is not there to supervise.

For a person with intact hearing, using a chainsaw without ear protection for greater than fifteen minutes at a time can be hazardous, since the noise of a chainsaw is able to easily exceed 115 decibels of sound, which is well within the threshold to cause hearing loss. Under no such constraint, Marissa has been tasked today with operating the chainsaw. Previously, the land around the cornfield which her father envisions to be cleared as part of his master plan to expand the crop area was all covered in woods. Over the last few days the workers have gone and chopped down all the trees, and now all that remains is the bramble. Marissa's job, in this heat, will be to use the chainsaw to disperse whatever heavy brush remains on this stretch of perimetered land.

Sweat adheres her shirt to her back as she silently clears away branches and vines. Out here, away from everyone else, with nothing else beyond this simple task to keep her thoughts occupied, Marissa begins to wonder about Tobias. How has *he* been handling their separation over the past several days?

My birthday is coming up soon, she realizes. It's right around the corner, just a few days from now. Will he be able to make it? Whenever her mother asks if there is anything special she wants to do for her birthday, Marissa has no idea how to answer, as she has not once thought to ask him.

Tobias, agreeable to the extreme, rarely imposes his own suggestions on what to do, and it had completely slipped her mind to bring it up the last couple times they were together. And since Marissa and her family pretty much live in the middle of nowhere, and just about all the kids her age left town as soon as they got the chance to go to college out of state, the chances of throwing a gigantic party are pretty much slim to none. *Maybe I could take dad's truck and drive around and go door-to-door the next town over*. Marissa chuckles at the thought.

The hours begin to tick by. Chips of wood and vegetative matter begin to accumulate on her clothes as Marissa lets this train of thought play out in her mind. She periodically shifts her weight from one side to the other to compensate for the heavy chainsaw. Letting go of everything but the minimal attention required to complete the task ahead of her adequately, she envisions a perfect birthday: an intimate picnic, just her and the Tobe-ster, sitting together in some beautiful, perfect place. A place where their privacy and tranquility can be absolute, where real-life problems no longer matter and their hearts are no longer touched by worry. If only it were possible.

Marissa's mind drifts backwards to the Sunday school stories of her childhood about the Garden of Eden. Before the fall of man, when it was just Adam and Eve living together and munching on fruit. There was a time when she was a child, hearing that story, that she would ask,

"Did they ever get lonely?"

She did not understand at the time how two people could so fully complete each other that they needed the company of no one else. She had not yet experienced the feeling of being lonely in a crowd.

How could they possibly *have been lonely?* She wonders now. *They had each other.*

Then, of course, came the temptation of man, when Adam and Eve were locked out of the garden forever because they betrayed the promise they made to God. Shortly after that, they disappear from the story altogether, so that the focus can be on Cain and Abel and all those silly hebrews. Now she wonders, *what ever happened to them? Were they still happy in the end, with each other, even after they got locked out of the garden?*

So absorbed in this thought is Marissa that she hardly notices when she reaches the end of the perimeter of the field, her task completed. Presently, she is approached by the tender presence of her mom, who waves her inside.

Time for dinner.

The sun begins to sink low into the horizon...

Songbirds call to each other from the tops of branches that sway in the summer breeze while down below a different sound, the sound of a half-broken car muffler, echoes through the trees. Fingers curl around the steering wheel of a rusting Ford Taurus which whips up and down rolling hills and negotiates sharp turns with a studied precision. Tobias is in a hurry.

Beside him in the passenger seat of the vehicle is a stack of important documents which he forgot to fax to the central office of his current client, Delco Westinghouse Transmission Services Incorporated, whose liaison is a man notoriously short on patience and whose central office closes in the next fifteen minutes.

"I am an *idiot!*" Tobias exclaims under his breath as he yanks his car into the now nearly empty Wisteria building parking lot. He throws the gear stick into park with the force of a naval seaman hauling an anchor, and rips the key out of the ignition. The setting sun casts his shadow long and thin in front of him as he runs around to grab the entire stack of papers in one swift motion and then dash through the double doors of the building.

The office building Tobias works at has just been renovated and every cubic inch of air inside carries the aroma of fresh paint, fresh carpet, fresh carpet deodorizer, fresh paint thinner, fresh paint primer, fresh air freshener, fresh wood finish; well, you get the idea.

It's a smell that hits you in the face as soon as you enter the lobby and your eyes immediately water. Going into any one of the myriad offices, which are each littered with twenty-five cluttered cubicles, throws an extra layer of stale Colombian office coffee and dust bunnies into the mix.

The building has offices on three floors, and fortunately for Tobias (given the hurry he's in this evening and the perennially unreliable nature of the elevators), his office is on the bottom floor. He only has the access code for this office, and no other. And there is only one fax machine tucked in the back corner of it. As Tobias pounces down the hallway, he makes a silent desperate prayer that no one is currently using the fax.

Mercifully, his prayer is answered. The office seems to be entirely bereft of other life.

Upon approach, Tobias sees that the fax machine has been turned off for the night, and he jams his finger on the power button, proceeding to do an impatient "pee-pee dance" as he hops from one foot to the other while it boots up.

Finally, the screen comes on and Tobias is able to key in the number for the Delco Westinghouse office. He claps his hands in excitement, and the sound ricochets around the walls of the room.

"This fax machine sucks," he breathes. "If I could help it, I'd never use one again."

A fax machine combines the sounds of a printer and standard telephone and amplifies them to be as annoying and ear-piercing as possible. Upon first being booted up, the user is greeted by a shrill electronic tone reminiscent of a furious bird's call being filtered through a megaphone directly into his/her eardrum. This alerts the user to begin the long and arduous process of feeding each document through the device's scanner, a process that seemingly cannot occur without the fax machine producing a series of loud noises both electronic and mechanical which only become louder and more unbearable the older the piece of equipment is.

This fax machine has been in the office for nearly ten years.

Unbeknownst to Tobias, on the opposite corner of the room, Tobias's coworker Kevin, a middle-aged Swedish gentleman, sips decaffeinated coffee as he tries to finish up his own set of late-evening work so that he too can finally go home. He did not hear Tobias come in, but now his concentration is sorely disturbed. He has placed himself at this secluded spot in the office intentionally to focus better on his spreadsheets, and now the intermittent beeping of that incessant fax machine seems to be mocking his concerted efforts at establishing peace and quiet.

"Man, I need another cup of coffee," he mutters to himself. *The real stuff, not this decaf crap.* Who could be using the fax this late at night, anyway?

Kevin turns up the volume on his radio, hoping soft rock throwbacks from the '60s and '70s will create some sort of audio counter-distraction from the horrible KEEEEAAUUHGH-HAAAAA EEEE EEE EEEEE EEEE EEEE EEE EEEE sounds filling the space around him. The vanity of this action is revealed in seconds as Kevin's music is drowned out by Tobias's own off-key singing of a different song, which is somehow loud enough to rise above all the rest of the din.

"*Girl you know it's truuuuuue*!" Tobias caterwauls in a falsetto that would embarrass a hyena. "*My heaaaart belongs to* — oh, you've got to be shitting me!" He exclaims as the fax decides abruptly in the middle of scanning a document to drop the Delco Westinghouse connection entirely.

Tobias gives the machine a swift kick and hurriedly re-dials the number for the office, gazing anxiously at his watch to see how fast the time is ticking away. After a repetition of the awful dial tone, he is surprised to hear another man's voice close behind him.

"A stirring rendition, Tobias," coworker Kevin says, politely applauding as he approaches. "But just a little bit pitchy."

"Oh my gosh!" Tobias exclaims, startled. "Kevin Ffff.... Falcon, right? I didn't know you were here, sorry! I, uh — nice name, by the way. I think we've talked maybe twice before, so I never mentioned it, but Kevin Falcon is a really cool name. Have you ever thought about forming a band?"

"If I do, unfortunately I might have to leave you off the shortlist for main vocalist."

"So what are you — what are you doing here this late at night?" Tobias asks, still flustered about the whole situation.

"Up until a couple of minutes ago," Kevin replies with a thoughtful scratch at his chin, "I was deeply invested in important paperwork. And what about you?"

"Sorry," Tobias says again, sheepishly, pressing the button to finish the scan. "I forgot to fax out all these documents, and now I've got to finish doing it in..." He glances at his watch. "...The next six minutes."

"Well shoot, best of luck to ya," says Kevin Falcon in a jovial tone. "Hey, for my sake, the quicker you get that done, the better, alright? Don't let me stop you!"

He gives Tobias a meaningful look and friendly wave of goodbye, then departs back to his cubicle and out of sight.

"What a strange guy," Tobias remarks to himself.

Kevin Falcon has been working at the office for longer than anyone else can remember, an enigmatic figure in the politics of the office. He is an undeniably diligent worker who knows the company better than anybody else, but he carries himself with a downright lackadaisical attitude befitting his former hippie past. He often tells people that he never stopped being a flower child; he just learned to smoke a little less and shower a little more. In fact, when he was a teenager he was a part of a communist paramilitary movement in Sweden and maybe even killed a few cops, but he's fuzzy on the details due to the holes in his memory from all the LSD he did at the time and probably wouldn't admit to it either. In any event, he was approached by members of the Weather Underground when he immigrated to the United States, but he turned the invitation down in order to try to go straight.

This is not information anyone else in the office knows about Kevin Falcon.

Tobias concentrates vigorously on the task at hand, his fingers doing the repetitive button-pressing motions practically in autopilot on one hand as he sorts and swaps out the documents with the other. Nary a second is available to waste.

Finally, with his palms sweaty and fingers starting to cramp, Tobias steps back as the final document is sent out into the ether. He exhales the stress of the night out of his lungs and takes a step back, stretching out all his extremities. The deed is done. Silence falls over the room.

"Did you countermand the self-destruct function?!" Kevin calls out from across the room.

"Huh?!" Tobias responds, quickly approaching the cubicle to make sure he heard him right.

"I'm just busting your balls a little bit, man," Kevin says once Tobias has come face-to-face with him. "Just, like, having a laugh. Hey, corporate put out a notice that they need someone to rep the company in a big conference in Omaha. Seems perfect for an aspirational self-starter, a young guy looking to be upwardly mobile, maybe kick his career into gear, you know? In other words, got your name all over it, maybe. You interested?"

"Yeah, maybe," says Tobias thoughtfully. "When is it?"

"It's in October, man. To kick off the announcement of the company's quarterly earnings."

"Well, I've got nothing planned."

"Smart guy! Alright, I'll put your name down. Hey, you're helping me out here too. That leaves me with just one less thing to do tonight. You leaving?"

"Yeah, I'm getting out of here." Tobias nods and leans against the wall of the cubicle, awkwardly trying to emulate Mr. Falcon's "cool" demeanor.

"Alright man, drive safe." With a flourish, Kevin spins around in his standard-issue lumbar-supported office swivel chair and diverts his undivided attention toward completing the rest of his extensive paperwork.

The night air greets Tobias like a snapshot of frozen time: warm and unmoving, completely still. He has to really strain his ears to hear the sounds of the crickets and the mating bullfrogs. Beyond a low level of ambient noise, it is silent outside. Completing the diorama, the lights that shone over the parking lot have all gone out except for the one closest to the door.

It is the sort of environment that makes a person feel palpably alone.

With a shiver that does not come from the temperature of the air, Tobias walks empty-handed to his car, and turns the radio on, sitting idly with the car geared in park and letting a throwback hit from the 80s wash over him for a solid minute. The song calls to mind a suppressed childhood memory that he struggles to get a grasp of. A picture begins to form in his mind; then, like a novice fisherman grappling with a fresh and still living capture, he loses his grip on the thought and it slips away.

The country roads take Wisteria's eerie silence factor and amp it up a notch. The only perceptible sound outside the car is that of Tobias's wheels kicking up trace amounts of concrete. A thick misty fog has descended over the road, making Tobias's surroundings inscrutable.

Car headlights cut through the fog only a negligible zone of visibility barely sufficient to reveal the next ten feet of road. Meager light from the crescent moon hanging in the sky barely adds anything more. What lurks in the shadows of the trees and the untamed meadows on either side of the road remains an uncomfortable mystery.

Have I ever seen that grove of trees before? Tobias begins to wonder. *What road am I even driving on right now?*

He slows the car down to create a mental map of all the turns he has taken up to this point. He is fairly sure that he has not taken a wrong turn at any point in the navigatory process. *I guess I could be wrong.* The only thing for it is to keep heading straight and see if there might be some landmarks against which Tobias can get his bearings.

The path ahead halts at a T-shaped intersection; the road goes on no further in Tobias's current direction, but he can turn either left or right. There are only mile markers and no street signs this far out in the boonies, so the name of this road is a mystery. On a hunch, Tobias narrows his eyes and hangs a sharp left.

Ahead lies a steep downward hill, one that requires Tobias to switch gears in order to traverse without slipping. About thirty feet down, the road disappears into an old covered timber truss bridge that looks about as secure as the sanctity of a prostitute's marriage. Tobias reasons, coasting on his brakes, that the bridge probably dates back to the days when this whole area was covered in train tracks, possibly a hundred years ago. An antique, in a decidedly less-than-new condition. *Do I really want to cross this possible death trap?* Tobias asks himself.

Yet his fears are overridden by the same niggling feeling that made him turn left, agitating him to press ever onward. Tobias takes his foot off the brake and the car crosses the threshold into the bridge.

CLICK.

In an instant, the car's headlights turn off of their own accord and Tobias's whole world is plunged in darkness. He cannot see anything beyond the steering wheel in front of him.

"WOAH!" he cries, feeling a nauseating rush of vertigo. There is a sensation of falling. In a singular instant, Tobias's head whips backward, hitting the headpiece on his seat. Then forward, bouncing off the steering wheel. He closes his eyes in pain and massages his aching forehead.

Behind Tobias's eyelids, there is light. He picks his head back up and opens his eyes. His car's headlights illuminate the scene in front of him: a beautiful, splendorous field of flowers and flowering trees, with bright and powerful moonbeams coming through the branches and lighting up the whole area. The moon seems brighter here somehow, together with the headlights casting everything in an ethereal glow. Seeing it all, Tobias is filled with an overwhelming urge to get out of the car and have a quick look around.

The color palette of this beautiful garden seems to encompass every shade in the known universe. No floral expert, Tobias can nevertheless recognize a cluster of brilliant pink petunias, a clump of deep auburn marigolds, and a gathering of several pearl-white daisies. Plus a number of flowers of every other color which are vaguely familiar by sight but unidentifiable by name. They stretch on into the horizon as far as the eye can see, these beautiful perfect flowers. The sky above is freckled by stars that shine as golden pinpricks against a rich dark blue expanse as vast as the field on the ground, with streaks of majestic royal purple strewn throughout. There is not a cloud in sight, and the air is pleasant.

Despite the lateness of the hour and his earlier trepidation, Tobias is overcome by a feeling of inner peace. His first thought is to thank God for this sudden discovery. And after some deliberation, his second thought is that Marissa would love this place.

July 1, 2014

Joaquin Anderson stands in front of Lance Morrissey's front door, weighing his options. Like yeah, he and Lance were friends a while back but like, the kid is totally nuts. So, there's an even chance whatever he wants to see Joaquin for is completely made up in his head, you know? It could totally be a complete waste of time, like. Like, *if he don't open this door in the next ten seconds, I'm turning around and going home.* He impatiently kicks the heel of his shoe against the concrete doorstep, a mild ache running through his feet, which have recently grown to be ever-so-slightly too big for his shoes.

Come on, Lance. Last night, Lance had called him all excited about something, so excited it was like he was giddy, and he'd said he wanted to show Joaquin something "really fucking cool" in his backyard. And like, Lance is a big fat liar and all. "Pathological", they call it. But sometimes he's gotta be telling the truth. Especially like when he's so excited like that, you know? Like it's easy to fake being sad, sure. Probably. So you can get people to pity you and all, but genuine like real excitement is hard to fake.

Last night, Joaquin had told him it was too late at night to like drop everything and just show up at his door but he swore up and down he would be here today, and it wouldn't be fair to the legacy of the friendship they used to have with each other if he listened to the voice in his head saying Lance is a crazy motherfucker and he'd backed down. But at this point right now he's wondering if *anyone* is going to come and open this friggin door.

But then the door opens.

Lance Morrissey stands in the doorway, his eyes unfocused for half a second before suddenly lighting up in recognition, as the vaguely apathetic expression on his face is quickly replaced by a look of unfiltered joy.

"My man!" Lance exclaims. "Wocky! I wasn't sure if you were gonna come today, man!"

"What's good, Lance!" Joaquin says, trying to artificially lift his own enthusiasm to mirror that of his friend. He glances inside the house, doing a quick scan left and right to see if everything looks the way he remembers it. "It's been a minute, homie!"

Lance laughs.

"Yeah," he says, nodding with his mouth drifting open slightly like he forgot to close it. He says nothing for multiple seconds.

"So, um... You finna let me in or what?" Joaquin asks.

"Oh yeah!" says Lance. "Come on in."

The boys enter the foyer of the Morrissey household.

"I thought you said we was going to the backyard for this thing," Joaquin says suspiciously as Lance walks past him and into the kitchen.

"We are," Lance responds simply, opening the freezer above the fridge and sticking his hands in. "But it's hot outside and I thought it'd be nice if we had these."

He pulls out two orangesicle pops and hands one to Joaquin.

"Oh thanks," Joaquin says, touched by this surprisingly lucid gesture of empathy. "I 'ppreciate it, man." He begins to unwrap his frozen pop and watches as Lance does the same. They both discard the wrappers in the kitchen trash can by the sink.

"Now!" Lance announces, raising his free hand in the air with the pointer finger outstretched. "To business!"

He leads Joaquin out the back door and they proceed into the unfenced backyard, standing still out on the grass for a moment together to acclimatize to the heat and the glare from the sun.

"You remember that, right?" Lance calls out, pointing to the ditch at the outer side boundary of the yard.

"Yeah, sure. Yeah," says Joaquin. "We were six."

The two of them approach closer. Lance crouches down in front of the two-by-four plank bridge and picks up the end of one of the planks, looking at the grubs crawling on the underside of it. Joaquin hangs behind him, with his hands shoved deep in the pockets of his red basketball shorts.

"And — oh, and how about this bridge, eh? You remember that too?" Lance asks with a note of desperation in his voice.

"It's just a couple of old boards, man. I'm surprised you even left them there, to be honest," Joaquin replies derisively.

"I had to," Lance responds simply. "Just in case if anyone decided to come back."

Lance slowly rises back to his feet and faces Joaquin, who feels a stab of pity.

"Just, just like show me what you wanted to show me, man," he says.

"Alright." Lance nods. Then he points into the mouth of the woods. "See that?"

"No." Joaquin looks a little more closely and his eyesight adjusts to differentiate between the intersecting shapes and shadows of the forest. "Wait. Shit. I see that! Damn, homie, that's kind of impressive actually!"

Joaquin's overlarge t-shirt, which says "TOO SWOLE TO CONTROL" in block letters despite his ironically stringbean-thin frame, flaps briskly in the breeze as he runs towards the fort in the woods to get a closer look. Lance picks up the rear.

Sure enough, the mysterious wooden fort remains exactly where it stood the day before. Lance keeps his eyes on it both to continually reassure himself that it really exists and to ensure that it does not disappear on him. Meanwhile, Joaquin walks around the circumference and admires the craftwork, taking in a full sense of the size, scale, and scope of the thing.

"Yo, this is so cool!" he exclaims. "I bet it's even weatherproof too like this thing could stay standing up for like years and years. When did you build it?"

"That's the thing," says Lance, trying to convey a fireside ghost story-esque tone of mystery in his voice. "I didn't."

"Oh... kay... so, when did your dad make it then?"

"You don't get it, Joaquin. He didn't build it either! It's just, one day this spot was empty, and the next day this tree branch fort was here. Like it appeared out of thin air!"

"Lance, my man, what the hell are you talking about?" Joaquin stops in his tracks and puts his hand out to rest it against the outer wall of the fort. "Why you always gotta unnermine$_{(sic)}$ yourself by saying dumb shit like that?"

"Go inside."

"Huh?"

"GO inside the fort!" Lance commands.

"Shit, alright, if you say so," Joaquin says, flashing a you-are-totally-crazy hairy eyeball at Lance as he obliges the instruction. He moves to stand in the center of the fort, underneath the highest point so that he does not have to crouch, and faces Lance.

"There's nothing in here, Lance," Joaquin says. "A lot of space, sure, but don't seem like much else."

Heart pounding with anticipation, Lance is eager to see what happens next from the outside.

"Okay, now try to come back out!" he orders Joaquin excitedly.

Joaquin scrunches his face up in confusion for a moment, but shrugs his shoulders in acceptance. He takes three steps forward — *crunch crunch crunching* on the dead grass and broken twigs strewn all over the ground — and emerges in front of the fort completely unscathed and unhindered. He raises his arms to the sky in mock triumph.

"Ta-da!" He exclaims.

"Nothing," Lance says under his breath dejectedly.

"Yeah, that's what I said," Joaquin replies. "There's nothing in there."

"No, I mean nothing. Like, as in, nothing happ—" Lance wrinkles his nose. "Man, fuck you Joaquin!" he explodes, marching up to Joaquin. "You must have did it wrong somehow! Go back in there and try it again!"

"Man, what the hell you talking about with this 'fuck you' business?" Joaquin exclaims defensively, backing away. "I'm not doing shit for you, you crazy as hell, Lance! Enjoy your little tree fort, asshole. I'm going back home."

He storms out of the forest as Lance panics.

"Wait!" Lance calls. "I'm sorry, I know I — I shouldn't've —!"

Before Lance can finish the thought, Joaquin Anderson briefly looks over his shoulder to flip him off, then runs away and disappears from sight.

October 11, 2033

There is a certain level of perverse absurdism that comes with living in Washington, D.C.

In the first place, it is one of the few locations in the world where you can witness rich folks beg shamelessly on the streets. Like, K-street and the slums are about a mile apart from each other and you can take a walk across town and first get harassed by an unwashed bum with a grubby raincoat and stale weed on his breath hassling you for some spare change, then ten minutes later get harassed by a different sort of bum with a professionally pressed hairstyle and perfectly manicured nails and perfectly tweezed eyebrows (psychological studies have confirmed this to be a sign of narcissism) wearing designer clothes, who demands that you sign his petition right now or front a stack of cash for some boutique economic interest or progressive social cause du jour. Washington D.C. is one of those distinctly Dickensian "tale of two cities" situations.

All of the typical hallmarks of liberal administration are on prevalent display in the residential areas of Washington, D.C. These include the astronomically high cost of living, the proliferation of crime both violent and financial, ubiquitously drugged-out vagrant population (symptomatic of the aforementioned cost of living), and a grotesquely enriched administrative class. Washington, D.C. is the sort of place whose wealthy denizens will drive down the slum streets in their pimped-out German or Japanese cars and remark to each other about the tragedy of the deleterious effects of laissez-faire patriarchal capitalism on the common man, and then get together and lobby for girlboss politicians to pass government regulations which only serve to make labor more expensive and thus more scarce and do the same to housing as well. Then they drive down the same streets the next year and see how the poor are even worse off than the year before and remark to themselves about the tragedy of the deleterious effects of laissez-faire patriarchal capitalism and so on.

Further, much of the city is now walled off behind security checkpoints and barbed wire, and a substantial portion of its spaces have been occupied by military patrols stationed there in the wake of the previous decade's civil unrest. All the extra security began as a temporary measure, but a supermajority of Congress had found themselves rather enjoying the extra protection, enough to include it as a permanent fixture of the national budget.

Finally, there is the egregious level of corruption that permeates the entire city. The usual suspects of campaign financing are abundant, and you will see repeated glimpses of it while walking the streets: lobbyists, foreign business tycoons, oligarchs, "philanthropic" foundations, political action committees, self-righteous celebrity gardeners, clowns.

The political system is one big game, and it is one that the young ambitious reactionary who calls himself John Nash has successfully been exploiting for the better part of the past four years. An avowed accelerationist, "John Nash" (a pseudonym he operates under while conducting business) has dedicated his life's work to bringing down the administrative state from the inside. Today's target is an interesting one: he has a 1:30 lunch scheduled with a disgruntled lackey from USAID. This man presented a most intriguing case (via electronic memo) to the firm for which John Nash works, and Nash was quick to seize the opportunity before any of his midwit associates could get the chance.

The sidewalks of Washington D.C. are covered in puddles and trash. The trash is old but the puddles are new, and John Nash weaves around them as well as between the pedestrians who shuffle around from place to place, fixated mindlessly on whatever lies immediately in front of them. It is hard not to view the typical person with a cynical twinge of contempt when you stand in full view of the tragedy of popular mediocrity. How is it possible for a man, or a woman for that matter, to travel through life with neither a plan nor a creed? To view oneself as purely atomic, with neither a connection to the continuity of the past nor a purpose for the future? No obligation, no higher sense of awareness?

Nash estimates that approximately 80% of the people around him on this street, or maybe more, are under the influence of some chemical or technological distraction. He passes by a group of ethnically unidentifiable ladies with close-cropped and neon-dyed hair, whose eyes are pink and gaits are sluggish. They lean on each other and one of them giggles, all three clearly having smoked a sizable amount of marijuana. The whole city smells like the stuff. He also passes by a grown man probably in his thirties, wearing a doggie collar-style choker and listening to something through translucent earpieces. Probably hearing, but not particularly listening, to a podcast or something, probably about, for instance, the latest and greatest popular streaming show. *All these people, moving so fast and yet going nowhere*, John Nash thinks, feeling a stab of disgust. *The degenerate moderns.*

The street ends at a corner, and right around the corner is the restaurant at which John Nash is about to meet USAID agent Garrett Johnson. It is a stuffy and overpriced Italian joint that Nash has visited a few times before, always with low-level bureaucrats who usually offer to pay the bill for both of them.

When the lunch or dinner partner offers to pay, Nash uses the first ten minutes or so of the meeting before they order food to gauge his feelings about the person he is doing business with. When it's someone he feels a good rapport with, he tends to order something reasonably affordable and small. The more he dislikes the person he meets with, the more expensive an item he will choose. This is true at every restaurant, and on one occasion Nash put an order in for a $125 sirloin at the fanciest steakhouse in town which the nebbish federal reserve employee he met with and despised had to pay for at the end of the night. John Nash does not drink alcohol, but that night he had also considered ordering a $70 cognac just to add insult to injury, which, had he gone through with the idea, he would have left on the table in front of him, untouched. He really abhorred that federal reserve employee.

Every new client represents a fresh start, and hopefully today's will at the very least make for better company.

John Nash forces himself through the heavy glass doors that constitute the entrance of the restaurant and squints, scanning the dimly lit booths in the hopes that his correspondent will catch his eye and wave him over.

"Do you have a reservation?" the restaurant greeter asks. She is a tall, pale woman dressed in a black trim-fit suit with jet-black hair pulled back into a tight bun and her lips adorned in ruby-red lipstick. Her lips stand out in stark contrast to the monochromatism of the rest of the ensemble, and when she poses the question Nash finds his eyesight caught on her mouth for a brief moment.

"I'm here for a client," John Nash says, flashing a charismatic but aloof smile.

Sure enough, a few booths down to the greeter's right a big, fat, balding man stands up and waves both hands theatrically. *Oh God, he's fat. Guy looks like an idiot.*

"Terrific!" Nash exclaims, pointing. "There he is."

"I'll let you get right to it," she says, beckoning to let him pass. "And don't forget to check out our wine menu."

"You got it!" Nash declares, beaming as he faces her and flashes finger guns at navel level. Then he turns around and adopts a slightly modified but equally cheesy expression to face his dinner partner.

"I'm Garrett Johnson," the man says, stretching out his hand for Nash to shake firmly, thinking grimly that Agent Johnson's grip feels like a dead fish hanging limp in his hand. Both men take seats across from each other.

"Yes, so I've heard," Nash replies. "And as I'm sure you know, I am John Nash."

"Oh, I figured as much," Johnson says proudly. "I recognized that mustache from the picture on your microcred!"

"Yes," Nash muses. "It is quite recognizable. Anyways, my micro-*what*?"

"Microcred, that's what they call it, right? The little encrypted data packet I was sent to prove you are who you say you are?"

"Well my friend, I can't say I've ever heard it get labeled with that particular name before, but I know what you're talking about. Good. Good. Now, to business! I read about your particular case. As you may imagine, I got where I am because I'm good at what I do and I have the connections to prove it. I can get you in contact with Blackrock, I can put you on the phone with Brownstein Hyatt Farber Schreck, you tell me who you want to get a hold of, and I'll pull the strings."

"NASA. I need NASA."

"Well." John Nash places his hands in scholars' cradle formation in front of him on the table. "Color me intrigued."

As the evening progresses, Nash's initial misgivings toward his dinner companion begin to fade away as he finds himself unironically enjoying Garrett Johnson's company and straightforward way of looking at things.

They are attended to by a waiter who is about as fresh out of the Italian mold as they come. The tips of his immaculately waxed mustache curl into an ouroboros, and his hairy arms do an unchoreographed, free-form dance through the air as he animatedly describes his favorite food and drink recommendations on the menu.

Presently Garrett takes generous sips from a Campari IPA whenever it is not his turn to contribute to the conversation, while John uses his pointer finger to lazily twirl the straw inside of his mostly full glass of cherry-flavored Italian soda.

"And she says to me, she says Mister Johnson she says that 'up in space all there is is a bunch of cold, dead rocks millions of miles away, no use to nobody.' Can you believe it? I mean that's really what she says!" Garrett recounts dramatically.

"Yep, this supervisor of yours sure sounds like a real piece of work. And, if I'm being honest, what an incredibly unintelligent thing to say!" John exclaims in earnest. "The space race was a pivotal component in the Western defeat of the Soviet Union, and it gave humanity just about everything from memory foam to cell phone satellites. Not to mention solar power, which pretty much wasn't a thing the way it is now until people had to outfit deep-space probes with them. And that's just off the top of my head! Just, the absolute —"

"More importantly," G.J. interjects, "Joseph Mulenga *wants* this. He told me so himself."

"You talked to him again? Describe this interaction."

"Well." Garrett suddenly looks abashed, head sinking into his shoulders ever so slightly as he takes a gratuitous swig from his ale. "I know I wasn't *supposed to.* I mean, they reassigned me to a dead-end project in the Balkans, man! The fucking Balkans! And anyway, I did my best. He's not going to be taking any Americans' calls as long as..."

His voice fades away and John scrutinizes him.

"As long as what, exactly?"

Garrett's voice drops down to a conspiratorial whisper and he leans across the table.

"Director Agrawal is *dead-set* on this embassy project that's been in the works for the past couple of years. She absolutely refuses to hear me out on anything else and says it's my fault I can't land the deal that literally no person could ever land because THEY DON'T WANT IT IN ZAMBIA."

His face screws up into an expression of contrition for having raised his voice and (presumably) attracted the stares of people seated in the surrounding area. Once again he falls silent, but Nash refuses to interrupt the silence, sensing that the momentum of the story that Garrett is clearly itching to share will carry the rest of this part of the conversation.

"She gave me the reassignment," he says. "But I was feeling stubborn. And I had a hunch. I went through a diplomatic back channel and sent Joseph Mulenga a message. I told him I wanted to help him revive the Zambian space program. I even mentioned that I was doing it against the wishes of my supervisor. And I said I wanted to help his people reach for the stars."

"He responded?"

"He did. But not right away. The message was left on 'opened' for seven hours before I finally got a response in the dead of the night. It was one sentence: 'You have my attention.'"

John takes a sip from his soda and lets the flavor of the sweet cherry syrup start flirting with his taste buds as he mulls this over for a few moments. Finally, he swallows and says:

"I think I might know why she's obsessed with the embassy."

Garrett perks up and meets his eyes with a quizzical frown.

"You do?"

"I might."

Garrett's face lights up with eager expectation. John presses his tongue gently against the palate of his mouth, just about to divulge, when he is suddenly interrupted by the power-walking footsteps of their waiter.

"Gentlemen!" He announces, beaming, with his hands raised apart as though moved by the holy spirit in the middle of church. "What are your stomachs crying out for this evening, eh?"

This is it. Critical decision time. John has scarcely so much as glanced at the menu since sitting down, and in a blind panic his eyes begin running laps up and down the pages of it, while his mind opens up several new tabs to consider each possibility in turn. Whether Garrett Johnson knows it or not, at this very moment once and for all John is about to cement a verdict of evaluation in his head that will either be *for* or *against* him.

The expectant silence that follows the waiter's question is terrifying. Just as the pause is about to enter its agonizing fourth second, Garrett plows on ahead and tosses John a lifeline.

"Oscar," says Garrett contentedly, "I think I'll go with the beef bolognese."

And suddenly the decision John is about to make becomes clear. *Beef bolognese. Can't get more basic than that, besides spaghetti and meatballs.*

Across from John Nash, here sits a man of vanilla appetites.

"And I will have the squid ink spaghetti," John Nash says airily, sliding his menu to the edge of the table. The waiter records the orders of both men on his notepad while Garrett makes a nauseated face.

"Don't worry about it, my friend," John entreats, placing a comforting hand on Garrett's forearm, which presently rests on the table. "My family is Lebanese. I have been having squid ink pasta since I was a little boy."

Garrett's head pivots and he fixes his gaze on the waiter.

"Yes, ah, and it is quite the hoot in Sicily as well!" Oscar the waiter adds. "My grandmother, she used to make it for me with rocky mountain oyster meatballs, yes?"

He chuckles heartily and winks at John as Garrett goes from white as a hotel bed sheet to a sickly shade of green.

"Thank you, gentlemen, that will be all," Oscar says as he sticks the menus under his armpit and returns to the kitchens with a flourish.

John watches the waiter leave and turns back to face his dinner partner once he is sure Oscar is out of earshot.

"Now then. Where were we?" he asks, interlocking his fingers.

Garrett's face is still frozen in a slightly mollified expression.

"Nash... is squid ink really... *edible*?" He asks, his eyes silently conveying a deep concern that he may have to call up an undertaker before fetching the bill for the meal.

"Of course it is!" Nash exclaims with a grin. "Don't knock it 'til you try it."

"No thanks," Garrett says, scratching at his cheek. "I don't need to stain the insides of my mouth and stomach black tonight."

"Are you going to continue to judge my culinary choices or would you like me to continue with the subject at hand?"

"Sorry. What were you about to say?"

John Nash's Story

"This happened to me back in the Spring. I'm meeting with this woman, she's from the Department of Energy, real fresh-faced and petite lady, just to give you a mental picture here. And right away, because, well, I got this sense that she was troubled about something, based on her body language and this sort of wringing motion she was doing with her hands; because of that, I figured that whatever she wanted to talk to me about had to be quite a big deal, on account of how nervous she was. So she tells me she wants me to set her up with someone who's an expert on actuarial science, like logistics and projections and that sort of thing. So I tell her, I say 'I can do this, but can you give me some more specifics about this thing you need an actuary for, so I can tailor my work to your needs?' And now here comes another red flag, because she does not give me a straight answer to the question. In fact, she does not even give me the whole 'It's Classified' sort of spiel that I usually get from defense contractors and the like. Instead, she starts talking in circles, first describing this thing she needs help with as an 'initiative', then she calls it a 'policy proposal', then she starts to go off on a tangent about the ratification process of international climate treaties.

"I let her ramble for a few minutes, uninterrupted, but it feels like the conversation is going nowhere. By the time I've started digging for the actuarial questions, she has already started talking about international politics, which is like the last thing I was thinking about. So I say 'let me get back to you on this whole policy thing, if that's all right.'

"Anyway, this whole conversation goes nowhere, because this woman is starting to look really upset by now; again she starts mumbling about some things that are not at all related to anything I asked her. So I cut the whole conversation short and tell her 'Look, lady, I don't do this kind of work blindly, so I need to know more details before I can do this. If you are going to have me get someone to consult with you or your department or team or whatever it is, you are going to need to tell me something specific that I can start with. Otherwise, this meeting today will bear no fruit and I will have to let you return to your supervisors with nothing to show.'

"Now, she gets real red in the face after this. I can tell she's young and inexperienced and that sort of thing, and probably just a basket of nerves at this point, and probably what I said or the way I said it was a little bit undiplomatic. But I managed to pry out of her a general sense of what's going on. Apparently, the way she told it, she was the liaison of a Dee-Oh-Ee team making up one part of a larger inter-agency effort — *the largest* inter-agency effort in American history, in fact — to get an international climate change initiative off the ground successfully. They're billing it as the world's very first quadrillion dollar initiative, to really pull out all the stops on averting a global climatological catastrophe. Ambitious stuff, to say the least."

"Hold on. Why haven't I heard about it?" Garrett Johnson asks.

"Because it's in the formative stages, and as far as I can tell, every detail about this project is on a need-to-know basis. The powers that be, as it were, are doing everything they can to keep the public from finding out about this proposal at this point in time. I think they are worried about popular backlash, protest, bad publicity, that sort of thing. This woman I was meeting with, she tells me that the world leaders are getting very, very worried about this great disaster looming large on the horizon. This proposal, or this plan, or whatever you might call it, involves taking all the major energy-producing infrastructure of every country that signs on to it, and putting it under international management. All in the hopes of forcing a quicker transition to renewable energy and that sort of thing. But the catch, of course, is that it will require seizing power out of the hands of many people and putting it, operatively, in the hands of very few.

"There are many countries that will have to denationalize and sell off their energy resources to the United Nations, and many very wealthy people and their shareholders who will lose everything they have once private control of energy is also relinquished. And, as far as I can tell, very little oversight with regards to this international body that will now control the oil refineries and the solar farms and the hydroelectric generators and everything else in between. A number of elements that could produce significant social backlash, obviously, if word were to get out.

"This woman could not tell me how many countries are so far involved in the logistical development of this agenda, nor which other departments and agencies in D.C. were involved, although I imagine the number for both categories is quite great, and now I imagine we have a good case for the USAID department — is that a redundancy? — Anyways, your department's involvement as well. Either she did not know, or she could not say, but at any rate it does not matter now. By that point in the conversation I began to wrap my head around the sheer scale of such an operation and produced the contact information for one of my best people, which she gladly took, and thanked me. A week after the meeting I found out this woman I spoke to was no longer employed by the Department of Energy, or in fact anywhere in Washington, D.C. for that matter."

"What happened to her?" Garrett asks incredulously.

"Her supervisor apparently caught word that she had spoken out of turn, 'said too much', as it were, and decided to let her go. Within a week, she had skipped town altogether. Next week after that, I had a long string of meetings with people who would suddenly clam up and tell me that they were not legally allowed to divulge any information about their projects, so I am assuming low-level personnel involved in this grand plan were pushed to sign NDAs, or something like that."

"How come you didn't get caught?"

"A combination of factors, I suppose. On the one hand, luck probably had to do with it. They couldn't trace the first woman back to me, and after her of course no one was really directly giving me any more information. Still, sometimes silence speaks louder than words.

"On the other hand, I have a certain level of protection that federal employees lack, because the firm I work for is privately owned. That's how I can sit here and tell you these things right now without fearing for my life. I have not signed anything. You, on the other hand, should be very careful what you do with this information. I told a lawyer friend of mine about this grand international scheme not long after I first found out about it, and he was outraged. Once the woman I met with was terminated, he paid a visit to the FBI, demanding that they make an inquiry into the situation. I told him this was a bad idea, but nevertheless he would not listen. I told him, if the FBI are involved in this scheme in any way, and they don't like what you are doing, they can ruin your life, try to discredit you, even put child pornography on your computer and charge you for having it. It's been known to happen before."

"And what happened to him?"

"He ignored me, and in July the feds seized his laptop. After an investigation, all the relevant files and legal information were mysteriously corrupted, but according to the agent-in-charge the rest of the hard drive was intact and had more than a terabyte of kiddy porn on it."

"Jesus." Garrett has a look on his face, a colloid mixture of both anger and disbelief. "I can't believe this kind of thing is just happening right under our noses like that."

"Welcome to my life, Mister Johnson," John Nash says solemnly. "On the bright side, here comes the waiter with our food now!"

John smiles, but only with his mouth, as Oscar returns with heaping plates of steaming, aromatic food.

"Smells delicious!" he says, while Garrett remains silent.

The two men enthusiastically dig into their meals, with very little conversation between them. Nash strategically avoids engaging with Johnson's obvious discomfort, instead hoping to let him pick the thread of the conversation back up on his own initiative whenever he feels he is ready.

Twenty minutes pass.

Johnson's fork clinks against his plate.

"OK," he says. "OK."

Nash says nothing.

"I've been thinking," Johnson continues. "And my question is, what the hell is the next move?"

"Well," says Nash. "I am going to help you do something that will jeopardize your standing within your job and fundamentally screw with a deluded international elite's plans for world domination." He leans down, dabs at his face with the corner of the black tablecloth, and returns to an upright position to face Garrett once more. "I think it's time we took a trip to Africa."

Morning, August 5, 1998

Marissa awakens gently, eyelids languidly fluttering open to take in the light of the new day. Brilliant golden sunlight radiates into the bedroom, filling her tender eyes with its glow.

A moment ago, Marissa was envisioning herself baking Bundt cake in the kitchen, immersed in the idea of touching the whisk and smelling the vanilla, licking the batter off her fingertip. Now she finds herself anchored to her bed, staring at the clutter in her room, which consists of a pile of clothes tucked in the corner and various odds and ends from her makeup bag strewn atop her vanity table. The smell of the vanilla lingers, which Marissa realizes is coming from downstairs. Her mom is probably putting the finishing touches on the cake.

It's my birthday.

No matter how gentle the transition, the shift from the realm of dreams back to reality is always a little bit jarring for a person who lives in a world of silence. It used to be hard to cope with, so several years ago she got in the habit of keeping a daily dream journal, filling out a new entry every single morning. Presently there are three notebooks bound and stacked on top of the nightstand to her left, the bottom two entirely filled with entries from the first seven months of this year. Marissa pushes herself up to a seated position and gingerly cracks her back, her long blond hair falling chaotically around the margins of her vision.

As Marissa sits up, she catches a glimpse of herself in the vanity mirror. Sure enough, her hair is a disheveled mess, and the clothes she slept in are not fit for anyone's witness but her own. As soon as this matter of daily routine is dealt with, she'll need to put in some serious work to look presentable for this long-awaited birthday reunion with Tobias. A hot shower, some eyeliner, and just a dab of rouge would work wonders to put a little bit of life back into her appearance.

Pencils and pens for the dream journal are kept inside the top drawer of Marissa's nightstand, the knob of which has a tendency to fall off under the slightest application of force. Marissa decides to forgo the delicate art of attempting to reason with this fickle knob, choosing instead to pry the drawer open by working her fingers around the edges.

Marissa retrieves a pen and, after giving it a vigorous shake, rests the tip of it on top of the open page in her journal, reflecting for a moment on both the content and significance of her dream. As these things go, dreaming about Bundt cake is awfully mundane, really, but the takeaway is quite clear. Baking is one of Marissa's choicest activities for inner peace. She has spent the past several days in a state of mental unrest, but the prospect of a tranquil birthday in the company of her loved ones has finally started to turn her mood around.

After scribbling down some punctuated musings about the finer aspects of the culinary arts, Marissa returns the pen to its resting place. Her attention drifts back to her room, where she catches sight of a pale face peering around the edge of the now-open door. Marissa jumps, her heart suddenly racing, then she realizes that it's only her mom.

< Good morning! > mom signs, appearing to her daughter with an enthusiastic smile and several smears of frosting across her apron.

< Oh! Hey mom, > Marissa responds with an exaggerated look of surprise. < You gave me a bit of a scare there. >

< Tobias called ahead this morning. He's looking forward to seeing you again. I know this summer hasn't exactly lived up to your expectations, but he told me he's got something really cool to show you. >

< Did he say what it was? >

Must be a birthday gift of some sort, Marissa reasons. She racks her brain for all the possibilities. *'Really cool.'* That sounds like the kind of thing Tobias would say as the lead-up to a big joke. Knowing his twisted sense of humor, it could very well be an ice sculpture in the shape of a giant frog. By the most literal definition, that would certainly qualify as "cool". Or a pair of socks dipped in chocolate. Or a sparkly pink unicorn pen. Tobias has been known to always go all-out with his gag gifts, at once both hilarious and deeply personal.

They have only celebrated one other of her birthdays together in the 17 months since they first met, but there have been many occasions on which Tobias has bequeathed to her little tokens of his appreciation. From the very start, he has always recognized that Marissa is not a materialistic person, and that the best sort of gifts in her eyes are ones that have a great deal of thought put into them. Marissa has never known anyone to use humor as a gesture of love quite like Tobias.

< I guess you'll just have to wait and see, > her mother says, starting to back out of the room. < And when you've freshened up, you'll find a delicious breakfast with your name on it waiting in the kitchen. >

< Would that be the cake I smell? Cake for breakfast, mom? I mean, I won't say no, but that would be quite the scandal! > Marissa replies with a giggle.

< The cake is in the oven. The breakfast is ready for you on the stove. >

With that pronouncement, her mom slips out the door.

Everyone really is trying their best to make me happy today, Marissa realizes. *It feels so great to be loved.*

One self-gratifyingly indulgent shower later, Marissa finds herself peering into the abyss of her closet, contemplating the perfect birthday outfit. Finding herself indecisive, she turns her head on a pivot and scrutinizes the outdoors. The vibe for today is unmistakably golden. The world outside is bathed in a healthy, vibrant glow. Returning her attention back to the closet, her eyes go unfocused, then her vision resolves itself on a beautiful yellow sundress bespeckled with a muted floral print that looks like hundreds of tiny daisies — absolutely perfect for such an occasion as this.

Marissa slips into the dress without a moment's hesitation and uses a length of matching yellow-colored silk ribbon to tie her hair up into a bun. After just a few more carefully applied touch-ups, she heads out the door and bounds toward the kitchen with an utterly contented wave of warmth flowing through her bones.

Sunlight streams through the kitchen's open windows, accompanied by a gentle breeze. The breakfast is to die for. Freshly poached eggs, cooked to perfection sunny-side-up; crispy maple-smoked bacon strips with just the right amount of that texture and flavor which can only be derived from a long, slow char in the smoker; fresh and lightly buttered toasted bread and an abundance of hot and cold fruit, granola and yogurt on top. Plus, to top it all off, glasses of the freshest, most frothy milk filled all the way to the rim. Both of Marissa's parents are already in the kitchen, dad leaning against the wall next to the fridge and mom standing by the stove, waiting expectantly for their daughter's reaction. After she gleefully helps herself to a heaping plate of food, they follow after her and each get a plate of their own.

Marissa and her parents each find a seat at the table, which is covered for the occasion by a cotton sateen tablecloth adorned in a pattern of isometric polygons. As mom prays over the food, Marissa squeezes her eyes shut and clasps her hands to perform her own ritual of silent prayer. Her concentration is marred somewhat, however, by the aroma of not only the food on her plate but also the twin tantalizing scents of chocolate and vanilla emanating from the cake baking in the oven behind her.

< Amen. > Marissa's hands go flat on the table.

The family begins to chow down.

< What do you think of all the food? > Marissa's father asks her.

Marissa swallows her bite of bacon and licks her lips.

< It beats cornbread, that's for sure, > Marissa responds.

At this, Marissa watches her mom pull an exaggeratedly pouty face, pretending to look indignant.

< Not that you haven't perfected the art of cornbread making to an absolute science, > Marissa reassures her. < But one does tend to get a little bit sick of having it at least three times a week. >

< We know you're tired of corn, > her mom replies. < That's why we put together this special treat for you. >

Marissa smiles but does not respond, her hands busy with silverware. After waiting for her daughter to finish taking another bite, her mom elaborates further.

< In fact, even though you're too kind to admit it, we know you're getting a little bit tired of Nebraska too, > she signs. < Your father and I, we're in a bit of a tight spot, although we've *also* been a bit *too kind* to admit it. Even to ourselves, sometimes. > She casts a furtive glance in Rob's direction. < But we think that with the help we've got from those workers your father hired this summer, we should be able to dig ourselves out of the hole. In fact, after this harvest season, if all goes well, we will have enough money to let you transfer out of state in the Spring. What do you think? >

Marissa drops her fork on her plate in surprise and her father, sitting across the table, does a startled jump at the sound of the clatter.

< Seriously?! > She takes a moment to process the news. < Wow. >

The sun appears to shine a little brighter through the kitchen window.

July 3, 2014

Lance Morrissey has spent every waking moment of the past 30 hours in a fit of inconsolable rage, the kind of rage that burns the hottest because it is so uniquely personal that other people could not possibly relate unless they walked around in your shoes and experienced everything you experienced in the same particular way you experienced it. The kind that, because of its personal nature, would be in no way diminished or abated simply by being described or related to any other person.

The sun has long since set and the time readout on the digital clock on Lance's nightstand has just crossed past midnight, which means it is now July 3rd, which means it has been four days since anyone told him that he is special and, technically, two days on the calendar since Jaoquin Anderson seemed to unequivocally imply that he never wanted anything to do with Lance ever again.

Other than his dad, who could Lance talk to about anything anymore?

Lance sits on the side of his bed and lets his feet dangle, hanging some indeterminate distance above the carpeted floor in the dark, with only the moonlight streaming in through the window behind him to illuminate the bookshelf against the wall in front of him. From within the recesses of his mind, Lance remembers that he committed Cora and Anastasia's numbers to memory, and he decides, now that those numbers have resurfaced in his cognitive processes, that it might be a good idea to go ahead and write both of them down, just in case.

Once he nails down the mystery of the people and creatures that live under his tree fort– once he really, properly gets it– he'll be able to eloquently plead his case to those two girls, and they can tell everyone else in the grade that Lance Morrissey is not crazy. Maybe he can even produce proof. And maybe that'll even be enough to get Jaoquin Anderson to believe it, too. And maybe, just maybe, when all that happens, Lance will finally receive the respect he deserves that has been denied him for so long.

Lance drops down onto his knees and shuffles to the bookshelf, feeling around the books with his fingers until he finds what he's looking for.

There it is! In a book about dinosaurs that he has not looked at since the end of Elementary school, Lance finds a scrap of paper tucked in between two pages as a makeshift bookmark. Wasting no tears over losing his spot, Lance plucks this scrap out of its place without a second thought and shoves the book firmly back where he found it. Then he grabs a pen off the nightstand and scribbles the names of his two classmates alongside their cell phone numbers. With this sensitive information secure, Lance takes the scrap and puts it back in the dinosaur book in the same spot he found it, congratulating himself on his subterfuge: now, no one will know anything is out of place.

Looking out the window now, Lance can see the edge of the treeline at the perimeter of his backyard. He can feel, tangibly, the presence of that damned immaculate tree fort, almost skulking in the shadows just outside the glow cast by the moon. He can feel it, almost, mocking him. Tomorrow, he resolves, he will go out there again. Alone. So long as that hidden world refuses to show itself to another soul, he will have to be alone. He will force the tree fort to relinquish its secrets to him once again. He will meet with Binnmerva and Zhanniti and all the other improbable creatures and demand answers from them. He will demand that they be forthcoming and comprehensive, these answers, and satisfactory too, or he will tell them that his services as designated Chosen One will be withheld.

Lance shoves himself under his covers, which have somehow twisted around each other. He angrily fiddles with them, wrenching his hands and kicking his feet. His bare feet brush against something vaguely sedimentary. Crumbs. Lance had brought a bag of chips onto this bed a week ago, and though the bag had long since been disposed of, these were leftover crumbs from that day. Forcing a long exhale, Lance gets back off the bed. He stands in the middle of his floor and places his hands on his hips, regarding the situation in front of him with consternation. The sheets are a tangled, crumb-infested mess. Not only that, but the Star Wars characters on his comforter are upside down due to its inverted orientation on the bedspread. The whole situation is entirely unacceptable.

In one motion, Lance grabs everything off of his bed and sweeps it all onto the floor, revealing the bare mattress underneath. He forces another protracted exhale. Time to reset.

Afternoon, August 5, 1998

As her birthday continues to unfold, Marissa's appreciation for everything her parents have laid on the line on her behalf grows ever stronger. After breakfast and cake are done, she offers to go out and help bear the burden of the day's farm chores, but mom and dad both rebuke her in no uncertain terms ('The day is yours. Please enjoy it!' is her mom's impassioned plea). They head out the back door to join Jorge, Tomás, Enrique, Juan, and Don Pablo in the fields, where the corn has started to reach an advanced stage of germination and now needs to be carefully monitored for any possible signs of blight. Tomás especially seems to have an eye for this sort of thing, his hot dog-sized fingers surprisingly nimble in pushing aside the outer stalks without damaging them, in order to peer at the cobs in the inner rows. The corn has grown past the height of Marissa's shoulders, but for the big Hispanic men, it barely reaches their lower chest. All except for, of course, the comparably diminutive Jorge.

Marissa heads in the other direction, out the front door of the house, armed with little knowledge other than the promise of her mother that Tobias will soon be coming along, bringing that aforementioned surprise with him, along with some sort of grand plan to keep the two of them occupied for the entire rest of the day.

Presently as she steps out into the golden sunlight and feels the crunch of gravel underneath her white loafers, a thought begins to creep into the corners of Marissa's mind. Hazy at first, more of an intuitive hunch than a complete thought, but gradually solidifying into a comprehensive and startling realization of what she is probably about to walk into.

Oh.

It should have been so obvious, from the jump.

Probably, maybe, no almost definitely certainly, she knows what surprise Tobias is about to spring on her.

He's going to ask me to marry him.

Like, duh. That's what all this coordinated fanfare has been all about. The birthday surprise, the sudden declaration from mom that life at the farm will be over soon, that she'll finally be able to leave home and go out in the world and actually *be a real woman* and not just a little girl anymore.

In a moment, months and months of accumulated fantasy have suddenly crystallized into hard reality. Marissa might very well be handed the chance to have everything she's been craving all this time. This is the best thing that has ever happened in her life.

And all of a sudden, it is also the most terrifying.

Marissa stops dead in her tracks. A gust of wind flicks at her nose as she considers the place where she stands. In front of her on the path is a flowering magnolia tree. It seems to beckon her ever onward. Behind her, the outstretched tendrils of a weeping willow. Its wispy foliage seems to be pleading for her to turn back around, mourning the lapsing of her childhood.

She could turn around now, go back home and tell mom and dad to tell Tobias that she's suddenly come down with something. A part of her wants to turn and run, now, from the fear.

Because what if I'm not ready?

Marissa shuffles backward a few paces until her upper back bumps up against the sturdy trunk of the willow. There she rests for a moment and does what 19 years of heartland sentiment have taught her to do when she can't make up her mind. She bows her head and prays.

Please, she thinks, *please, God, whatever you think I should do, please.* She turns around, resting her forehead against the tree's bark. *Please let me make the right decision.*

Exactly 200 seconds later, Marissa's fingers are enclosed around the handle of the passenger side door of Tobias's Ford Taurus.

She swings the door open and affixes her soon-to-be fiance with a critical eye.

< Well, you certainly dressed for the occasion, > she signs.

Tobias shrugs.

< I think I look pretty cool, > he responds, pointing his chin to the sky with pride.

Presently, Tobias is wearing a bow tie and a tweed jacket, looking like he just left a meet-and-greet for preppy economists. A musky scent hangs around him like a cloud. Clearly, he got a little heavy-handed this morning with a bottle of cologne. The smell is far from entirely unpleasant, however.

< I *was* thinking about turning around before, but now I might just have to for this crime against fashion, > Marissa tuts, feigning disgust.

< Turning around? Earlier? Why? > Tobias does that eyebrow raise thing he always does when he senses Marissa is withholding information from him.

< Just feeling a little nervous. >

< Why would you be nervous? Is everything alright? What's wrong? >

Tobias unbuckles his seatbelt and leans forward, trying to get a closer look at his girlfriend's expression in the light.

< Never mind. Forget it, > Marissa responds, sliding into the car and taking a seat.

< You sure? > Tobias flashes another worried look.

Marissa buckles her seatbelt and avoids his gaze, pretending to suddenly find the road in front of them incredibly captivating.

< Just drive. >

And so Tobias does, although a slightly nervous grimace never drifts too far away from his eyes or mouth as he deftly maneuvers the car, first past the usual neighborhood sights, and then into a hidden entrance between two trees, which leads onto a back road Marissa has never seen before.

There's not a whole lot of "new" in Nebraska, so Marissa finds herself a little bit in awe at the fact that beyond this turn there exists a whole part of her hometown whose existence she has been entirely ignorant of.

All the streets here have no names. No names, and no numbers, and all the roads look the same: dirt, rocks, trees. But the confidence Tobias is exuding at present suggests that he will nevertheless have no trouble reaching his destination.

After a few more minutes of backroads travel, Tobias puts the car in park at the top of a hill and looks at Marissa.

< Took me a few days to nail down exactly how to get here, > he explains. < I found it by accident the first time. >

< Where is 'here' exactly? >

< You'll see. > Tobias looks excited. < Get ready to have your mind blown. >

He puts the car into drive and grips the steering wheel with awesome determination. Then he takes his foot off the brake and places it squarely on the accelerator, stomping down with all his might and sending the car down the hill at a top speed easily exceeding 80 miles per hour.

Marissa feels a scream escape from her throat, the car vanishes into the gaping maw of a covered bridge, and the world goes black.

The darkness disappears and the world comes back into focus, awash in light and color. Tobias turns to his right and regards Marissa, observing her frozen mid-wince with eyes squeezed shut, chin tucked downward, and hands clasped on the back of her head. He taps her on the shoulder gently and she comes back up to look at him. He gives her a friendly wave along with an apologetic smile. She gives no visible response and continues to stare blankly ahead.

< You alright? > He signs to her.

Once again, no response. Marissa continues to stare at him. A muscle in the corner of her eye twitches.

< Marissa, what's going on? >

There is a dull ringing in Marissa's ears. She screws her eyes shut.

This is not supposed to be possible.

She suffered from tinnitus for a while after the incident that had deprived her of hearing, but it gradually went away. It's been a long time — almost a decade — since Marissa has experienced *anything* of the sort.

Something is touching her shoulder. It's Tobias, it would have to be Tobias. The ringing intensifies as she opens her eyes and tries to focus on him.

He's signing something now, but Marissa can't get her thoughts organized enough to follow along. The ringing is starting to resolve itself now; it's expanding into a wider spectrum of noise.

Marissa continues to stare at Tobias. He signs something else at her, and after she again fails to respond, he thumps his fist on the steering wheel.

Marissa jumps.

Holy shit. This can't be happening. *I just heard that.*

It was muffled, but that was a *real*, tangible sound. And she just *heard* it.

Tobias continues to watch Marissa as she holds her gaze on him. Then, to his complete surprise and bewilderment, she begins mumbling under her breath. It's incoherent at first, barely audible and without form, but within a few seconds her mumbling becomes louder.

"What the hell is going on?" Tobias asks out loud.

"Heh," says Marissa.

"Marissa?"

"Oom."

"Marissa, can you... Can you hear me?"

Now that he's asked the question out loud, it feels completely stupid. But to his utter surprise, Marissa nods. She screws her face in concentration.

"Hello, Toby," she finally says.

Tobias instantly bursts into a massive grin. He flings his seatbelt off and does a bit of an awkward jig inside his seat, shaking his fists and kicking his feet a little bit, clearly unable to contain himself at the miracle presently unfolding in front of him.

"No way!" He exclaims. "No way!"

He chuckles to himself. Marissa watches him, feeling a little bit overwhelmed. Their eyes meet and Tobias's chuckle transforms into hysterical laughter. Marissa finds that she can't help but join in. And so, together, they quietly laugh for what seems like a very long time. Without inhibition, without reservation, just the sheer impossible joy of the moment. Tobias's laugh is warm and inviting, tenderly heartfelt. This is the first time Marissa has ever heard it. It's better than any birthday present, better than a ring. This is quite possibly the greatest gift Marissa has ever received.

"Let's get out of this car," Tobias finally says, struggling for breath.

"Yeah," Marissa says, eager to finally turn a hearing ear to the outside world once again.

Outside of the car lies a utopic paradise, full of natural beauty in resplendent hues. The car is parked amidst a perfectly undisturbed field of flowers, which stretches out into the horizon along gentle rolling hills. At the center of it all, some 100 feet away from where Marissa now stands, is a babbling brook. Marissa moves to approach it and gazes into the waters. Some flower petals float lazily on the surface, but other than that the water is clear and pure. In fact, it looks clean enough to drink from. A number of flies and beetles buzz around the waters, and Marissa, despite being no particular fan of bugs, nevertheless finds herself delighted to hear the sounds they make, along with the steady trickle of the water.

Marissa finds a nice spot by the edge of the brook and sits down among the flowers. She folds her legs into a pretzel and lets her fingers drift idly along the petals. This particular patch is a brilliant blue — cornflowers, by the looks of it — and their petals are silky soft against the flesh of Marissa's fingers. She closes her eyes and takes several slow, deep, deliberate breaths, allowing herself to feel truly grounded where she sits.

Hearing — the sensory input Marissa has spent so long without — now paints the picture around her as she gives her vision a rest. Distant birdsong calls from an unseen source, avian frolickers telling each other secrets only they can understand. The water in the brook continues to babble, contributing its own set of mysterious stories. Now, behind her, soft footsteps parse through the grass. Without even looking, Marissa knows it is Tobias. She does not open her eyes or say a word as he takes a seat next to her.

"These flowers are the color of your eyes," Tobias says.

"They're beautiful," Marissa replies as she continues to listen.

"Yes, they are."

Tobias gingerly takes Marissa's hand from the place on the ground where it rests by her side, and holds it in his own. She opens her eyes and looks at him. His eyes are deep and earthy. They contain a story all to themselves, belying an intellectual curiosity, a humorous warmth, and — somewhere buried below the surface — a bittersweet tragedy that has yet to be spoken aloud or shared.

"What do you think?" he asks her.

"I'm overwhelmed," she replies. Marissa studies Tobias's piercing gaze, wondering when he will pop the question.

"It occurs to me," Tobias says pensively, "that this is the first time we've ever been able to have a conversation out loud. Do you know, I've sometimes wished we could do this. But now that we can, I don't even know what to say."

"I'm a little out of practice myself," Marissa admits drily. "I forgot what my own voice sounds like."

She thinks for a moment.

"Let alone yours," she adds.

"How did you think I'd sound?" Tobias asks. "Does it, you know, does it live up to what you imagined?"

"I don't know," Marissa says thoughtfully. "I guess maybe I imagined it was a little deeper or something. Your voice, I mean."

"Yeah?" says Tobias. "Huh."

The two hold hands and sit in silence for several moments as the birdsong and the noise from the water and the bugs continues to drone on. A gentle breeze creeps in and leaves a lingering tingle down Marissa's spine.

"What do you think of this place?" Tobias asks.

"It's marvelous," Marissa replies.

"Yeah, I think it's marvelous."

"But it's not like how you described it."

"Oh? How did I describe it?"

"My mom said that you said it was 'cool'."

Tobias nods and chuckles.

"Then maybe I was underselling it," he muses.

Marissa uses her free hand to toss a pebble absentmindedly.

"Tobias, do you believe in miracles?" she asks.

"Since I know you can now hear me answer it, I think my response to that question given the events of today is gonna have to be yes," Tobias replies.

"I had a teacher in school once who said that everything was random and that we're, you know, that everything just ended up the way it was by accident, and I think I've always known that just wasn't true," Marissa says. "Felt it in my bones, like, I guess it's just a foregone conclusion. I know things happen for a reason. They just have to."

"Everything is caused by something," Tobias responds. He smacks his lips. "We invoke randomness as an excuse for not knowing what's really going on."

He sits and thinks for a few seconds.

"I studied statistics once," he says at last. "And they always talk about, like, flipping a coin or rolling dice as the perfect examples of randomness. But I had a thought that if you flipped the coin or rolled the dice in the *exact* same way every time, like, every micro... you know, movement, every tiny motion exactly the same, perfectly replicated, then you would have to get the same result every time."

"Right," Marissa says, nodding slowly.

"Let's say you roll a three on your dice. It had to, you know, turn, a specific number of times while it was in the air, and then it had to land on the table in that specific orientation. If you could invent a robot that would make the same roll with mechanical perfection, the dice would turn in the air the same number of times every time, and you would always roll a three. And it's the same thing with that coin."

"And if you didn't know that a robot was rolling the dice?" Marissa asks rhetorically.

"Then when you rolled a three over and over and over again you'd probably assume you were getting really darn lucky," Tobias replies.

"Yeah, exactly," Marissa says. "So you agree that everything happens for a reason?"

"Well, for some reason, yeah. Whether it's all part of some prearranged plan or... or whatever, I'll probably never know." Tobias uses his free hand and starts fidgeting with the flowers in front of him, pulling some out from their roots and playing with their petals. Then he continues his musings. "I believe there is a God. I was raised on the Sunday school Bible stories. I don't know how you have your hearing back, but I'd bet He's got something to do with it. But whatever the plan is, I just don't know."

Marissa and Tobias's hands separate and slowly drift apart. Marissa uncrosses her legs and stretches them out in front of her.

"Tell me again," Marissa says slowly. "How did you find this place?"

Tobias tosses a handful of flower petals into the water and Marissa watches the current carry them downstream and past her.

"By accident at first," he says. "I was driving home on a foggy night and I got lost."

"Accident, huh?"

"Well, now you mention it, okay. Maybe not. Maybe it was meant to be."

Tobias throws up air quotes at the last three words and Marissa smiles.

"So what do you want to do now?" asks Tobias, rising to his feet and wiping some dirt off his knees as he does so.

"Why don't we explore the place a little bit?" Marissa suggests, pulling herself up to a standing position as well. "It's so crazy back at home, and I could stay out here all day."

"Yeah," says Tobias agreeably. "We could totally do that."

With scarcely a further word exchanged, Tobias and Marissa spend the next hour scouring the beautiful flower garden to uncover its secrets. One thing that jumps out to both of them as they continue to explore is the great abundance of edible plants in the garden's outer perimeter, where the flowers meet the edge of the thick and impenetrable woods. Marissa spots raspberry bushes, several clusters of honeysuckle, and even some Jack-in-the-pulpit which she had learned to distinguish by the hooded pocket on its side; these are starting to develop spots of bright red berries, typical for the season.

Tobias, meanwhile, stumbles upon a patch of tall grasses which, upon being uprooted, reveal small bulbous onions hiding just under the soil. After cleaning one off with his shirt and giving the matter some deliberation, he eats from it, finding its taste bitter but not altogether unpleasant.

Suddenly Tobias screams as his reverie is interrupted by an unexpected and entirely unwelcome touch on his lower back, which comes roughly and without warning. He whips around, ready to fight the culprit, but is surprised and relieved to find that it is only Marissa. He drops his guard and apologizes.

"It's just — you know how I am about getting approached from behind without warning," he says.

"Right," Marissa says soothingly. "Didn't mean to startle you."

"What's up?" he asks. "You know, I noticed there's a lot of edible plants in this field. You've got the knack for foraging that I don't have, but I'm pretty sure this is an onion." He holds up the bite-marked plant so that Marissa can see it.

"Right on the money," Marissa agrees.

Tobias scrutinizes her carefully.

"You've had an idea, haven't you?" he says. "I can, like, see it in your eyes. What are you thinkin' about?"

"Toby, it's been a long time since I last heard music," Marissa says. "And we've got a car, and the car's got a radio."

Tobias's eyes light up.

"Yeah!" he says. "Hey, that's a great idea! I could put something on, we could jam out. That'd be awesome."

The two walk hand-in-hand back to the Taurus, Tobias leading the way and both of them skipping along merrily.

"You've missed out on all the hits for, what? At least the last decade? You've been robbed!" Tobias exclaims as he puts the key in the ignition and switches the stereo on.

Marissa slips into her seat on the passenger side of the car as the radio bursts out a crackle of static and picks up in the middle of the chorus of a soft rock song from 1992. She takes deep breaths as the lead guitarist's infectious chords and the main vocalist's wispy words, touched by the slightest tinge of a Scottish accent, wash over her.

"Del Amitri, I'm pretty sure," Tobias supplies helpfully as Marissa nods along.

"God, I forgot how much I missed music," Marissa says wistfully. It colored all of her earliest memories, but all the time spent without it had turned those memories into a fevered haze. She begins to hum along to the melody, voice unsteady and warbling at first as she re-adjusts to the intervals between pitches. Tobias joins in, and after a couple of repetitions they belt out the lyrics to the chorus together and continue in a haphazard but nevertheless rhapsodical fashion until the current song comes to an end and acoustic noodling, marking the start of the next song, begins to fade in.

"Tobias," Marissa says, turning to look at her boyfriend.

"Yeah?" he responds, turning to meet her.

"This is going to sound totally cliche, but this really has been a *perfect* day. I mean, this place, it's *beautiful*. And I feel like we kind of glossed over this almost, but the fact that I can actually *hear* things, that's literally nothing short of a biblical miracle. I'm not even going to begin to guess how that's possible. For all I know, this could be a dream. But I really hope not."

"Does it feel like a dream?"

Marissa thinks the question over for a moment, and it actually troubles her.

"No," she says self-consciously, crossing her arms and tapping her fingers.

Tobias slowly reaches over and pokes her in the cheek with his pointer finger.

"Boop!" he exclaims.

"Tobias, you dork!"

"See? Not a dream."

"Nope, not a dream. A genuine, honest-to-God, miracle. The bigger miracle? The fact that today I haven't even once thought about corn or the harvest season or my dad's weirdly violent Mexican workers, or any of that stuff. Not once! Not since we got here, at least. Um, but there's just one thing that I'm not sure about."

"Yeah?" Tobias asks, confused. "What are you not sure about?"

"I thought you would have popped the question by now, honestly," Marissa confesses. "I didn't– I'm not sure if– well, I thought it would be awkward to bring it up but, you know, if you're afraid, that's totally cool. I'm afraid too! But now would be the perfect time to ask me, you know? And you know, I would say yes!"

"Uh, the question? Oh, holy shit!" Tobias goes white as a sheet. "You mean, you thought I was going to ask you to marry me?"

"Yeah, this was really, uh, shaping up kind of like, in the direction of a proposal, you know?" Marissa struggles to explain. "My parents, they said I don't have to work on the farm any more, if this harvest season goes well. I have an actual future now. And I want to spend it with you! And this was literally the best birthday ever. So I kind of thought..."

"Damn. I mean, uh–" Tobias clears his throat and picks his next words very carefully. "Dang. Darn. Wow! I– I do not have a ring. I was not planning to ask you to marry me today. Not because I don't want to! I'm not– like, I'm not holding out or anything. I'm not– you know, un-commited or anything like that."

"What's up then, Tobias?" Marissa asks.

"Honestly, I'm afraid," Tobias confesses, holding his hands out in the air, palms facing the ceiling of the car. "I don't want to rush into anything."

"I'm confused," says Marissa. "Lots of people get married at your age. You've got decent career prospects. You're almost 22,

I'm 20 now. I mean– by all means, I respect it, but I just. I don't know. We've known each other for far more than a year now. I just– I guess I just thought that, you know, the time had come and this was it."

"Yeah." Tobias goes silent and stares very hard into the horizon. The radio continues trailing along, with a female vocalist performing staccato vocal lilts that punctuate the otherwise tense mood in the car. Tobias switches the music off and the car falls into stone cold silence. Finally he continues talking.

"I know I can't wait forever," he says. "But I'm just not ready yet. I– you know I'm a very guarded person, and I really can't help it. Things happened to me when I was younger– it... being married opens the door to a domain that I'm afraid to explore. I don't know what might happen."

"You've mentioned your past before, although I still don't know the full story. I can only fill in the blanks in my mind," Marissa says. "But whatever it was– even if you don't feel comfortable talking about it right now– we can deal with it together. We can have that conversation, I can help you process whatever it is. Letting it fester? That won't– that's not gonna solve your problem. You know I'm always available to listen. Especially now, more than ever. Now I can *really* listen. So just, whenever you feel up to it, lay it on me."

Tobias stares into Marissa's soul with the force of a thousand suns.

"I love you," he whispers, seeming to be holding back tears. He puts the car in reverse. "Let's go back home."

"OK." Marissa nods and lets out a slow, forceful exhale. She turns her head and fixes her gaze on the scenery passing by out the window, falling almost into a trance.

The field of flowers passes out of view and the world goes dark for a moment until the car re-emerges from the mouth of the covered bridge. Juxtaposed with the Edenic scene they've just left, this part of the forest looks so much more comparatively drab, even gloomy. Whatever spark of magic was in the air is now gone.

The car continues to drift noiselessly through the woods, taking Marissa back down the familiar roads of her childhood as she passively watches.

Finally it pulls up in front of the dirt road leading back to the farmhouse, that old pockmarked dusty track that has seen cattle and trucks and so many other things tread upon it.

Tobias regards his girlfriend with a careful eye while she continues to look out the window, away from him. Girlfriend. A word that becomes more awkward the older the two of them become. One day, he will have to call her something different. Fiancé. After that, his wife.

What a weighty word.

"This is it! End of the line!" Tobias announces, trying to put some cheer back into his voice as he throws his car into park. "I don't know when we'll get together again, might be awhile because I'll probably have to do a ton of paperwork to make up for this spontaneous 'sick day', and besides I've only got so many I can use in a year anyway, so... you ok?"

He gives Marissa another poke and at last she turns to look at him. The expression on her face is deeply forlorn, a bitter mixture of disappointment and fear.

< I can't hear any more, > she signs. < I can't hear the birds, I couldn't hear the car, and I can't hear you. >

October 14, 2033

John Nash and Garrett Johnson sit across from each other in the first-class compartment of a Boeing 787. Nash, sporting a cream-colored suit and a pair of aviators, is cool and collected. He sips from an olive-topped martini and allows himself to savor the relaxing journey. His companion, on the other hand, is taciturn and sick-looking. Garrett's legs jiggle nervously and his doughy complexion has dropped a few registers into more pallid territory. He hums tunelessly to himself and fidgets with his hands.

"What's the problem?" Nash asks coolly.

"I can't stand altitude changes, I'm sorry. And the turbulence..." Garrett tenses up and feels a cold shiver run a lap down his spine.

"Just relax. We're fine."

Garrett nods but his body language remains unchanged.

"Do you want some gum or something?" Nash asks, preparing to reach into his breast pocket.

"I'll be fine. How much longer is it?"

John Nash looks at his watch, which currently has a widget enabled tracking the path of the flight.

"We'll be touching down for our layover in two hours, Garrett. Now try to relax."

"Okay."

Nash shakes his head and ignores his friend's neuroticism, taking another sip from his martini. *This is what happens,* he reasons. *A man goes 40, maybe 50 years living a completely unremarkable life. What does that make him? A weakling, scared to death of his own shadow.*

Gazing across the aisle that divides the passenger compartment of this plane lengthwise, he locks eyes with Jeanette

Emberley, the consultant from NASA he hand-picked for this assignment due in small part to her expertise in astrophysics and in larger part to her being the niece of Joseph Mulenga's brother-in-law, a factor that could play favorably if Nash's suspicions of the Zambian politician's soft nepotistic tendencies prove to hold true.

Jeanette's resting face is stern and unreadable, giving a mildly acquainted observer the sense that she is permanently regarding the world with an air of cool disdain. However, as she reciprocates eye contact with Nash, her dark features soften somewhat as she gives the man a reassuring nod, communicating without words that she is comfortably equipped for the business ahead of them.

Returning his martini back to its cupholder, Nash leans back in his seat and closes his eyes. The plane's flight is actually unusually smooth. The turbulence Garrett mentioned seems to be a figment of the anxious agent's paranoid imagination. He could probably get a brief snooze in, before the plane touches down. In fact, that doesn't seem like a half-bad idea.

"Wake me up when we're in Africa," he tells Garrett, before his thoughts go fuzzy and he drifts off into a pleasant slumber.

Compton, 1990

"Shit nigga, this the bullshit you pull that pisses me off. You be sayin shit like this and you ain't even really sure, you don't got no proof or nothing, and you expecting me and everyone else to believe you."

"All's I said is I think Dante a opp."

"You said you THINK Dante a opp, AND you be saying don't give him none of his cut on the next deal. Like you saying you *think* he a snitch but you be acting like you *know* he a snitch, so which is it, huh? Either you blowin' hot shit out yo ass, or you holdin' out on us with real proof."

"Man, 's just what I believe."

"What you believe, Carlo? Fuck, man, when you husslin and shit you can't afford to just go around believin shit just cuz you read sum'n somewhere and you think that, like, maybe this nigga Dante a opp because he be acting in a way that you thought you overheard is how opps act. Like, trust is a two-way street in this hussle and we can't be alienating niggas without proof. You know who can afford to go around believing shit they ain't got no proof for? White bitches who don't gotta worry about if the shit they believe is real. We sell to these white crackhead motherfuckers running around like the feds got bugs all over the place or the feds got niggas who can control the weather and shit, and the reason they can afford to believe that bullshit is because it don't matter if they wrong. Conspiracy shit."

"You sayin we shouldn't be vigilant? Ain't got to keep a eye out for snakes in our midst?"

"Nigga, you cracked in the head or some shit? I'm saying, like, the opposite of that, damn it. The only reason them white motherfuckers get away with believing the shit they be sayin is because it don't matter if what they say ain't true, they ain't gotta own the consequences of what they out here tellin people. When you live like us, allies is few and far between in this bitch, you *can't* be too careful. But you gotta verify the shit you believe. You can't be noiding out and shit thinking every nigga plotting to end you."

"Shit man, pipe down real quick. White kid about to pass by."

Tobias roams the unfamiliar downtown streets with a chill crawling up and down his spine and a general sense of unease threatening to unearth the contents of his stomach. Every dark corner could be concealing a bevy of unknowable dangers, and it feels as if the entire city is holding its breath in anticipation. His eyes dart around the shadows, darting away from windows lit by the pulsating lights, desperate to spot any sign of a lurking enemy. As he passes by a dark alley between two ramshackle apartment complexes, Tobias takes notice of two men dressed in black standing there, having a hushed conversation with each other. Perceiving that they, too, have become aware of his presence, he averts his gaze and fixates straight ahead of him, continuing at a steady pace onward.

Until now, he had never considered that he might go to a city as dangerous as Compton at night, but the feelings that Tobias has been saddled with for the past 18 months have been so overwhelming, so devastating, that he feels almost obligated to continue on his current course, now that he is so close to a resolution.

It has been a rough time.

Shortly before his twelfth birthday, something extraordinary and almost medically unprecedented happened to Tobias, as he grew from 4'10" to almost six feet tall in the course of just a few months. The skeletal growth was too much for his skin and muscles to handle, and it put him in excruciating, immobilizing pain. After a few days of life as a bed-ridden invalid, Tobias tearfully demanded that his parents try every medical technique available to get him sorted out. And so they did, lining up experimental hormone treatments, homeopathic brews, physical therapy sessions, and even a few elective surgeries. The doctors, nurses, and therapists did what they could, but the entire process was long and devastating, both physically and emotionally.

Tobias spent those months at home, mostly curled up in bed. All his school materials were either mailed in or periodically dropped off at his house by other students. Finally, when it seemed the growth had slowed down to a rate somewhat approximating normalcy, Tobias returned to school and attempted to readjust to normal tweenage living.

Unfortunately, the deck was stacked against him from the start.

In the first place, because of the delay from the mailing and a number of cognitive and motivational side effects from the treatments, Tobias found himself being several weeks behind his classmates on the concepts in his classes, and struggled to keep his grades above failing level. He felt out of place amongst his friends, many of whom had grown apart from each other in his absence, and his new hyper-awareness of his body made him feel freakish and exponentially more socially awkward. His nerves prevented him from being able to maintain even the most basic of chit-chat, and within a couple weeks he was almost entirely alone.

Tobias roamed the halls of his middle school, towering above everyone else, feeling like a freak. In all other respects besides his height, he was a late bloomer; his voice had yet to drop, his muscles had not filled out, and he hadn't even had his first crush on a girl. To make matters worse, the hormone treatment he was on had caused subcutaneous breast growth, which he hid under gigantic hoodies that made him unbearably hot in the late spring and summer months.

Gradually he began to wonder if he was queer.

The realization, or the aftermath of the recognition of this self-perception, brought along with it an additional heap of issues. Self-loathing mingled with self-disgust, a toxic brew which festered and turned into elaborate acts of self-harm. Acting out, picking fights, seeking dangerous risks, tempting a death sentence by decree of Murphy's law... Behind the backs of his fraught and overworked parents, Tobias stopped going to classes, falling in with a group of truants whose alternative lifestyles (goth, alt, stoner, and so on) were so aesthetically shocking to polite society that passers by were far more likely to take exception to his association with them (a factor Tobias had full control over) than his own emergent homosexuality (a factor which Tobias believed he had no control over whatsoever).

And as for his parents – God bless them – they tried their best to make sense of their son's behavior. Tearful admonitions for Tobias to just stay in school, to stay away from those bad influences, to just get a grip(!) were made in vain as their son, acting more out of concealment than rebellion, would often disappear without so much as a by or leave and refuse to breathe a word about where he was or what he was doing.

Tobias had a friend named Luisa – at the time one of his closest confidants, actually – who afforded him a great deal of pity and empathy. Leaning over her lunch platter, she once told him in hushed tones so that no one else in the cafeteria would hear about her older cousin, a family pariah that she knew virtually nothing about other than that he lived in uptown Compton and had a boyfriend. The subject was dropped and almost forgotten about until, one week later, she proudly slid a slip of paper across Tobias's table at the start of first period with the address of her cousin's apartment written on it. When Tobias got a chance to ask her about it later that day, Luisa refused to elaborate on how she had procured this address until he made a promise to her that he would indeed go there and talk to the guy.

This is the sequence of events that has brought Tobias to where he is now, standing in front of a dingy pharmacy, squinting at a damp scrap of torn looseleaf, and anxiously peering into the wet, smoke-filled alleyways around him. The pharmacy is positioned directly across the street from Tobias's destination, a crucial piece of intel related to him by Luisa after she had gotten ahold of a street-level map of the city. Its fluorescent storefront lighting casts the street whose name is inscribed on the scrap in a sickly yellow glow. Scanning the feebly lit darkness, Tobias at long last sees the metal number for Apartment 11. Success!

Even at this time of night the city is filled with a glut of people. Pedestrians bustle by as drivers speed down the road, deftly navigating between the rows of parallel-parked beaters sequentially arranged in front of the apartments and in front of the pharmacy. Homeless crackheads in dirty clothes panhandle in front of the buildings on either side of the block, and at the corner of the street a listless prostitute sways from foot to foot. In the midst of all of this, a scared 12 year-old Tobias finds himself a crosswalk and makes ready to ford the sea of humanity.

As he walks past the vagrants lounging outside the buildings on this street in piles of their own filth, Tobias can't help but feel a mixture of fear laced with pity. Head held high, he assumes a posture of confidence and single-mindedness as he blocks out the feeble groans of the city's woebegotten and strides onward.

Upon arriving in front of the eleventh edifice on the block, Tobias is surprised to find the entrance to the apartment building unlocked, opening with barely a touch. Inside, the dimly-lit landing smells like wet carpet and two diverging staircases avail themselves to him. One goes up into shadow, the other goes down into darkness. Inferring that the unit belonging to Luisa's cousin, 3C, must be on the third floor, he takes tentative steps up the escalating stairway.

The boards on the stairs creak under Tobias's unsteady gait. Releasing a breath and hoping not to wake a soul, he eases the pressure on the balls of his feet and quickly scurries up the next two flights.

Unit 3C is tucked in the back corner opposite the apartment's third landing and wreathed in a haze of darkness. Timidly, Tobias taps gently on the door and waits for a moment. After a beat, he recoups his courage and knocks more confidently once, twice, then thrice.

"Yes?" a muffled voice calls from inside. Tobias listens to the sound of his own exhalation and remains silent. Then the door swings open, basking him in stark yellow. A portly man stares up at him.

"And who are you, darling?" the man asks. He wears a patterned tank top, a scruffy mullet, and an even scruffier goatee. He peers at Tobias through shaded glasses.

"Toh- my name is Tobias," the boy mumbles to the stranger. "Luisa sent me?"

The man shifts his posture and beams, showing yellowed teeth.

"Tobias! Yes, please do come in, hon!"

The man opens the door a little wider and beckons Tobias to follow. Immediately inside is a lounge area with a green sofa, a coffee table in front of it, and an analog television set placed against the wall, presently playing a cheap-looking movie Tobias does not recognize. Directly to one side of the lounge is a kitchenette and dining area, while in the opposite direction lies a short hallway with a closed door buttressing either side.

Tobias trails Luisa's cousin, who positions himself to block the door they had just entered through and watches him expectantly. Feeling pressured to initiate further conversation, Tobias clears his throat and speaks.

"Luisa said you could help me with some questions I have, about, like, myself."

The man bares his teeth again.

"I think I can, bud. Why don't you start by telling me a little bit about yourself?"

Tobias shifts his weight, feeling uncomfortable with the uneven dynamic.

"Um..." he says. "You go first."

"I'm Francesco. You can call me Frank," the man says. "I'm Luisa's cousin, and as you probably guessed, I'm gay." Frank grins, showing his teeth again.

"Okay," says Tobias.

"Don't go looking at me any different for that, dear!" Frank admonishes. "There's absolutely nothing wrong with being a queer, even if not everyone tends to agree."

"How do I, um- How do I know if I am one?" Tobias asks with trepidation.

"*One* what?" Frank asks jovially. He removes his tinted glasses and drapes them on the neck of his tee. "A homo? A fag? A stark raving fairy? That's what you're here to find out, right?"

Shifting uncomfortably on his feet, Tobias nods.

"Please, take a seat on my couch. Make yourself comfy, darling!" Frank cries.

Tobias makes his way over to the couch, which is covered in tatters and smells a little funny. Meanwhile, Frank rummages in the kitchen for a moment. Taking stock of his environment, Tobias decides it probably wouldn't be too much of a social coup de gras to put his feet up on the coffee table, and proceeds to do just so. A drop of puddle water from the street wicks off his shoe, but quickly disperses on the table's wooden surface in a matter of seconds as Tobias watches.

Just then, Frank drops a glass bowl on the table between Tobias's feet. Tobias notices for the first time patterned stains on the tips of Frank's fingers. The bowl is filled with clumps of dry vegetative matter that Tobias infers to be cannabis or something similar.

"Have you ever been high before?" Frank asks conversationally as he sits down next to Tobias on the couch, pinches some hash from the bowl, and begins working it into a piece of rolling paper.

"No, never," Tobias answers. "What's it like? Is it scary?"

"Honey," Frank chuckles drily. "Everything's scary until you go through it. Then it's just another thing that's happened."

He pointedly produces a lighter from his pocket and proceeds to wave the flame around the unpinched end of his rolled joint. He takes a deep sup from the blunt and sighs, exhaling the smoke with a flamboyant flourish. Tobias watches laconically. Then Frank pinches the joint between his fingers and wordlessly offers it to him.

"Please," Frank says as Tobias hesitates. "Take it. Take a load off, hon. It'll be so much easier to speak your mind when you aren't burdened by the droll misery of sobriety."

Convinced by this appeal and hoping for a painless exit from his own fear, Tobias accepts the offering and tokes from it. The smoke tastes hot and acrid in his mouth and he splutters for a moment before making eye contact with Frank and drawing a deep inward breath to consume it.

"Rock on!" Frank exclaims. "Now hit it again! Hey, have you seen this?"

While Tobias adjusts himself to the sensation of hitting the joint for a second time, his attention adjusts to the TV, which presently depicts two men dressed in airline pilot uniforms taking off their pants to begin performing anal sex with each other.

"Um, I've never watched this kind of stuff before," Tobias says sheepishly.

"It's educational, babe!" Frank insists. "How does it make you feel?"

"Uncomfortable, I guess," Tobias confesses.

As Frank adjusts the volume to make the pornographic film louder, the previously closed bedroom door creaks open and a slim-built black teenage boy steps out. Tobias notices a faint greenish bruise just under his eye.

"Markus!" Frank barks when he sees the interloper, causing both boys to jump. "We aren't ready for you yet! Now stay in there until I say we're ready! Damn you!"

Markus wordlessly backs into the bedroom and shuts the door once more. Frank sits back on the couch next to Tobias and clasps his shoulder firmly.

"Now please don't worry about that," Frank drawls. "Markus forgets himself sometimes, that's all."

At a loss for words, Tobias finds his head becoming flushed and his heart rate elevated.

"Please try to relax, Tobias," Frank says, not unkindly. "Look, you still have the stink of the street on your clothes. Why don't you slip out of them and get comfortable."

This statement was worded as a polite question but something about the way it was conveyed suggested authority and a threat of force. Tobias shrugs off his dingy, wet jacket but stops himself from proceeding any further with additional disrobing.

"Can I go to the bathroom, Frank?" he asks, trying to sound brave.

"It's right across from the bedroom, darling," Frank answers.

Tobias stands up, feeling unsteady on his feet, and gingerly steps away from the strange man he is presently trapped with. The whole situation now becoming increasingly unwelcome, he finds himself on the brink of tears by the time he closes the bathroom door behind himself. Sliding a pin lock closed on the door, he sits down atop the closed toilet seat lid and collects his thoughts.

It is alarmingly obvious to Tobias that this grown man intends to make sexual advances towards him and may become violent. He could try to burst out of the bathroom and make a run for the exit, but there is no present certainty of escape. Compounding the problem, Tobias has just foolishly left his jacket, containing the remainder of his bus fare in its pockets, next to his captor.

There is also the question of this mysterious Markus. Luisa had described Frank as having a boyfriend. Could this be him? Maybe Frank has a rotating group of male suitors. Markus doesn't look many years older than Tobias is now. Is Frank a pedophile??

The dire reality of his situation sinking in, Tobias raps his feet anxiously against the carpeted bathroom floor as he looks around for objects he can leverage to his advantage.

Frank knocks on the door.

"Is everything okay in there?" he calls.

"Yes, Frank. I'm fine! Just give me one minute!"

He forces himself to his feet and examines his surroundings. They are sparse: a bar of soap and a toothbrush by the sink. A loofah and more soap in the shower. A couple of towels draped across a rod hanging up in the wall. A mirror above the sink.

Frank knocks again, more impatiently this time.

Making a split decision, Tobias pries the metal towel rod out of its holdings and carefully slides it up his sleeve, attempting to make as little noise as possible. Then he quickly unlatches the door and wrenches it open with haste.

Frank leers up at Tobias expectantly. There is malicious hunger in his eyes, a predator locked onto prey. Tobias steels himself.

POW!

Tobias brings his arm up, then slashes it down, fast and hard. The towel rod connects with Frank's skull and causes him to stagger backward, backing into the wall behind him with a hard thud.

Markus emerges again. His eyes meet Tobias's and the two have a moment of mutual understanding.

"Markus, I told you to stay in that room!" Frank jeers.

"Fuck you," Markus growls.

Markus brings his hands into a ready position and shoves Frank backward with all his might. Frank raises a fist to retaliate but Markus anticipates it and dodges, reciprocating with a right hook that meets its target with force. Tobias scampers past the kerfuffle, handing the towel rod off to Markus like an olympic baton as he passes. The latter boy immediately begins putting his new tool to use.

Tobias rushes over to the couch and grabs his jacket. Just as he is about to bound away, he realizes with dread that one of the sleeves is caught on an exposed nail in the upholstery. Suddenly, Frank is imposing himself on top of Tobias, pinning him down by the shoulders. His yellowed teeth and reefer-laden breath briefly overwhelm the young boy's senses as he wriggles and screams to escape.

His fingers brush against something cold. The hash bowl has skittered toward him as Frank has pounced, putting it just at the edge of Tobias's reach. Frank relinquishes control of one of Tobias's shoulders, now using his freed hand to work his own belt. This gives Tobias just enough additional range of motion to grab the hash bowl. He swings it with all his might and clobbers Frank in the head, causing cannabis to disperse everywhere and the glass to shatter.

Frank howls in pain. Markus, who has recuperated from whatever set him back previously, tackles Frank and pins him to the ground, rallying him with punches. Tobias wrestles his jacket free and dashes out of the apartment unit.

Skittering down the stairs, it isn't long before Tobias finds himself back in the night air. Even the urban decay is a welcome sight relative to what came immediately before. Tobias sprints past the homeless, no longer afraid of them. He enters the pharmacy across the street and asks to borrow its phone. He calls parents – not his own but Luisa's – and tries to collect himself across the twenty minutes they promise it will take them to arrive. He tells the concerned pharmacist nothing about his experience, nor does he admit to Luisa or her parents anything other than that the city gave him a bad vibe.

Returning to his angry and terrified parents, Tobias invents a story about a sleepover he forgot to announce having led to an argument that drove him back home.

At school the next day, Tobias refuses to tell Luisa anything about his experience except that her cousin Frank had made him uncomfortable.

Toby will never speak a word about the events of that night to Luisa or anyone on Earth again. Not even Marissa, not for several years to come. But they will continue to haunt him, returning in idle moments between waking and sleeping, for the rest of his life.

October 15, 2033

The tired bureaucrat rests his head against the glass of his seatside window and gazes out between clouds at the spots of grassland, farm plots, and scattered cities that make up the Zambian countryside far below. After their last layover at Cote D'Ivoire, he and his companion John Nash had been transferred into a considerably smaller and less comfortable airplane.

Back-to-back days in flight and barely a moment of sleep have done hellish work to his frayed nerves. USAID Agent Garrett Johnson tries to distract himself by thinking about football. All to no avail. He can't stop thinking about the faces of his daughters, Catherine and Lia. Back home with their mother, so far away...

After an interminable time, the plane begins its descent. As it noses beneath the clouds and circles over Kenneth Kaunda International Airport, Johnson finds himself breathing deeper in awe. He'd expected little more than a crumbling shack and dirt instead of tarmac on the airstrip. Instead, the scene laid out on the fast-approaching ground below is that of a bleeding-edge, modern airport with freshly paved runways and beautiful, glittering buildings making up the terminals. The whole area around the airport bustles with cars, departing planes, and foot traffic. Even the trees in the immediate vicinity seem to be a little greener.

"Wow," he breathes. "It's a lot nicer than I expected."

Jeanette Emberley, who sits beside him, explains:

"The airport has gone through a few renovations in the last couple decades. It is one of the hidden jewels of Southern Africa. People all over the continent take connecting flights for business here. And they are planning to build new terminals soon."

"Huh," says Garrett. "Whatdaya know."

With a jolt, the airplane's wheels touch pavement and its engines scream into full reverse thrust. Garrett banishes the rising anxiety in his chest that the runway will be too short and focuses instead on collecting the feeling back in his legs to stand up in a short moment. His neck is stiff, and he rolls it, trying to get all his bones back into their proper alignment.

The plane shudders to a stop. In no time at all, John Nash is in the aisle, bracing his arms against the outer edge of Emberley's seat and the seat in front of her with a smile.

"We made it, my friends. Please, let's bring our best selves out of this airplane as we prepare to greet the honorable Mister Mulenga."

At the arrivals gate, Joseph Mulenga welcomes the men and their entourage jovially. A tall man with a remarkably round head, he peers at his guests through tiny-lensed glasses while they approach and greets them with a hearty belly laugh.

"Here are my Americans!" he roars, his voice rich with good humor. "Now which one of you is de space man?"

Dressed sharply in a dark suit and pan-African styled kufi hat, Mulenga commands respect. Nash and Johnson, who stand at the front of the American delegation, glance at each other for a moment before Johnson speaks.

"That would be me," he says in a burst of confidence. "We talked about a week ago, and that was about which— um, that was what we talked about."

Joseph Mulenga laughs uproariously.

"Come with me, my friends," he finally says. "My drivah is waiting."

John Nash, Garrett Johnson, Jeanette Emberley, and the three other Americans who make up their coterie follow the big man out the airport and into the gathering dawn.

Joseph Mulenga's driver has brought a white and lightly mud-speckled twelve-seater bus to the outside of the arrivals gate. He and Mulenga help their yankee visitors with the stowing-away of their luggage, then return to their seats at the front of the bus while the rest of the assembled party files in. The doors roll closed, the driver pulls away, and Mulenga speaks again.

"Dis airport is a one half hour away from de city of Lusaka. That will give us plenty of time to talk."

"You have a very beautiful country, Mr. Mulenga," John Nash says earnestly after a moment.

Outside the window, small towns and pastures go by. As do people, dressed in colorful clothing and going about their day with sprightly energy.

"We are a proud country, but we are quite poor," Joseph Mulenga admits. "Between de airport and de city, there is not much going on. I want to look out on this journey and see big African projects dat my people can be proud of. I want dem to have jobs, jobs which pay well and give dem purpose."

"Hey, that's what we all want, right?" Garrett Johnson offers.

"One of these big projects, maybe de biggest, hm? I see it in my mind's eye. Dis space program you talked to me about, eh? De idea of Africans, reaching out and touching de stars, dis is what excites me. I believe it will excite my people," muses Mulenga. "I am prepared to go a long way with dis team, but I need to know who each of you are."

Garrett speaks up first.

"Well, you know who I am already, of course," he says.

"Of course," agrees Mulenga. "And miss Jeanette Emberley, I have met before. She is my second cousin or something like dat."

"Well, um, I guess the next person you should know is my friend John Nash. It was his idea for us to fly here, and he assembled the rest of the team."

Mulenga swivels his shoulders to peer intently behind himself at the mustachioed Levantine sitting next to Johnson, as if only now seeing him properly for the first time.

"Mister Mulenga," Nash says. "I've read a lot about you. It's an honor to meet you properly, face-to-face, today. I've brought some of my best contacts with me. They'll do your country right, I guarantee that."

He outstretches his hand for a professional shake, and Mulenga meets it with a vice grip. After a second of intense pressure, he taps John's hand with his free hand and lets the man go.

While John Nash clenches and unclenches his fingers in muted pain, Joseph Mulenga's attention shifts.

"How about de rest of you?" He asks. "Miss Emberley, are you still working for NASA?"

The woman seated directly behind Nash nods.

"And how about you?" he continues, addressing the blonde woman seated next to Jeanette.

"I'm Jenny Sabelle," the next woman answers. "I studied particle physics at Oxford, then I went on to NASA. I used to work with Ms. Emberley, but now I head quantum research for Stardust Systems."

Mulenga considers this and nods at the man seated behind her.

"And you?" he asks.

"Mark Fallon," the next man says with a flourishing wave. "I'm with the government affairs department at Stardust Systems."

"How interesting," Mulenga says with a big, charismatic smile. "And finally... you."

The stocky man hidden in the back corner of the van speaks up.

"I'm Eddie Wu," he says after a moment. "I am also with Stardust Systems. I head up our projects and logistics division. Oh, my boss expresses his regret that he couldn't make it today, but he says he looks forward to meeting you sometime in the future."

Joseph Mulenga chuckles to himself.

"Stardust Systems... Who is my mysterious benefacta?" he wonders aloud. "And what does he want with Africa?"

July 5, 2014

Lance Morrissey's second successful visit to the strange world under his tree fort began thusly.

The previous day being Independence Day, his father had taken him to see a parade in town and then fireworks down at the park, during which time Lance had protested loudly about how bored he was and the unfairness of it all, to no avail. By the time they had returned home, a fierce summer storm was blowing in which rattled the shingles of the house and drenched the land in torrents of water.

Now, on the morning of the fifth, Lance finds himself sloshing through his muddy backyard in hopes of trying one last time to validate the prior week's events to himself.

Last night, the wind had come and knocked over many of the branches and some of the trees in Lance's backyard, but its enigmatic conical fort still stood strong, not a single component out of place. Fearing some unseen spectator might again spoil the magic, he glances behind himself to ensure he is unobserved before wasting no time in forcing himself into the fort and spinning around.

The ground beneath him gives way, and in Lance's next conscious moment he opens his eyes to find himself in a new place.

His knees are pressed into a dirty wooden floor. Rising to his feet, he brushes hay and gray dust off his shins before taking in his surroundings. He finds himself on the shabby back porch of a ramshackle tavern. Aside, he hears the distant sounds of clinking glasses and conversation within the building. Next to him is a post with a tightly knotted rope attached. Following the rope with his eyes, he turns to see a giant lizard standing a few paces behind him, which passively bleats in a low rumble upon making eye contact. It bears a saddle on its back whose horn is tied securely to the other end of the rope. Presently, the docile creature grazes from a small trough of hay.

Awash with excitement and relief, Lance rushes forward to stroke Gilead's Gorrpaa on the cheek while its attention is affixed to its meal. Startled, the creature rears onto its hind legs and whips its thick skull against Lance's hand, causing him to yelp in pain.

Something thrusts open the back door of the tavern behind Lance, and a familiar blue elf steps out.

"Lansamor!" Gilead shouts, his tone concerned rather than accusatory. "What in blazes are you doing?"

"I'm sorry!" Lance says sheepishly. "I just wanted to pet your Gorrpaa."

Gilead shakes his head, straightens out his long white beard, and steps forward into the sunlight.

"Gorrpaas are skittish critters, my liege," the wizened elf admonishes. "You aren't to startle them with sudden movements, and they especially hate to be touched when they're eating!"

"Sorry," Lance says again. "We don't really have them where I come from back at home."

He steps closer to his pointy-eared friend, whose eyes sparkle at him with mirth.

"Oh sire, say no more about it!" Gilead insists. "How can a young man learn if he is never taught? Which reminds me... my dear Binnmerva is waiting for you in the hall of heroes! Your return this day heralds that it is time for your next lesson."

"Are we going to see her now?" Lance inquires.

"All in good time," Gilead assures him. "Do you know where we are now?"

Lance takes in his surroundings once more. The wooden porch he and Gilead now stand on only extends a couple meters in each direction from the rear wall of the tavern. Beyond it, a purple cobblestone pathway stretches in a few directions to scattered homes and buildings made from copper-hued wood and large stones. A few snout-nosed men in robes and cloaks intermingle with a diversely-colored group of elves in the distance. The whole tableau is strange, but not entirely unfamiliar.

"Kind of," Lance answers. "But not really."

Gilead moves next to Lance and leans against the wooden railing of the porch. He shields his eyes from the bright sun as he scans the distance and waves to a distant villager, who presumably waves back. Remaining in place but returning his attention to Lance, he gestures outward.

"We passed through this village during your first visit here," Gilead reminds him.

"Oh, right." The memory of it is coming back to him now.

"The hall is not too far from here. Once my Gorrpaa has finished breakfast, the ride will only be a matter of a few pleasant minutes."

Lance shuffles his feet.

"How long do we have to wait before that?" he asks anxiously.

"Please have patience, my liege," Gilead pleads. "Come into the tavern with me, meet some of my friends here, and we will be underway soon."

He begins to walk back toward the tavern, but Lance does not move. Keeping his eyes on the road ahead, he asks:

"How long would it take to walk if we left now?"

Gilead laughs and shakes his head.

"Oh, I dare not," he says. "My wee legs could not take the strain. Come inside. Sit with me. It shall not be long."

Gilead and Lance sit together at the middle of three long wooden tables situated in the center of the busy tavern. All around them, patrons gossip and laugh and take generous swigs from their heaping flagons of drink. Long flowing tapestries hang from the walls. A strange bird nests in the rafters. A fire crackles in a fireplace on the farthest wall.

Lance finds that he appears to be the only human being in the whole place. Thinking back to his previous visit here, Lance reminds himself that the residents of this land come in three typical forms: impish elves like Gilead and Skanot, ranging in hue from deep scarlet to alabaster; bulky green-skinned pig-people like Binnmerva, who range slightly in tint but generally look homogenous; and anthropomorphic bird people like Zhanniti, who strut with prideful postures. There seems to be no bad blood between the members of these groups: all across the tavern, they intermix with one another joyfully like members of one big eccentric family.

Gilead trades old stories with an eyepatch-clad eagle, and a helmeted hawk too. A drunken pig man listens to them talk and guffaws dramatically at various times. Lance tries his best to sit tight and listen, but his attention wanders and he soon finds himself fidgeting impatiently.

Most of the tavern is dimly lit and smells like beer and sweat. The sunlight that streams through the windows of the bar, on the other hand, is warm and inviting. Every once in a while, a strong breeze carries in a pleasant aroma from outside. Gradually, Lance finds his attention pulled toward the nearest window as he tunes out the conversation around him.

The golden leaves almost glimmer outside as they quiver on their branches and catch the rays of the sun. Occasional passerby cast shadows through the window, some on Gorrpaaback, some on foot, and others still carried on the gentle breeze at a low altitude by their wings. Lance watches them go by for a minute with mild disinterest before something catches his eye that makes him rise to his feet without a conscious thought: a familiar-looking blonde-haired woman strolls along past the window, before turning where she stands and meandering towards the treeline.

By the combined spark of genetic instinct and deep-rooted memory, Lance recognizes in an instant that this can only be his long-lost mother. He takes one last look at Gilead, still deep in conversation and oblivious to Lance's behavior, before swiftly exiting the tavern and giving chase.

Evening, August 5, 1998

Marissa plucks a stray leaf off the fold of her dress as she traipses away from the road, Toby's Taurus disappearing behind her into the expanding twilight. This has probably been the single greatest day in her life, but its imminent end depresses her. As does the unceremonious return of her deafness. The enormity of the miracle she experienced in "Eden" with Toby is still rather too large for her to fully process, and the pain of being so swiftly deprived of it once again sinks to a depth of comparable magnitude.

Dusktide shadows deepen around Marissa as she crosses through the forest and past the threshold of her family's most recently developed stretch of land. Stumps of felled trees bespeckle this small reprieve between endless woods and endless corn, a constellated monument to her father's optimism about the farm's future. As she looks up to the twilight stars, Marissa remembers the birdsong of the garden, and her heart aches at its absence.

Rows of corn stretch extravagantly in the direction of the setting sun. A month away from harvest, the maturing stalks are like soldiers standing at attention as Marissa, their visiting general, passes through the throng. Amused at the thought, she salutes the corn, and imagines it saluting back.

The evening air is hot, thick, and still. Beads of clammy sweat stick to Marissa's forehead and palms. By the time she has made it out of corn-land, a weariness has settled into her bones and discomfort creeps into her shoulders.

The door of the barn next to the farmhouse is wide open, the interior lights creating a shell of illumination around it. Her parents are away at dinner, but the air stinks of booze and tobacco. Enrique and Don Pablo, two of her father's hired workers, stand in the entrance of the barn and watch Marissa hungrily as she approaches. Empty and half-emptied beer bottles are strewn on the ground around them.

Marissa watches the two dangerous men with cautious interest. As she gets closer, Don Pablo makes some sort of comment to Enrique, who nods. When Marissa is some twenty feet away, Enrique purses his lips and whistles.

In an instant, Juan and Tomás slide out of the shadows and move behind her. The stench of their breath, a foul mix of liquor and cigarette smoke, announces their approach before the two men seize Marissa and start brusquely escorting her into the gaping mouth of the barn. She screams and drags her heels in protest, but there is nothing she can do against their strength. She watches with desperate terror while Don Pablo and Enrique remove their belts just as she is thrown to the ground on her knees by Tomás and Juan.

Like the stings of hornets, Marissa is pelted by the metal buckles on the two men's belts as they whip her viciously. Juan keeps her arms pinned behind her back while Tomás starts clawing at her dress to remove it. Blind with pain and rage, Marissa thrashes about and sobs uncontrollably. She feels a pair of giant hands shove her to the ground, then her face plants into hay and concrete. Someone is on top of her, breathing heavily, fiddling with something.

Her head restrained, eyes foggy with tears, unable to hear, too weak to fight back, the only thing Marissa can do is pray for her terrible nightmare to end.

Where are my parents? Where is anyone?!

Marissa realizes with horror that her bare rear end has now been exposed to the night air. The man on top of her shifts his weight and something brushes against her butt.

NO!!

PLEASE!

Every muscle in her body tenses for what is to come next.

Suddenly, there is a rapid motion above her, and the weight pressing her to the ground is released in an instant. Marissa throws herself into what she estimates to be the safest possible direction, re-secures her underwear, and rubs the tears out of her eyes as quickly as she can to see what is the matter.

Jorge, the runt of the men, has appeared on the scene to intercede on Marissa's behalf. A shovel in his hands, he has just knocked Tomás out cold, which accounts for the interruption in the men's efforts to rape her. In fact, the remaining three assailants are attempting to close in on Jorge at present, while he swings the shovel around with all his might and slowly backs away to keep his distance.

Marissa summons her remaining faculties and switches into survival mode, scanning her environment for resources that can help her. The first thing that catches her eye is a glass bottle just at the edge of her reach. The next thing she notices is a jug of Roundup pesticide attached to a pump hose, which is tucked against the wall nearest to where she sits.

Juan, Enrique, and Don Pablo have their backs turned to Marissa, their attention completely captured by his antics with the shovel for the time being. Jorge, for his part, looks terrified and overwhelmed. Things could get ugly for him, and fast.

Marissa scampers over to the Roundup jug and begins vigorously adding pressure to the container via the handle at the top until it cannot pump any longer. Then she scoops up a glass bottle and hurls it at the back of Enrique's head with all her might. It shatters dramatically, and the three men turn around in anger, whereupon Marissa immediately showers their faces with Roundup.

The effect of skin contact with the toxic chemical is immediate and salient. Juan and Don Pablo shriek and wither in pain.

Enrique puts his hands over his eyes and howls, dropping to his knees.

After a moment, the three men gather enough wherewithal to run away from Marissa, Jorge, and the unconscious form of Tomás. Jorge encourages their haste with additional brandishes of the shovel.

Upon being fully satisfied the men do not plan to regroup and return, Jorge directs his attention to the bruised and shell-shocked Marissa.

"Miss, are you okay?" he asks, although Marissa does not need to read his lips to see the deep concern etched across his face.

Marissa shakes her head. How could anyone be okay after an ordeal like this?

Jorge escorts Marissa inside her house and locks the door behind them, then rushes for the living room phone while Marissa sits on the couch. She tries to communicate with him in sign language, but Jorge shakes his head, not understanding her meaning. So, she speaks aloud, hoping her voice will not be too garbled.

"No police," she says, before Jorge can dial a number. "Call my parents, tell them to come home."

Jorge nods solemnly and moves to comply.

Marissa trudges upstairs and showers every part of herself thoroughly. Then she collapses into bed and falls into a deep, deep sleep.

October 16, 2033

Joseph Mulenga and his visiting American delegation sit around a large ovoid conference table perched at the top of a high-rise in the business center of Lusaka.

Accompanying Mulenga on the Zambian side is his personal attache, Moses Nyiramba, who diligently types notes on the meeting's proceedings into a tablet embedded in the desk. At this moment, Garrett Johnson is speaking.

"Speaking on behalf of the United States Agency for International Development," he is saying, "I want to extend America's strong support for your nation and its people. We welcome the twin strengths of diversity and inclusion, and we are eager to walk hand in hand with Zambia as it takes its place on the world's stage."

Mulenga reclines in his chair slowly, letting it creak under his weight for a second and remaining in that position while observing the rest of the people in the silent room.

"Okay," he says after a moment. "I have heard all of this before. What is your plan for my people?"

"My plan?" Garrett asks.

"Yes, yours!" Mulenga says impatiently. "You and your country. Your agency, your government – what are you going to do for dis nation, and what are you asking for in return?"

Garrett purses his lips and thinks, then speaks carefully.

"As you gathered– as you probably guessed– we are putting together a partnership between private and public American entities to facilitate the, um, proliferation of foreign direct investment into this country, with particular focus on, um, securing objectives pertaining to, uh, space... investment... and jobs. Aaand we are looking forward to establishing a trade relationship and diplomatic goodwill between our nations, and collaborating against our common adversaries."

Mulenga nods slowly and considers this. Meanwhile, John Nash, who sits to the other side of Agent Johnson, whispers in his ear.

"This is boilerplate stuff," Nash insists in a hushed tone.

"What?" Garrett whispers back.

"If you want to capture his attention and get leverage in this negotiation, you need to be more inspiring."

"I don't know how to do that! I have to follow the guidelines from my supervisor."

John Nash tuts and straightens his tie. Then he clears his throat and sticks his finger in the air, waving it in little circles to get the attention of the rest of the room.

"Honorable Mister Mulenga," he says. "If I may be permitted to speak?"

"Speak freely," Joseph Mulenga urges him.

John Nash's eyes flit around the room, sizing up everyone in it: doughy flake Agent Johnson to his right, a handpicked team of lackeys to his left. The only one who isn't yet eating out of his palm is Mulenga, but the allegiance of this backwater folk hero can be captured from the proper angle. Taking his measure of the man, Nash launches his spiel.

"Well," he begins. "Let me share this theory I picked up from an online friend of mine."

He stands up and reaches into the pocket of his taupe-colored suit jacket, producing a reticulated metal rod. He pulls at its ends and it quickly extends until it is about three feet long. Moving away from his seat, he begins to pace back and forth as he continues talking.

"This friend of mine, who shall here remain nameless, has a theory that as individual civilizations rise and fall, they are also part of a process in which civilization itself as a global phenomenon expands and recedes. Consider the following."

He stands by a map projection which occupies the rearward wall of the conference room and taps on the Mediterranean basin with his metal stick.

"The Greco-Roman era of civilization," he declares triumphantly, "Marked a period of great social development around the world, beginning here. It eventually spread into other places around the world. But after the Roman Empire fell, it was only a matter of time before the reach of other Empires began to recede as well. For one reason or another, the entire world went into a dark age at about the same time."

He adjusts his position.

"Then, of course, some centuries later, we have the European Renaissance. This brings us the Columbian Exchange, and imperialism, and the colonization of the New World. This is the second era of civilization, which we are in now. We've seen a transfer of power from Europe to the Western hemisphere, various struggles between regional interests, a great time of nationalism and independence movements and so on. But let's not kid ourselves."

Nash casts a meaningful look at Garrett Johnson, who so far seems enraptured by the diatribe. He also steals a furtive glance at Joseph Mulenga, who is listening attentively. The populist leader's scribe finishes tapping away at his onscreen keyboard and looks up, waiting for Nash to continue. And so he does.

"What my American friend will not admit— cannot admit, because of his station— is that any long-term promises made on the part of the United States are all but worthless. One would have to be extraordinarily naive to expect America to hold up her end of any agreement in the several decades to come," Nash provocatively proclaims.

"Hey!" Garrett Johnson shouts. "Don't say that!"

"Sorry my friend," Nash says with a bashful smile, "but it's true. Yes, America's situation is declining, and I'm afraid to say it's not going to get any better. Her social services are headed towards bankruptcy, between generations of unsustainable fiscal policies and an anticipated wave of climate refugees from the global South. Eventually, the government will lose its legitimacy in the eyes of the people and the nation will balkanize. But, and here's the thing—"

Nash eyes up Mulenga again, whose expression is difficult to read. There is something haughty about it, but also a hint of concern. His lips are pressed in a thin smile, but his brow is furrowed.

Nash returns his focus to the map and points at China.

"The Chinese are scrambling for influence wherever they can find it. They want to expand their control over territory because they know their home demographic situation is unsustainable, as is their domestic political situation. Their aging population is sick from pollution, restless with anger at their own government, and dying. The bigwigs in Beijing think that colonialism will save them. But of course they will struggle with keeping their colonies servile. It isn't the 19th century anymore. That time has passed. No, China is on its way out, too.

"This anonymous friend of mine that I mentioned earlier believes that the world is headed for another dark age. A high-tech dark age to be sure, but a dark age all the same. The major powers of the world will be collapsing under their own weight and world technological progress is going to slow down. The process has already started, and there's no turning back now. The question we have to ask is, what comes next?"

Nash scratches his chin and points his stick at Africa.

"Ladies and gentlemen," he says, "I believe the third era of civilization begins with Africa. This is a continent of boundless potential. Humanity began here, and it has played host to a great number of caliphates, kingdoms, trading empires, and so on. But it has always been held back by one thing or another. Corruption, ethnic strife, foreign occupations. You name it. But I see a path forward. I see Zambia leading the charge out of the darkness. I see you, Mister Joseph Mulenga, carrying your people into the light!"

He collapses his metal pointer and returns to his seat. Garrett Johnson politely applauds, while the other Americans in the room remain in silence. Joseph Mulenga laughs with gusto.

"What a guy, huh?!" he exclaims, thumping his scribe on the back and gesturing forth. "Dat was a great speech. But again I am looking for a plan."

John Nash nods.

"You're about to hear it," he says. "I will defer to Miss Jenny Sabelle."

He points over to the blonde woman at the end of the table.

"Please," he directs. "As we say in America, spill the beans."

The woman nods and begins to speak in a clipped British accent.

"About a decade ago, a man spoke with me and brought me along to lead highly experimental research efforts in quantum science. That man was the head of a large company, and the research I produced for his company became the bedrock of what is now known as the Stardust Initiative. We have been able to successfully produce quantum tunneling technology that allows us to fold bits of spacetime together and cross very long distances very quickly."

She pauses, unsure how much she can reveal. Mark Fallon escorts John Nash and Garret Johnson out of the room, and she continues as he returns to his seat.

"Ours is a company of considerable resource, but it is limited by the need to keep many of its operations secret."

"Why secret?" Joseph Mulenga interrupts.

"Sorry?" Dr. Sabelle asks.

"Why do dey operate in secret?" he asks again.

Mark Fallon, his hands steepled together and his head resting on his fingers, speaks up.

"I can answer that," he says. "First, the technology being used is highly proprietary. We don't want any competitors to get ahold of it, so we prefer if they don't know about its existence in the first place. We also don't want the regulatory agencies to know about it, or they'd slow us down with a bunch of red tape. And there are other reasons as well, but those are also secret. So. Lately, our boss has been talking about wanting to open a quantum tunnel in outer space and sending a team of astronauts through it. Um, Jenny, back to you for this one."

"Right," she says. "Now, obviously, we can't be open about the nature of this mission, which is why we decided not to go with an American team for this project. You can imagine the scrutiny that would entail. Instead, if your country is willing, we'd like to use a set of Zambian astronauts and send them through the quantum tunnel to explore a distant planet."

"There has never been a Zambian astronaut before," Joseph Mulenga muses.

"Well," says Dr. Sabelle, "Now there will be. The plan is to present it to the public under the guise of an orbital lunar mission. We'll have the Zambian press report it to the international community and Zambian workers assembling the craft and the rocket to our specifications."

"How will you keep de story going when the astronauts are in space?" Mulenga asks.

"Actually, it really will be a lunar mission! We'll send a team of, say, eight into space and have half of them go into orbit around the moon to keep up appearances. The other half of the team will detach from the spacecraft halfway along the journey and enter the quantum tunnel. So, in the span of a single day, Zambia gets to join the club of countries that have sent men to the moon AND it gets to be the very first to send men to the surface of another planet. How does that sound?"

"What will happen to de people on dis other planet?" asks Mulenga. "Is it safe? Dey will not be stranded?"

Jenny Sabelle responds cautiously.

"It... should be safe, yeah. They make camp on the planetary surface, spend a night collecting data, and then leave the next day. On their way out of the quantum tunnel, they rendezvous with the returning lunar crew and all go home safe and sound!"

Joseph Mulenga weighs this in his head and then finally nods slowly.

"Okay," he says. "Supposing I am on board with dis big spaceship idea, how much money are you looking for from us?"

Eddie Wu, the final American present, speaks up to answer this question.

"Money isn't our concern," Wu promises. "We just need your people to build it and ride it."

Joseph Mulenga chuckles.

"And say hello to de aliens, no?" he quips. "De first handshake between a black man and a green man, that will be quite de spectacle."

His smile fades and he stands up, all business.

"Dis meeting is concluded," he announces. "Thank you for visiting me today."

"When will we hear your decision?" Agent Johnson asks.

"You will hear it soon enough," Mulenga vows. "In de meantime, make yourselfs at home here in my country. I will talk to you all later."

One by one, the Americans file out, thanking the man for his hospitality.

Golden Forest:
July 5, 2014
(Relative Time)

Locks of flaxen hair flit to and fro. Lance catches glimpses of it between thorny thickets and spiraling shrubbery, along with flashes of the back of his mother's white gown as it comes into view in the distance and the sunlight catches it.

Fleeing like a frightened animal, the figure becomes ever more elusive the harder Lance gives chase. Branches scrape his face and snag on his clothes, but he pays them no mind as he swats them away and continues at a full-tilt sprint.

"Mom!" he calls.

The woman does not stop, does not turn around, will not even slow down.

"Mommy!" he calls again, his voice breaking.

But his mother only seems to be further and further away.

Eventually, she rounds the corner of a gigantic gnarled tree, some twenty feet in diameter. By the time Lance rounds the same tree, she has vanished, as if into thin air. Like she was never even there.

Lance steels himself and grinds his feet to a halt, just as his breath catches up with him. He bends over and wheezes from the exertion. Then he straightens up and looks around.

In every direction: nothing to see but rocks and vegetation stretching out into the horizon.

"Hello?" he shouts. "Anyone?"

There is no response. Somewhere, a bird leaves its perch atop a tree and flies away. There is not a sound to be heard save for the quiet rustling of leaves in the breeze.

Lance takes stock of his situation. His shoelace is untied and his bare kneecap is trickling blood. There is also the matter of his being completely lost in a strange place with no one in earshot to come to the rescue.

First things first. He sits down and ties his shoe.

Returning to his feet, he is just about to shout for help again when sharp talons jab into his shoulders and he is violently yanked up into the air. Shrieking in pain, which quickly gives way to fear as he sees the forest grow smaller and smaller beneath him, Lance whips his head around wildly to ascertain what is going on.

"Hold on tight, kid!" a bright feminine voice calls from above him.

"Zhanniti!" Lance shouts in relief. "Is that you?"

"Of course!" she says. "Don't worry bud, I've got ya!"

"Where are we going?" he asks.

"Why, to the hall of heroes, of course!"

Zhanniti spreads her wings to their full span and glides into a masterful swan dive, causing Lance's stomach to do a somersault. Nevertheless, he is confident in his own safety, trusting completely in the steely grip of his avine friend.

It is only a minute longer before Lance's wild ride comes to an end and Zhanniti takes him for a graceful descent in front of the crisscrossed and vine-laden iron bars that encircle the hall of heroes.

She comes to a hover in the air by the main gates so that Lance's feet dangle only a few feet above the ground, then her talons release all pressure on his shoulder and he dismounts, feeling ruefully that he had started to enjoy that method of travel and kind of wanted to fly around for a little while longer. Seconds after Lance comes to his feet with a solid thud, Zhanniti joins him and walks by his side as they enter the manor grounds.

"So where is everyone?" he asks.

"Oh, they're waiting for ya inside," Zhanniti says casually, then her voice drops to a hushed, conspiratorial tone. "Now just between you and me, ya may want to brace yerself. You're in for a spot of trouble from the others. They're not well pleased."

Lance takes the lead as the two of them walk up the meandering path through the limestone-paved courtyard of the manor grounds. Finally, they step up to the manor's great wooden front door.

Lance shoves the door open and blinks as his eyes adjust to the difference in lighting. As his sight comes into focus, he sees Skanot, Binnmerva, and Todd assembled before him, looking severe. Skanot, who takes center-stage, intones in a solemn rasp:

"You have let us down this day, young Lansamor."

Excuse me?

"What the hell did I do?" Lance asks with an angry snarl.

"Our friend Gilead made a very simple request, that you stay by his side. Instead, in your impatience and foolishness, you took off into the woods and almost got yourself killed!"

Immediately on the defensive, Lance looks around for someone to back him up. Binnmerva is shaking her head, Todd bares his razor-sharp canines, and Zhanniti casts a bashful sideways glance at him, apologetic but unwilling to intercede.

"Look, Skanot, I was chasing after my mom, okay?" Lance says.

"My liege, you need to abandon these thoughts about your mother," Skanot commands, fiercely. "You have a sacred and solemn duty. When one of us instructs you, you are to do as we say."

"Man, fuck you and your duty!" Lance explodes. "You can blow it out your ass! I'm not sitting around in some shitty bar while my mom is out there, waiting for me."

"You would do well to hold your tongue, boy!" Skanot returns with equal fury. "You are here at our pleasure. Need I remind you, if you wish to stay in this land any longer, you ought to do what we say. Otherwise, we will cast you out forevermore!"

Binnmerva shakes her head again, indignantly.

"We have so many wonderful things to show you," she says sadly. "All you have to do is be patient. All will be revealed in time, including the truth about your mother. Please don't ruin this for yourself."

Todd barks and scratches his ear.

"Lansamor," Skanot says, his tone now more conciliatory. "We were going to spend today teaching you how to harness your power. But instead it seems you need a different sort of lesson first."

"Power? What power?" Lance asks, eagerly.

"That is a question you will have to wait until tomorrow to get answered," Skanot says flatly. "Because today's lesson is about the importance of patience. Good things come to those who wait, my liege. But until then, your challenge is this. After we are done here, Todd will show you to your bedroom. You are to spend the night on the grounds. Do not talk to anyone, and do not leave your quarters. You are to spend your time in silence and solitude until the dawn breaks. Do I make myself clear?"

"You want me to spend the night here? What about my dad back at home, won't he wonder where I am?" Lance asks, confused.

"As long as you are here, almost no time will pass for the people back at home," Skanot explains. "You could spend years in this realm and only a few hours will have passed for everyone else. Now, please, follow Todd and prepare yourself for this night's task."

Skanot and Binnmerva leave the foyer, chatting with each other in low voices.

"Good luck!" Zhanniti says, before departing and following the other two champions.

Todd leads Lance in the opposite direction, down a couple of corridors past exotic portraits and suits of armor, and up a narrow spiral staircase. The staircase opens up to a claustrophobic hallway, and at the end of it, the door to Lance's dormitory hangs ajar. Todd beckons to it and Lance nods, preparing himself for the next stage in his journey.

The Next Day

The furnishings in the room Lance had been escorted to proved to be exceedingly comfortable. Situated on the top floor of the enormous manor, a large curtained window overlooked a great deal of the land, and Lance had taken a few minutes to stare out through this window shortly after arriving to spy on the miniature flora and fauna far below.

A large wooden bookshelf backed up against one of the walls, containing a multitude of leather-bound books with strange letters etched into their crispy, yellowing pages. Next to the bookshelf stood an ornate armoire, which Lance had opened to find a number of robes made from brown, teak, and gold fabric. Lance found a large, flowing one which fit him appreciably and put it on over his clothes, then continued searching around the room.

The bed, a queen-sized number with a wooden post at each corner, was adorned with amethyst canopy curtains and twelve pillows of various sizes and shapes. The bedspread was covered in a black and violet checkered pattern. After first laying eyes upon it, Lance had tested the bed with a belly flop and found that the mattress was comfortable, with a decent amount of give.

At the end of the bed stood a wooden trunk, which Lance had opened to find a collection of maps, tabletop games he did not recognize, and various tchotchkes and trinkets. He spent a couple hours poring over each of these objects, until his eyes finally grew heavy and he decided to sleep.

After the sun came up in the morning and shone through the window onto his face, Lance had spent a little while longer lounging in the bed, feeling that this punishment really was not so bad after all, before he finally slipped the robe off and left it on top of his sheets, then proceeded out into the hall to find the manor's other inhabitants.

Presently, he stands in the empty foyer of the hall of heroes, waiting to see what will happen next.

Down one adjoining hallway comes the echoing sound of hobbling footsteps. In a few seconds, the elven form of Skanot emerges, looking considerably less stern than the day prior.

"Come with me," he directs, and Lance complies.

The aged elf escorts Lance down a fresh set of labyrinthine corridors. A thick shag carpet covers their path, hued in murky magenta. Skanot makes conversation as they walk.

"How did you find your lodgings?" he rasps.

"Oh, Todd showed me," Lance answers helpfully.

"I meant, what did you think about them?" Skanot clarifies with some exasperation.

"Oh. They were good, yeah. The bed was super comfortable. Also, I liked the maps."

"You would do well to become familiar with those maps before your next excursion, Lansamor."

"Way ahead of you, Skanot."

In fact, Lance had committed most of the relative locations of this land's big landmarks to memory. He now had a solid grasp of where the hall of heroes stood in relation to the village, and to the base of the mountain, an intriguing-looking cave in the midst of the forest, as well as the lake that he first washed ashore next to on the occasion of his first visit.

Skanot and Lance pass by an open-faced kitchen. A pleasant aroma wafts out of two great brick ovens set up inside. As the smell reaches Lance's nose, his stomach rumbles and he realizes how hungry he is.

"What's cooking in there?" he asks. "It smells great!"

"You'll soon see!" Skanot says cheerfully. "Our Carfassan chefs are preparing a banquet."

"Carfassan? Oh... you mean those elf guys, right?"

Skanot looks startled and deeply offended by Lance's comment.

"Elf?!" he exclaims. "What in the heavens are you talking about?"

"Oh, you know..." Lance says. "Big ears, pointy noses, beady eyes. That sort of thing. Like you! Elves!"

"I will forgive this iniquity because I know things must be different where you come from," Skanot says, his voice on edge. "But around here, that kind of talk is deeply, horrifyingly racist."

An awkward, stilted silence follows. Lance and his escort complete the rest of their journey without speaking to each other. Eventually, they arrive in a room with green and gold walls that Lance recognizes from his first visit to the manor. The fireplace is lit and Zhanniti and Binnmerva sit patiently by it on a lavish sofa, waving hello as Lance and Skanot arrive.

"I hope you're ready to listen to us now, dear," Binnmerva says.

His face hot with embarrassment, Lance smiles sheepishly, thinking about his outburst the previous day.

"Did ya have a comfortable sleep?" Zhanniti asks.

"Yes. The bed you have here is way more comfortable than my one at home," Lance says.

"Oh wonderful!" Zhanniti exclaims. "Splendid."

She begins preening her wing feathers while Lance sits patiently in another sofa opposite the two woman-creatures. Skanot observes his calm demeanor with visible satisfaction, then begins to speak.

"In order to dominate the beast," he begins in even tones. "You must call together allies. And in order to gather allies, you must find your Authority. It resides deep within you. You must gather it up and allow it to outwardly manifest."

"What does that mean?" Lance asks.

"It is written by the oracle that when Lansamor addresses the multitudes, no being shall fail to listen. He will stand at the pulpit and give his commands, and every person shall obey. The prophecy says that you will be the greatest and most powerful of all leaders, with every thinking creature at your command."

Lance takes this in and nods with some satisfaction. He thinks back to his peers at school and their constant disrespect, their willingness to disregard everything he says and act as though he doesn't exist. How satisfying will it be when they have to do whatever he says!

"How does that work?" he asks Skanot.

Skanot walks over to where Lance sits and places his palms flat on the boy's temples.

"Close your eyes," he instructs. "And tell me to take my hands off of your head."

Lance screws his eyes shut, feeling Skanot's weathered and clammy hands pressing firmly on the sides of his skull.

"Okay," he says. "Take your hands off my head."

Nothing happens.

"You have to mean it!" Skanot insists. "And keep your eyes shut!"

Lance can feel Skanot pressing down a little bit harder now. The sensation is mildly uncomfortable.

"Take your hands off my head!" he says again, louder this time.

Skanot increases the pressure in his hands further and begins to dig his sharp nails into Lance's flesh. Lance winces.

"No," says the Carfassan plainly. "Not like that."

"Let me go!" Lance whines, his voice cracking.

"Pitiful!" scoffs the elf. "Hardly the bearing of a leader."

Skanot's nails dig in deeper. His hands feel like ice. Lance's skull aches with a roaring pain that makes him hardly able to think. For a moment, he wavers in and out of consciousness. The pain in his head is all he can focus on, and his burning desire to have it gone. It is singular.

"Let. Me. **GO.**"

On the last syllable, a second voice seems to rise out of Lance's chest. A deeper, fuller voice that is not his own. Though Skanot does not relent in his contact on the boy's head, he no longer feels it. He feels instead that he has been displaced from his body, somehow, and that some other being is now in control. He opens his mouth once more and moves his lips, but this other being's voice is the one which presently rings out.

"**You will take your hands off of my head, NOW!**" The voice roars as Lance opens his eyes and sees Skanot stumble backward. Shaking as if having just been jolted by an electric shock, the wizened creature looks suitably impressed, but also a little bit afraid. Behind him, Zhanniti and Binnmerva look disturbed.

Skanot recollects himself and addresses Lance.

"So the prophecy was true," he says in awe. "You are indeed the leader that we sought."

To cajole his frightened female friends, he turns and speaks behind himself:

"Have no fear, my fellow terrestrial Guardians. The day that was promised to us approaches. The beast will indeed be taken out of the pit!"

Zhanniti spreads her wings to their full breadth and flaps them in delight. Binnmerva flashes a toothy grin.

"So what's next?" Lance asks.

"Now," says Skanot, "we have a banquet to eat."

October 17, 2033

Joseph Mulenga wicks a fat bead of sweat off his prodigious forehead and sits back in his chair.

"I will need to talk to de president," he says, his voice faintly hoarse from a dry mouth. "I am not opposed to dis idea at all. But we will draw up de list of demands we expect to see met."

His conversational partner, Jeanette Emberley, takes a gentle sip of dark roast coffee and sets her mug on the small table between them before returning to an erect, stately posture.

"Name your terms," she says. "The feasibility of this project is contingent on your approval, so the ball really is in your court."

"Our governing coalition represents a diverse set of interests," Mulenga explains. "As much as it is possible, we expect your company to use Zambian materials, hire Zambian workers, and spend private money. You will support our economy and we will pay it back with our support for your project."

He clears his throat and coughs. Jeanette Emberley sits, silent and inscrutable. Mulenga continues.

"Dat is just to give you an idea of what to expect in the negotiations," he says.

"Consider it done," she replies coolly.

Mulenga nods, satisfied.

"There is just one last point I would like to talk to you about," he says.

"Oh?"

"Stardust Systems. I would like to know who dey are. I wish to meet this CEO of yours."

"You'll have your chance, Mr. Mulenga, I promise. He'll see you when the time is right."

The Hall of Heroes

The Carfassan banquet had been exquisite. Great tables piled high with delicacies of every kind, from fall-off-the-bone meats to juicy pies and the ripest fruits and vegetables. It had taken all of Lance's willpower to restrain himself from totally pigging out.

"So what's next?!" he asks Binnmerva excitedly, a crumb of pie falling out of his mouth.

She smiles sweetly while a Carfassan waiter approaches, bows, and removes their empty plates.

"You'll have one more test," she says, "And then you will be allowed to leave."

"But I don't want to leave!" Lance exclaims. He crosses his arms and sighs.

"Don't get sulky on me, child," Binnmerva warns him. "I'm too old to tolerate that nonsense."

"Okay, fine." Lance concedes the point and tries to adopt a more positive attitude. "So what's the deal with this test?"

Skanot's gruff voice is audible behind him, and Lance whips around while the Carfassan speaks.

"You're about to find out. Come with me."

"Where did you come from?" Lance asks, bewildered. "How long were you standing there?"

Skanot ignores this.

"Come with me," he orders again.

Lance stands up without further complaint and follows Skanot out of the banquet hall.

Together, they proceed down a lavender-carpeted corridor that gradually declines in elevation and grade. The temperature drops as they walk and Lance feels the air pressure shift behind his ears.

"Are we going to see the clockwork elf again?" he asks, thinking back to the end of his first visit.

"Eventually," Skanot says, ignoring the slur. His hooked nose bobbles in the air as he walks ahead of Lance briskly.

"So what's going on with this test Binnmerva was talking about, exactly?" Lance asks, starting to jog a bit just to keep up.

"You will need to prove your mettle to earn your escape," Skanot explains. "What did you think about your experience in the commons room?"

"Are you talking about when you almost skull-crushed me to death?" Lance asked. "Because I thought that was really unpleasant."

"That is not what I am *not* talking about," Skanot muses. "More specifically, I am curious if you have any thoughts about what happened when you made me let go."

Lance thinks back to the strange voice that came out of his mouth, the one that was loud and deep and not his own.

"Honestly, I still don't really understand that part, yeah," he says. "What exactly did I do to make that happen?"

"Prophecy dictates that Lansamor will be known around the realms for his sheer Force of Will," Skanot recalls. "His voice shall be that of a dragon, and he shall use it to compel millions."

Lance considers this and replays the experience in his mind's eye.

"My words didn't work until I got control of my thoughts," he realizes aloud. "Once I was able to focus my whole entire mind on that one single thing, I was able to tap into that power."

"You are becoming wise, my liege," Skanot says approvingly. "Hence the importance of discipline that we have tried to instill upon you."

"So if I get my focus right, I can basically make people do whatever I want?" Lance asks. "That sounds pretty awesome!"

"With some caveats," Skanot clarifies. "Some people may build a mental resistance. But if you can keep at it, your power will grow. Which – and here we are – brings us to your test."

They have arrived at a set of giant stone double doors, flanked by torches, with iron handles in the center. Skanot motions to Lance, and each of them grab one door handle apiece. After some forceful tugging, the doors pop out of their positions and slide the rest of the way open smoothly.

"Go ahead in," Skanot directs Lance. "I will be right after you."

Lance salutes sarcastically and enters the dimly lit vaulted dungeon just beyond the threshold. Rather than follow him in, Skanot slams the entrance shut, leaving Lance submerged in inky darkness as the hollow echo of the stone doors reverberates around him.

August 10, 1998

Robert Miller scrubs voraciously at a stubborn tomato stain adhering itself to a glass pan in the sink. His wrists ache from the pressure and his brow furrows with concentration. It is a humid Monday morning and the air inside the house is still. Ordinarily, the workers play music while they perform their duties in the field, but the farm has been quiet while they work for the last few days.

Rob stares out the open window above the sink and squints past the harsh sunlight. He can see the cornfield: Tomás is moving methodically down the column of corn and examining every stalk. Even from inside the house, the man's swollen purple bruise is visible. It obscures the entire left side of his face. Rob finds himself staring at Tomás and scrutinizing him while he labors.

There's something weird about that, he thinks to himself.

He and his wife had returned from dinner the previous Wednesday to the scene of a total fracas. Broken glass bottles scattered on the ground in front of the barn. Most of the men complaining about their "*ojos*," and Tomás with his nasty bruise.

And there has been a palpable shift in the mood on the farm. Marissa has been eating less and sleeping more. The working men no longer whistle jovially while they work, nor gather in the evenings to listen to salsa music and drink. In fact, they seem to keep their distance from each other, and especially refuse to speak to or even stand near Jorge, the smallest among them.

Clearly, something had happened. The problem is, no one on the farm seems keen on fessing up to what it was. Don Pablo had fed him a story about the men getting too drunk and wrestling each other too hard. Marissa's account of her own behavior had been a sadness about Tobias.

Clearly, there is more to the story.

Rob dries off the dish and flicks his hands on the towel before stowing it back in a drawer by the stove. He looks out at Tomás again, still diligently engaged in the work, then shuts the curtains and walks away.

The Dungeon

Lance blinks slowly as his eyes adjust to the murky darkness and his mind races to process the deception to which he has fallen victim. He now stands in a vault-like chamber made of stone. There is no light, save for a few small glimmers escaping into the room through cracks in the wall.

Deep in the gloom, Lance's eyes adjust to take in the hazy gray form of a motionless object. After a second, he reasons that this must be a table, and he stumbles over toward it. He places his palms flat on its top and feels along its rough mahogany surface. There is a large unlit candle standing in its center, a fact Lance only becomes aware of after his hand brushes against its metal base and feels its tall waxy stalk. It is too dark to see more than a few feet in front of him, and nothing is visible in detail except at a very close quarter.

The air in the room is chilly and slightly damp, and a vaguely putrid smell clings to it, as though something had once died here a long time ago. It is an uncomfortable setting.

Moving away from the table, Lance outstretches his hands and begins to feel around the wall in vain hopes of finding a light switch. Very much in doubt that there is even a whiff of electricity in this desolate place, he is primarily motivated by the anxious need to do something with himself to justify being here and perhaps learn more about the nature of this test.

As he shuffles sideways and leftward along the perimeter of this rather claustrophobia-inducing space, he notes the rough and jagged texture of the stone that composes its moisture-speckled walls. Now rounding the corner, he approaches the two stone doors from which he originally entered. They are almost flush with the wall into which they are laid, with no discernable knob or handle.

Moving past the door and now rounding the other corner, Lance notices the unpleasant smell permeating the room has started to intensify. He continues to shuffle sideways.

Suddenly, the back of Lance's head grazes against something sharp and he hears a metal chain rattle above him.

He whips around and looks up. In the darkness, slowly swinging, is a meat hook, lightly crusted with oxidation and old blood. Lance yelps and backs away.

At the other end of the room, some twenty feet away, a hitherto unseen door creaks open, blinding Lance with a sudden flood of light. Between his fingers, he sees a spindly bipedal figure slip into the room and then quickly slam the door shut, casting it back into blackness.

Lance dives under the table in a flash, hoping the creature did not see him. Hoping further still that it cannot see in the darkness, cannot hear his ragged fear-filled breaths or thumping heartbeat.

The creature in the room exhales huffily, then produces a faint light and begins to walk toward the table in the room's center. Lance tries to hold himself as still as a statue while the light approaches closer and the heavy footfalls of the being carrying it get louder. The skin on his legs begins to go clammy from contact with the cold, uneven stone floor.

After several seconds, heavy-booted feet come to a stop by the edge of the table. A second later, the room slowly fills with warm light, and a familiar voice rings out.

"My liege, why are you sitting under that table?"

It is Gilead, who has just lit the candle in the center of the table with a match and now affixes Lance with an expression splitting the difference between confusion and dry amusement.

Feeling a sense of rank humiliation, Lance crawls out from underneath the table and stretches out his joints.

"I was just inspecting the floor down here," he says after a moment, lamely. "Look at how dirty it is!"

He holds out his outstretched palm, which is covered in dusty soot. Gilead makes a point to ignore this.

"It is time to administer your final test, my lord Lansamor," Gilead says, brandishing a bronze key from the pocket of his sleeveless overalls. "This key unlocks the door behind me. You must convince me to give it to you."

"Okay," says Lance. "Can you hand me the key?"

"No."

"Please?"

"No. Not like that. You know what you need to do."

Lance takes a deep breath and closes his eyes, then pictures Gilead's key in his mind, forcing everything else to go blank. He pictures the shape of it and the feel of it in his hand, its weight and its texture.

"**Gi**ve me the **k**ey now!" he roars, in an uneven voice that is mostly his own.

Opening his eyes, he sees Gilead has not budged. The elvish man shakes his head.

"Come on, gimme!" Lance says, trying to reach for the key. Gilead holds it high above his own head and wiggles it around in the air, tauntingly. He chortles with contentment as Lance grabs at the air with each hand, backing away from the boy slowly.

"Ho ho!" he laughs. "Too slow!"

"Come on Gilead, this isn't fair!"

The Carfassan continues to back up slowly, jubilance etched in his face.

"You want the key, Lansamor!" he says with glee. "I know you– URK!"

Gilead's foot stumbles on the uneven stone floor, and he falls backward onto the meat hook behind him, instantly impaled through the flesh on his exposed upper back.

"Gilead!" Lance exclaims with horror. "No!"

"My liege, help!" Gilead pleads.

"What should I do?" Lance frantically asks.

Gilead dangles a few inches above the floor, his booted toes kicking frantically. With horror, Lance can see that his wriggling movements are only digging the metal hook deeper in his back.

"Gilead!" Lance says again, vigorously. "**Stop moving!**"

Like it did in the common room earlier, a powerful voice speaks through his mouth that is deeper and more commanding than his own. The candle in the room flickers. Gilead goes completely immobile, his body as stiff as a board. Lance cannot tell if the wizened creature is even breathing.

He rushes to Gilead's aid and begins to inspect the scene. The barbed tip of the suspended hook seems to be buried a couple of inches beneath the surface of his skin.

"I'm sorry, Gilead. This is probably really gonna hurt!" he announces. "But I gotta do it."

There is no response, verbal or otherwise, from Gilead's limp form. Lance grabs each of his arms firmly and yanks him off of the hook in a single tug, shocked at how light the strange man seems to be.

Strange-colored blood oozes profusely and thickly from the wound on Gilead's back. Lance helps him gently into a supine position on the floor.

"Gilead, are you alright?" he whispers.

Again, the Carfassan does not respond. A pool of shiny blood starts to collect underneath him. His unblinking eyes look glassy and unfocused.

"Please!" Lance yells. "**Say something!**"

Gilead slowly comes to. He lifts his head slowly and weakly.

"I am in pain, my liege," he groans hoarsely. "And I do not think I can move."

"How can I help you?" Lance asks frantically.

"Through that door is an entrance to the chamber of the clockwork guardian," Gilead wheezes, his voice thin. "It will send you home, and in its providence it may deem it prudent to help me."

"What do you mean, prudent?" Lance asks. "It can save you, but it might not want to??"

"Nothing transpires... that the guardian does not account for," Gilead chokes out. "Please... my liege... take the key and leave me here. Either the guardian will help me..."

His voice trails off as his eyes flutter closed. Lance grits his teeth and pries the bronze key out of Gilead's clenched fist. Then he stumbles over to the wooden exit door and jams it into the lock.

Throwing the door open, Lance again illuminates the room in a powerful warm glow. The light being cast from ahead seems to pulsate in intensity and shift in hue. He turns back to steal one last glance at his dying friend. On the table, the candle Gilead had lit extinguishes itself while Lance watches, and a small wisp of smoke travels away from the wick, into the air.

A cold feeling inches across Lance's back, triggering an involuntary shudder. Then the feeling is gone.

Lance crosses the threshold out of the dungeon and shuts the door behind him. Ahead lies a long corridor whose geometry seems to warp in on itself: where Lance stands now, the walls are vertical and orthogonal to the floor. Further ahead, the walls, ceiling, and floor seem to spiral inward and collapse at a point in the horizon which is flooded and drowned with light.

Unsure what will happen next, Lance begins to step forward.

August 14, 1998

T.G.I.F., Tobias thinks to himself. The final day of the third week of his new job at the Wisteria office is coming to a close, and about time too. In exchange for a meager pay increase, the tradeoff for this new position has been more work hours, more ruthless and antisocial coworkers, tasks that somehow manage to be more pointless and soul-crushing than the last job, and a cantankerous elderly Japanese supervisor who barks orders in a completely incomprehensible gibberish accent.

Presently, Tobias is completing a task that involves combing through thirty pages of spreadsheet data and transcribing it where relevant into a quarterly investor report that he will spend next week retooling and reformatting after new data avails itself over the weekend. He is hunched over his cubicle desk and squinting at a word processor software open on his Sony Vaio, whose hardware is brand-new but whose operating system is still running a corporate-approved version of Windows 95. The document he has been typing into has crashed three times since his lunch break, and his fingers are starting to ache from the constant typing.

Tobias looks up; there is the sound of an impatient knuckle-tap on the exterior wall of his cubicle.

"Toby, why aah we stirr wating for you ratest revisyon of dis report? Da work day armost oba!"

It is his supervisor, angry and hyper-caffeinated as ever.

"Sorry, Mr. Toubayashi," Tobias says affably. "It keeps crashing! I promise I'll send it to you in less than an hour."

"For keeping me wating, I expect dis draft to be exserent!" his supervisor retorts.

"You got it, sir," Tobias promises.

Never one to overstay his welcome or belabor a point, Mr. Toubayashi grunts and promptly leaves.

Tobias points his eyeballs back at the screen of his laptop, but quickly finds it difficult to retain his focus on the words in its open document. The interruption from his boss having disturbed his concentration, his inner monologue keeps dancing between reading back his own report and vocalizing a series of unbidden anxious thoughts.

Tobias pushes himself back from his desk and stretches out his lanky limbs. He stands up, gathers a few errant scraps of litter from around his cubicle into a pile, and tosses it into the nearest trash can.

The Wisteria office is swanky and modern. Cubicles are arranged in an ergonomic grid formation, with rounded corners for ease of mobility. There are twenty-five on each floor. The lighting is cool-hued and bright and the furnishings minimalist, except for a few plastic plants sporadically arranged by the support pillars of each big room. Central air-conditioning keeps the office's indoor temperature perpetually on the brink of being too cool to be comfortable while wearing shorts, a marked contrast to the stuffy heat of Tobias's last office. When he started working here, the building had just been renovated, with the addition of a third floor making room for new hires. Over the last couple weeks, the obnoxious new paint smell that tormented Tobias when he first started working here has abated somewhat, or perhaps he has simply become tolerant toward it.

Tobias walks aimlessly around the office, taking in its open floor plan and quiet chill. His coworkers are all diligently rapt on their tasks.

Built predominantly into the East-facing wall of this floor is a large window which overlooks the side parking lot. Tobias finds himself magnetically attracted by it, walking toward it without a conscious thought.

The view is unimpressive. In one direction lies a quaint gathering of other small to midsize office buildings, dealing (at a guess) in IT and actuarial science for regional businesses. In the other direction lies the highway, which is ultimately shrouded in forest. Tobias unconsciously transfixes his gaze upon the distant trees while he stands here and peers through the glass, gathering himself.

For a moment, he wants to flee, feeling in some sense like a battered and cornered animal, desperate to escape. Then he fantasizes elaborately about going postal on his boss. Then he squashes these primal thoughts and considers his future more practically.

Is this menial grunt work any way for a man to spend his early twenties? The social opportunities here are a dead-end, the professional opportunities a long shot, the money appreciated but useless with nothing to spend it on but gas and rent. He feels that he is not only a prisoner here but a coward as well, trapped in a cell not by a guard or by chains but by his love for the familiarity of the prison and his fear of the world beyond it.

He thinks back to Marissa, whom he has not seen in nearly ten days. She must be miserable.

The Clockwork Chamber

The clockwork elf looks exactly as bizarre as it did at the culmination of Lance's first visit. Its shifting ephemeral form is difficult to comprehend, with vaguely anthropomorphic, androgynous features constantly dissolving and reforming in geometric patterns. As Lance enters its domain, it speaks to him in a resonant voice that rattles his skull and does not seem to emanate from a discernible source.

"So, you have passed the test," it says.

Lance takes in his surroundings, something he failed to do on his first visit to this place given the pace of everything that had been happening at the time. The room itself is plain, its slate-colored walls featureless, but intriguingly the clockwork elf seems to be rooted to the floor as if it had sprouted there. It reminds Lance of the fungal growths he learned about during a biology unit at school. He remembers learning about the underground mycelium network that fungi use to communicate with each other and gather information, and briefly wonders if the elf might be woven in a similar manner into the fabric of this realm. It is a passing thought, as he quickly remembers the dreadful sight of Gilead lying in a pool of his own blood.

"Right, the test, yeah," he says dismissively. "But what about Gilead? Aren't you gonna save him?! He's dying back there!"

"He is already dead," the elf states flatly. "And he is not yet alive."

"What?" Lance is bewildered.

"He is still dying, and he is just being born. I see all these things at the same time. It makes no difference to me."

"Well it makes a big difference to me!"

"Irrelevant. You and I are the only real things here."

"Huh? I don't understand."

"That is just as well. Are you ready to leave?"

Lance glances around and considers the question. Is there more he could do before he goes? Does it matter? He could always return later—

As if having read his thoughts, the clockwork elf interjects.

"Know that when you go, you will not be able to return to us for a year or more."

"And why the hell not?" Lance demands. "Why can't I come back whenever I want?"

"Because it is written."

"Written?"

"In the prophecy. Let he who hears this accept it."

"Is there anything we can do for Gilead? Anything at all?"

"Nothing." The clockwork elf's word on this matter seems final. Lance swallows his feelings.

Unlike every other person or creature he has ever met, this being seems singularly incapable of changing its mind. No kind of acting out will have an effect. Best to play it straight.

"I'm ready," Lance declares. "Send me home!"

"It is done."

Within a single attosecond, before one synapse of Lance's brain can send an electrical impulse to another, he is standing outside the tree fort in his backyard as though he had been there all along.

The sun is still high in the sky, a faint breeze blows, and the call of a distant thrush rings in the trees.

Lance enters the back of his house through its sliding glass door. His dad is seated in the living room watching financial news on the television and drinking an iced coffee.

"Hello, daddy," Lance says.

His father seems only half-interested in the world beyond the scope of the Dow Jones Industrial Average at the moment, so he responds without much engagement.

"What's up, Lance? How's it going?"

"Oh, nothing. I just played outside again!"

"Well, congratulations. Would you mind keeping the noise down for the next couple hours? I have a headache."

"Sure thing."

Lance stomps loudly up to his room and feels around his bookcase for the scrap of paper he left there a few nights prior. Within a few seconds, he has found it. Then, more delicately, he sneaks back down the stairs, careful not to make a peep, and pokes around the kitchen.

Under a stack of papers, he finds his dad's cell phone and wallet. He grabs the phone and pockets it, then puts the papers back in their place to conceal his theft.

Sneaking back up the stairs once more, Lance stretches out on his bed and places both his dad's phone and the paper on his pillow. His heart is beating out a symphony in his chest and his head is light with manic, giddy energy.

He dials the number of Cora, his classmate.

The phone rings twice, then she answers.

"Um, hello? Uh, who is this?"

"This is Lance."

"Lance?"

"Yeah, Lance Morrissey. From your English class."

"Ohhh! What do you want, Lance? Wait, hey, how did you get this number?"

"I found it on the school's website."

"Oh."

"But that's not important. I'm calling because I need you to do a favor for me, okay?"

"Okay...?"

Lance takes a deep breath and taps his mind into its proper place. He thinks about how he will phrase what he says next. Then he moves his lips, and a commanding voice speaks:

"**You are going to tell everyone that you kissed me. On the lips. You got that?**"

"Everyone...?" Cora's voice comes through the phone a bit unsteady, which Lance correctly attributes to her post-hypnotic trance state.

"**Everyone**," he says. "**When the school year starts you will tell all your friends. And you will say that you liked it.**"

"Yes, Lance." Her voice is still monotone, but she sounds resolved to comply. "I liked it."

"Alright, cool!" Lance laughs to himself and hangs up the phone. Then he blocks the number and takes a minute to delete the call from the phone's records list.

Now to repeat the process with Anastasia.

August 16, 1998

Her family has just returned home from a pleasant post-church lunch outing. It is the first time since her birthday that Marissa has had the wherewithal to dress nicely, get made up, and look pretty. It is the first time since she said good-bye to Tobias that she has felt any kind of emotion besides languor or fear.

Marissa sits cross-legged on her bed, reading *Little Women*. Her tabby cat, Henry, excuses himself into her bedroom through its ajar door and hops up onto the bed next to her. Arching his back, Henry stretches out all his paws, then begins making himself comfortable next to her. Marissa gives his head a gentle scratch with her free hand. Within a few seconds, the cat begins to vibrate contentedly.

It is this arrangement – book open on her lap, cat purring on the bed – that Marissa loses herself in for perhaps an hour or more until she is interrupted by a tap on the knee.

< Hi, mom > she signs.

< Sorry to interrupt you, Mare, > her mom replies. < I am glad to see you're feeling better. >

< Does it show? >

< Yes. There's color in your face again. And you look relaxed. >

< I'm looking forward to the end of the season. I just can't wait to leave. >

Marissa's mom nods sympathetically, remembering her promise about college.

< In the meantime, > she signs. < Could you be a dutiful daughter and muck the barn? >

Marissa dog-ears her book and folds it up, dropping it on her pillow.

< Yes, mom. Of course. >

The cow stalls are mucked on a rotating basis. With thirty cows on the farm, each farmhand removes manure from 15 stalls over the course of a day. This task, if performed diligently, can be performed within just a couple of hours. The manure is collected into a giant pile, where it is later machine-separated into liquid and solid components. The liquid component is sprayed periodically onto the corn crop while the solid component is accumulated, bagged, and sold at the local farmer's market every couple of weeks.

Larger farms have a mostly automated process for handling this task, but the Miller family farm isn't built for it. This predilection toward manual removal of manure is one of many unfortunate inefficiencies driving the obsolescence of small family farms. When it comes to the Miller farm in particular, Rob has an instinctive skepticism toward large industrial machines. His luddism is driven in no small part by the fact that his daughter's hearing loss had been caused by a close encounter with a piece of threshing equipment that had severed Marissa's auditory nerve when she was only six years old.

Upon arriving at the cow barn in a pair of boots and denim overalls, Marissa is relieved beyond measure to find that the other farmhand set upon the task is Jorge, who waves politely when he sees her. She flashes him an appreciative smile.

Jorge and Marissa make short work of the barn. Within an hour and a half, Marissa returns inside her house and finds her mom, preparing dinner in the kitchen.

< Can we call Tobias? > she asks. < I want to see how he's been doing. >

Her mom wipes chicken fat off her fingers.

< Sure, > she replies. < Let's see if we can reach him. >

She dials his number and waits. The phone rings once, twice, then three times. No answer. Marissa's mom shakes her head. Marissa resolves to try again in a week.

August 23, 1998

One week later, a storm cell crashes across the Midwest, causing a temporary power outage on the farm and destroying a small fraction of the crop. With phone lines down, Marissa does not have a chance to call her boyfriend. Disappointed but undeterred, she vows that she will give it another try next Sunday.

August 30, 1998

Another week has gone by at the pace of a tedious crawl. In the past seven days, Marissa and her mother have finished repainting the exterior fence, while her father and the workers have cleared away the corn stalks felled by the storm. This evening, Marissa and her parents have just finished cleaning and decluttering the entire kitchen.

"I'm thinkin' of crackin' open some whiskey. Marcia, d'you want any?" Rob asks his wife.

"Ooh. I... may... have a glass," Marissa's mom says, stifling her enthusiasm for a Sunday drink.

Taking her meaning in the affirmative, Rob nods and heads down to the basement, where his off-the-books distillery resides. Marcia Miller locks eyes with her daughter and smiles.

< Mom, > Marissa signs. < Let's call Toby again. >

Intermission

"As the tears streamed fast down poor Jo's cheeks, she stretched out her hand in a helpless sort of way, as if groping in the dark, and Laurie took it in his, whispering as well as he could with a lump in his throat, 'I'm here. Hold on to me, Jo, dear!'

"She could not speak, but she did 'hold on', and the warm grasp of the friendly human hand comforted her sore heart, and seemed to lead her nearer to the Divine arm which alone could uphold her in her trouble.

"Laurie longed to say something tender and comfortable, but no fitting words came to him, so he stood silent, gently stroking her bent head as her mother used to do. It was the best thing he could have done, far more soothing than the most eloquent words, for Jo felt the unspoken sympathy, and in the silence learned the sweet solace which affection administers to sorrow. Soon she dried the tears which had relieved her, and looked up with a grateful face."

- Excerpt from Chapter 18 of *Little Women* by Louisa May Alcott

"These libtards think gay puppet shows in Zambia are soft power. Soft power isn't real. The Chinese don't fund gay puppet shows in Africa. They build ports and railroads. That's real."

- Post by @CyberPunkCortes on X.com, February 7, 2025 6:52 PM EST

"Let no one in any way deceive you, for it will not come unless the apostasy comes first, and the man of lawlessness is revealed, the son of destruction, who opposes and exalts himself above every so-called god or object of worship, so that he takes his seat in the temple of God, displaying himself as being God."

· 2 Thessalonians Ch 2, v. 3-4

November 4th, 2036

John Nash settles comfortably into a well-cushioned seat shaped like a banana and watches the show play out on an LED screen set inside the wall across from him. Together with USAID agent Garrett Johnson, he is at the recording studio of Africa's biggest entertainment, culture, and events podcast, which is broadcasting live from South Africa to an audience of as many as 71 million subscribers. At present, Joseph Mulenga is being interviewed by the host about his country's coming rocket launch, while Nash and Johnson sit in a room off to the side and watch it simulcast on the screen in front of them.

Also present is a man with shaggy light-brown hair and a scruffy beard, who sits in the corner of the viewing room and watches the proceedings silently and thoughtfully. He seems to pay the other men no mind as he does so.

Nash is relaxed and casual. His brown suit jacket is unbuttoned to make way for his expanding waistline. The past three years have been good to him. His consulting work has been highly successful, he has accomplished a number of small to mid-sized personal and professional goals, and the success of the Zambian space program has caused the anonymous owner of Stardust Systems to furnish his bank account lavishly.

Joseph Mulenga is speaking.

"De United States Agency of, eh, Intanational Development and de U.S. State Department do deserve *some* of the credit," he says. "Just a little bit, eh? A tiny bit. We owe so much more to our brothers and sisters, the ones who dared to dream and gave us dey skills and hard work."

"And who would you say gets the *most* credit?" the podcast host asks, prying for a controversial answer.

Mulenga answers in a heartbeat.

"Dat would be our forefadda, Edward Makuka Nkloso. He had de dream first, before all of us. He wanted to put an African on Mars, eh? Today, he'd be so proud to hear about the Afronauts of this twenty-first century. At last, we're going to make his vision a reality, bwana."

"And you'll be one of them, right?" the podcast host prods.

Mulenga laughs.

"Yes, dat is right!" he says. "And I am blessed to be joined by Africa's finest scientists as well."

Back in the viewing room, Garrett Johnson turns to John Nash and beams.

"How do you feel about all this?" he asks. "I'm so proud of Mr. Mulenga, isn't it awesome?"

Nash's expression is unreadable.

"Yes..." he says. "Quite so."

"I wonder how many times in history a sitting politician has gone to space before," Garrett says thoughtfully, scratching his chin and pulling out his mobile device to look it up. "Oh hey, did you know that John Glenn was a Senator? He walked on the moon, I'm pretty sure."

"He did not," says Nash. "He only went into orbit. He was too old for the moon. And Mark Kelly was an astronaut-turned-Senator too. But neither of them were in space when they held their terms in office."

"That's so cool," Garrett Johnson says wistfully.

John Nash releases an exasperated sigh.

"How come you never get excited about anything, John?" Garrett asks. "The entire time I've known you I've almost never seen you get excited about stuff."

"The sorts of things that excite me, Agent Johnson," Nash says, "you wouldn't understand."

"Okay then..."

Garrett Johnson continues looking up more trivia while John Nash affixes his attention back on the screen.

"Can you tell us a little bit more about the mission?" the podcast host is asking.

"To start with, there'll be, eh, six of us. Tree Zambians to step foot on the moon, and tree more to do de work between Earth and de moon, looking for Near-Earth Objects. The two teams will split, but we'll meet again after a few days, at a spot we've already set."

"How fascinating! Has anything like this been done before?"

"No, dis idea is brand new."

"Amazing!"

Johnson looks up from his device to interject.

"I'm confused," he says. "What exactly is the deal with the team that isn't going to the moon? I haven't found as many details online about what those guys are doing."

"Call it a state secret," Nash explains. "Only a small amount of that data will be released to the public. No livestreaming or anything like that. We might never find out exactly what it is that they're doing."

"Oh, okay. Huh."

A question occurs to John Nash.

"Garrett, I never asked. Do you like working at USAID?"

"Huh? Oh, yeah, I guess I like it okay. I like meeting and talking to people and I get to do lots of that every day at work."

"Do you know, when I started in politics, your agency had been whittled down to a small team? It's interesting to have seen it grow again. Many people think what you people do has no value."

"Do you think it has value?"

Nash considers this question and its appropriate response carefully.

"Well, Garrett," he says. "I suppose that depends on who you are and how you look at it."

Garrett Johnson, ignoring the fact that John Nash had completely sidestepped the substance of his question, seems satisfied by this answer.

"Yeah," he says. "I never thought about it like that but I guess it's true."

John Nash estimates that the man sitting next to him has an IQ somewhere between 80 and 90. The median Chinese third grader could run circles around the poor dullard.

Joseph Mulenga's interview continues for another half-hour. Just as it ends, Garrett Johnson gets a message from his supervisor asking him to leave the venue to check in for a meeting.

He and John Nash shake hands before he exits.

"Agent Johnson, we may meet again some day or we may not," John Nash says. "But it has been a pleasure working you these past few years."

"Yeah, um, yeah, man!" Garrett Johnson says enthusiastically. "I really liked working with you too."

"Right."

"Okay, uh, see ya!"

Garrett Johnson collects his belongings and leaves. John Nash stretches out his extremities and yawns.

In a moment, Joseph Mulenga enters the room and greets Mr. Nash enthusiastically with a mutual clasp of arms - a Spartan handshake between two would-be warriors.

"How did I do, eh?" Mulenga asks. "Did I look relaxed on de camera?"

"I think you were great," John Nash answers truthfully. "You have a commanding presence even on screen."

"Thank you, thank you, my friend," Mulenga replies graciously. "Well, I must be off now..."

Nash interrupts his farewell.

"How do you feel about going out into space? I have to be honest, I kind of envy you."

Joseph Mulenga laughs heartily.

"I put on a brave face, eh?" he says jovially. "But I am scared shitless. Dis is no easy thing."

"Well, I'm sure you'll do great," Nash says. "Get out there and make your people proud."

Joseph Mulenga replies with a slight bow and leaves to greet his entourage outside.

John Nash hangs back, leaning against a brightly-colored wall, to check the AI data aggregator on his smart watch. It has collected a sampling of analytical data from the initial impressions of the podcast and is outputting a report on viewer demographics, major social media talking points, and other assorted curios of value. He takes in the information silently for a second before his concentration is interrupted by an unfamiliar voice.

"It seems like you've been enjoying the show."

It is the third man who has been sitting in the room all along, silent up 'til now. John Nash looks up in surprise.

"Are you talking to me?" he asks.

"That depends," the man says. "Am I speaking to John Nash or Samir Abdallah?"

A jolt of fear shoots through Nash's spine and his heart rate instantly accelerates.

"Excuse me?" he asks.

"The nickname is cute," the man says. "A clever reference to a famous mathematician with a singular life. But I know who you really are, Samir."

Nash stands stock still, feeling compromised.

"And what is that supposed to mean, exactly?" he asks defensively.

"You've worn many hats, haven't you?" the mysterious man asks. "Consultant, political insider, reactionary accelerationist, pseudo-intellectual... The list goes on and on. But there's one hat you've been unable to take off for the last three years. I call it 'useful idiot.' What do you think?"

"Excuse me, who even are you?"

"I'm the guy who pays your bills," the man says simply. "Haven't you been wanting to meet your boss all this time?"

"So that means you're—"

"Yes, I am the owner of Stardust Systems. I'm also the CEO of its parent company, Lansamor Industries. And I want to thank you for the work you've done for me, but now it's time to take you off the board."

Off the board?

It sounds like a threat. Bewilderment gives way to resolve. Samir shakes off his paralysis and begins to make for the door.

"**Run into traffic and kill yourself**," Lance Morrissey commands as Samir Abdallah exits the building.

Seconds later, pedestrian onlookers in Cape Town look on with shock as a fat Lebanese man runs out into the street to intercept the path of a speeding cargo truck and dies instantly.

June 5, 2015

Geography. For Lance, it is the final period of the final day of his seventh grade school year.

And what a year it's been! Through a great deal of guile, and very little additional hard work, Lance Morrissey has managed to finish out the school year with straight A's and an award for exemplary performance from the principal of LFMMS. He has never been more socially popular, maintaining a circle of close friends and devotees no smaller in number than ten at a time and rotating members out whenever he tires of them. He now has his own cell phone and three girlfriends. Two of them are in class right now with him, one hugging his right arm and the other resting her head on his left shoulder while he sits on the carpeted classroom floor and talks to Mitchell Creevy about sports.

"–really think I could play football?" Lance is asking.

"Yeah man!" Mitchell says earnestly. "You've totally got the right build for it."

Lance glances from side to side.

"Melody and Grace," he says, "What do you girls think? Do I have a football player build?"

The girls hanging onto him begin competing with one another to wax effusively about how athletic Lance is. He smirks, content to watch them vie for his favor. Later he will have to ask the same question to Anastasia, his third girlfriend, to see what she has to say about it.

Yes, it has been a tremendous year for Lance Morrissey. Being able to coerce people into doing his bidding has reaped so many benefits that he has begun to lose track. He can issue demands to his teachers to exempt him from punishment, or correct a bad grade on a test, and in almost every case, they do it! And the social perks have been enormous. Never has it been so easy to convince his peers of a lie or pit them against one another for his own benefit.

It has also been a learning opportunity. Over the course of the school year, Lance has learned all the rules and limitations of his persuasive power. Its effectiveness increases the longer a target spends time in his presence and builds rapport with him. It works on students, teachers, and even parents alike. The only caveat is that he can issue commands to a maximum of a few people at a time – Lance could not, say, get on the school PA system and demand that everyone dance naked. He has to be able to concentrate his influence on each person individually, with diminishing returns if there are more of them.

In fact, during October Lance did try to do exactly that, and after being kicked off the intercom by the principal's assistant, it took a great deal of mental fortitude to convince her not to punish him. The incident had also become a temporary source of social embarrassment, although Lance has since had plenty of opportunity to successfully play it off as a joke.

More than anything else, Lance has sharpened his skills in social deduction and manipulation. He has become hyper-attuned to the cues of others and brilliant in his ability to nudge their minds into a favorable direction with just an idle phrase. In many cases, he does not even need to use his otherworldly power at all to make people do exactly what he wants. His fellow middle schoolers at LFMMS, with their sordid insecurities and developmental awkwardness, are particularly easy prey.

Among other favorable changes, over the last year Lance has also become three inches taller and the pitch of his voice has dropped half an octave. Where before he saw himself as quite small and mousy in relation to most of his peers, he now comes across as more mature and even slightly physically intimidating. This has aided in his ability to get the things he wants, to say nothing of the added boost in self-confidence. It has also – as is the case right now – given people like Mitchell Creevy cause to call attention to his potential for athletic prowess.

"Lance, we totally gotta hang out sometime this summer!" Mitchell says. "I can teach you the rules of the game and we can put a scrimmage together. If, you know, you think you'll be free?"

Lance makes an exaggerated thinking gesture with his thumb and pointer finger.

"Hmmm," he says. "I'll have to think about it. I think I'm going to have a pretty crazy summer. But maybe I'll text you."

In truth, he has no intention of hanging out with Mitchell Creevy unless the jockish boy proposes a plan himself. Lance has found that refusing to approach people directly, and instead nudging them into approaching him, has helped to make him appear more aloof and desirable. Constantly being the one demanding attention from others makes a person come across as desperate. You have to make them come to you.

In any case, whether they play football this summer or not is of no relevant concern to Lance. What he really looks forward to, more than anything else, is the chance to go back to the tree fort and return to his other life as Lansamor.

He has been aching for it all year.

Just one more month to go.

Morning, September 5, 1998

*P*BRRRRRRRRRRRRRR! The air compressor box hums loudly as Tobias dashes around to the back of his car, rubber hose in tow, to inflate his rear tires.

Crouching down on the gravel, Tobias struggles to unscrew the cap on his car's wheel. A drop of sweat drips down his temple.

"Come on, come on!" he shouts impatiently, glancing nervously at the tire inflator over his shoulder, unsure when its timer will run out. The small plastic cap between his forefinger and thumb is stuck, and try as he might, he cannot budge it.

"Ugh!" Tobias grunts, as the cap finally unsticks and falls out of his grasp, skittering and bouncing on the ground before finally coming to a stop behind him. He pivots on his heels and plucks it off the gravel, then stows it in his pocket. Now, back to the task at hand. *Finally.*

Just as Tobias secures the tire inflator nozzle onto the wheel's pin, the air compressor sputters to a stop. He sighs deeply and straightens up, then dashes back around his car in the *other* direction to feed a second quarter into the air machine.

Despite the pleasant temperature of this slightly overcast late summer morning, Tobias is all nerves today. After recovering from a bout of pneumonia which had set in the previous weekend, he had returned to work later in the week to find a backlog of tasks and an angry supervisor waiting for him. The combined strain of long hours, minimal sleep, and constant reprisals from his boss and coworkers has eaten away at his self-esteem and made him into an anxious wreck.

In just a couple hours, he will be reunited with Marissa for the first time in a month. But given everything, the thought of what might happen fills him with fear and trepidation rather than hope. What if she's still angry with him? What if he says the wrong things? What if too much time has passed over the last month and she doesn't love him anymore?

These thoughts had put a knot in his stomach when he woke up today, and he has been trying his best to distract himself with work on his car in the intervening hours that have since passed. Perhaps if his car looks impressive and drives her smoothly, it will distract Marissa from any of Tobias's current shortcomings. It's an irrational thought. But it gives him something productive to focus on. After hosing down his car outside his house and clearing its interior of trash, he had brought it to the gas station to fill up the tank and, now, to complete his list of tasks by topping off the air in each of its tires.

Tobias finishes filling his last tire up with air to his car's manufacturing specification and stands still for a moment, thinking. The rubber hose in his grasp hangs limply toward the ground, still emitting air while the timer inside the compressor continues to run down.

Tobias considers his car for a moment. It has been more than a year since his humble Ford Taurus has looked so pristine. Then he considers himself, scrutinizing his appearance in his car's rear view mirror. His hair looks disheveled. Is it too late to get it cut? He checks his watch. Maybe not! The nearest barber shop is just a few miles down the road. Yes, he should definitely have time, and plenty of it...

Two hours and twenty-three minutes later, the clouds have rolled in and rain has started to fall in a steady drizzle over the town.

Back in the Miller house, Marissa sits on the couch in her living room and frets.

< He's late, > she signs to her mother, who is watching daytime television.

Her mom, fixated on the TV screen, does not perceive this. Marissa waves more emphatically to catch her eye.

< Mom, Toby is late, > she signs again.

< It's raining, > her mom observes, pointing out a nearby window. < The roads are muddy. >

This is true, and certainly a factor that might slow a person down, by a few minutes at least. Still, Marissa can't help but worry something bad has happened. Surely, Tobias can't have forgotten about their plans?

Marissa is briefly disturbed from her thoughtful stupor by a huge vibration that rattles the walls of the house. Sitting on the recliner across from the television, her mother trembles and looks out the window. In a few seconds, Marissa puts two and two together, realizing that the weather has started to become more inclement and a roll of thunder has just moved in. Before her eyes, the rain outside intensifies and a gust of wind whips the trees in her backyard.

Marissa watches the rain for a minute, transfixed, biting on her pointer finger absentmindedly.

Suddenly she feels a hand tap her knee. She looks up.

< Answer the door, > her mom signs, jerking her head in the direction of the entryway of their house.

Still feeling out of step, Marissa shakes her head vigorously to recenter herself as she picks herself up off the couch. Then she trudges sluggishly out of the living room, through the kitchen, and down the hall to answer her front door.

Tobias stands on her front porch, looking sheepish and soggy. He smiles awkwardly when Marissa opens the door and proffers a wilting, bedraggled bouquet of flowers.

< You cut your hair? > Marissa asks, noticing his freshly buzzed scalp.

Her boyfriend nods and steps into the house. Marissa takes the flowers from him as he crosses past her and enters her kitchen. She watches and follows after him as he opens her fridge and grabs a glass bottle of root beer.

< Do you mind? > he asks.

Marissa shakes her head, so he pops the cap off with his pocket knife and takes a swig. Marissa observes him with a placid expression.

"Ahhh!" Toby says, before placing the bottle back on her kitchen table. < So how are you? >

Marissa considers how to answer this question, but her thoughts are sluggish and her brain uncooperative.

< I'm OK. >

While Marissa watches, Tobias scratches his back and shakes his sweatshirt, trying to displace loose pieces of hair that had gotten stuck there during his haircut. Marissa's mom enters the kitchen and greets him, then directs him to hang up his wet raincoat in the hall closet.

He returns to the kitchen to scrutinize Marissa, who has not moved from her spot, more closely.

< Are you sure you're OK? > he asks.

< I think so, > Marissa replies, forcing a toothless smile.

Tobias is unconvinced. He takes another sip of root beer and squints at her.

< Let's get out of here, > he suggests.

Marissa points casually out the window with her thumb, where the storm rages outside unabated.

< Forget the rain! > Tobias signs dramatically. < Come with me. >

He beckons extravagantly, grabs his root beer bottle, and begins to head for the front door.

Marissa follows him with some exasperation, stopping with her hands on her hips in the middle of the hall as Tobias waits for her by the door. She throws open the hall closet and grabs his coat, holding it up for him to see.

Tobias scoffs and throws his hand out lazily to indicate disregard. Marissa puts the coat on herself instead and shuts the closet door.

As they step outside together, lightning flashes up in the clouds.

Guess we're going on an adventure in the rain, Marissa thinks as she follows Tobias to his car, which is parked at the edge of the road, several minutes of walking away from her house. *He's gonna catch a cold.*

January 17, 2037

Joseph Mulenga sits in a small operations room with five of his fellow Afronauts. A few of them are deep in conversation about gravitational trajectories and delta-V. Everyone present is clad in a gray flight suit accented by the four colors of Zambia's flag. On a screen above where they sit, technical data beyond Mulenga's comprehension flashes and scrolls by, providing readouts on the day's atmospheric conditions and rocket's fuel status.

Mulenga is restless. With less than a half hour to go until the team enters their rocket and makes ready to blast off, the looming prospect of saying goodbye to the Earth and embarking to parts unknown has finally broken through his steely nerves. The ticking countdown clock set in the bottom corner of the room's readout screen only compounds his worry.

Dr. Miriam Beauty Nwanga, the flight captain of the lunar team, approaches Mulenga with a small glass of icy water and offers it to him.

"You look like you need it," she says good-naturedly.

"Thanks," the politician replies, accepting it and taking a gentle sip. "I'm feeling very out of place here."

"You are doing a very brave ting for your people," Nwanga encourages him. "Dis is true leadership."

Mulenga lets out a humble chuckle.

"I appreciate it," he says. "But, truth be told, I do not know what I am getting myself into."

Dr. Nwanga, having piloted an orbital test flight a few months prior, places a hand on Joseph Mulenga's shoulder gently to comfort him.

"Take it from me," she says. "No one does until dey do it. But you are a brave and strong man, eh? You have what it takes to do dis ting."

Mulenga considers this perspective and tries to internalize it.

"Miriam, do you know what my part of de mission is supposed to do?" he asks.

"Yes, of course," she replies. "Dey briefed us separately but we got de full story."

"So you know dat we are traveling to another planet?"

Dr. Nwanga regards Joseph Mulenga with an expression suggesting that he might be cracking up.

"Mister Mulenga, I hate to contradict you, but dat is not what your team is doing," she says.

Mulenga frowns and blows a gust of air out his nose. Dr. Nwanga elaborates.

"Dey showed us your flight path and everyting. Your team will orbit at de L4 Lagrange point between de Earth and de moon and take compositional reading of passing asteroids and comets. Den you will rejoin us a day later and return to de Earth."

Mulenga glances around and leans in conspiratorially.

"It isn't true," he whispers. "We have a different mission than dat."

"Really? Who else knows?" Dr. Nwanga asks.

"Sorry?"

"Who else knows about dis other mission? Why was I not told?"

"Only a very few people. De engineers who built our flight systems and a handful of Americans who came to Zambia a few years ago. Plus my crewmates and a handful of technicians."

"Why de secrecy?"

"Dey don't want anybody to know. Even de Americans who came were later fed a different story. Dey probably don't remember what was originally said in dat meeting."

"Joseph..." Nwanga sounds concerned. "Are you sure about dis?"

Frustrated, Mulenga massages his brow and sighs deeply.

"Docta Miriam, why would I lie?"

"A very good question. But why would *they*?"

Joseph Mulenga looks away from Miriam Beauty Nwanga and stares at the countdown clock, with only nineteen minutes remaining. He suddenly feels very lonely.

He motions to his crew mates, Jeanette Emberley and Madoda Tembo, who are talking to a different member of the lunar orbiting crew. They approach in his direction and he sidesteps them into a huddle away from eavesdropping ears.

"What's going on?" he asks. "Why don't dey know about our part of de mission?"

"We were told to keep it a secret," Madoda Tembo explains simply.

"Yes, but why?"

Jeanette Emberley responds in a lowered voice.

"The technology we're using to cross to the other planet still isn't known to the public," she explains. "Its reveal is conditional on this mission being a success. It's just basic op-sec."

"Do you remember Garrett Johnson and John Nash?" Mulenga asks her. "De Americans who first brought dis idea to my attention?"

"Who?" asks Tembo.

"Of course I do," Emberley replies.

Joseph Mulenga drops his voice to an urgent hiss.

"John Nash turned up dead a couple months ago. Garrett Johnson went missing last week."

Emberley looks shocked.

"What?!" she asks, drawing eyes from elsewhere in the room.

"Shush! Keep it quiet. I don't know who may be listening."

Madoda Tembo, the pilot of the mission, raises his hands to chest-level and beckons his comrades to settle down.

"Listen," he says. "Strange as it is, dat could be a coincidence. Dis is not someting we should be tinking about right now. We need to focus on dis launch."

The three of them glance over to the countdown clock. Only ten minutes remain until blastoff. Tembo is right: now is not the appropriate time. In five minutes, they will exit this room and cross over to their capsule. Then they will strap in, make final instrument checks, and communicate with their mission control team back in Lusaka. As is tradition, there will be one last countdown, then their spaceship will blast off, headed for parts unknown.

There is an 8% chance the rocket will explode before exiting the atmosphere.

Joseph Mulenga guides his companions back to the fray with the lunar team.

"Is everyone ready to get started?" Madoda asks his counterpart on the lunar team.

"I think we are!" Dr. Nwanga replies brightly. "Mister Mulenga, any final words for de good of de orda?"

Mulenga clears his throat and briefly considers raising the alarm about his true mission to the rest of the lunar team. Instead, he puts on a brave face and tries to embody a confident, inspirational swagger.

"When I was a small child, I flew with my father to de city of Harare in Zimbabwe. De city was in great trouble and de people needed his leadership to know dat things wa gonna be okay. I had never been on a plane before dat day. I was so scared. Dat day, I cried and I screamed. I begged dat we should stay home because I was so scared of de airplane." Mulenga pauses, steadying his breath. "But my father squeezed my hand and he told me not to be afraid. De entire time, walking trew de airport, he did not let go of my hand. We walked together, rode de plane together, helped de people together. I learned I did not need to be scared."

He reaches out, linking arms with Dr. Miriam Beauty Nwanga and Madoda Tembo, who each stand on either side of him.

"Let us join togetha as we enter dis rocket and show de world dat Zambia stands united!"

The three members of the lunar crew link up their own arms with each other, then the two team leads join up. All six Afronauts leave together as an enjoined row and march out of the operations room.

As they step out onto the catwalk leading to the spaceship outside, a drone-powered camera records their procession and streams it to the major mass media outlets of the world. Joseph Mulenga nods at it as they pass by.

July 5, 2015

The summer sun beats down on the Morrissey household like a cruel prison guard. Lance's father taps out a rhythmic beat on his laptop while the TV in their living room blares a warning about the day's record-breaking heat index. Sitting up in his air-conditioned bedroom, Lance stares impatiently out his window and watches the air shimmer. Behind him comes the quiet sound of gently rattling metal. The noise comes from his pet rabbit, Stardust, guzzling down water from the bottle suspended inside its cage.

Last time Lance had visited the strange land beneath his backyard tree fort, he had been told not to return until a year had passed. Of course, since then, he had paid several visits to the fort, but the ground beneath it had remained unyielding each time.

Today officially marks the passage of a full year since that last visit. Now, Lance reasons, only a little time remains until he will be granted access to that other world. He had tried it one last time when he first woke up this morning, but still to no avail. Since then, he has compulsively been alternating between glancing at the clock on his phone screen and looking out the window. Last year, he had entered the tree fort around 11 o'clock in the morning. Today, the wait feels interminable.

At exactly 11:01 am, Lance kicks the back door of his house open and sprints across his backyard. Reaching the tree fort before the sun's heat has a chance to touch him, he spins around quick as a flash inside it and drops to his knees.

His kneecaps land in a viscous and satin-sheened mud. A pleasant breeze ripples his shirt.

Rising to stand, Lance does a full rotation on the spot to take stock of his surroundings and orient himself.

Where did you put me this time?

Surrounded by golden-leaved trees and tangled underbrush, Lance reasons that he must not be too far from the village, and somewhere in close proximity to the part of the forest where he had chased after the apparition of his mother. The mud on the ground indicates that this spot must be low in elevation and close to water. Sure enough, Lance focuses his hearing and begins to perceive the faint trickle of a babbling creek nearby.

Lance judges that his best bet to get to where the action is would be to find the village. Given that it is situated at a relatively high point of elevation, the most rational course of action is to head uphill.

Sure enough, the ground in the opposite direction of the flowing water seems to be inclined at a slight positive grade that continues for quite some distance. Lance points himself this way and begins his jaunt in the direction of the rising sun. Based on what he remembers from the maps in the hall of heroes, he is probably in the South-West quadrant of the forest; the village is to the East and the manor somewhere to the North.

It takes only a few minutes before Lance arrives at the outer limits of the village, indicated by the sound of talking and bustling nearby. He pulls his phone out to look at the time, but the screen refuses to turn on. There's simply no way its battery could be dead, but his device might as well be a brick for all the good it does him. Lance reasons that interference with outside electronics must simply be one of the many quirks of this place.

Lance wanders into a small butcher's shop, where cuts of unidentifiable meat are hung on hooks and displayed on shelves. A few pedestrians filter in and out of the shop, seemingly oblivious to his arrival. He approaches the counter, where a fat piglike man in an apron has his back turned and is paring a sirloin with a large knife.

Lance raps his knuckles on the countertop and announces his presence.

"Yo!" he says.

"Huh?" the butcher grunts, turning to face him and wiping juice off his blade onto his stained cloth apron.

"You know who I am?" Lance asks.

The butcher sizes him up.

"Er... 'fraid not," he mutters.

"It's me!" Lance announces triumphantly. "I'm Lansamor!"

"Don't think we've met," the butcher replies thoughtfully, scratching his hairy chin with a webbed finger.

"Oh. Well, do you know a Carfassan named Skanot? Or a... Malyumpkin-ite... named Binnmerva?"

"Come to thinking of it, yeh!" the butcher says with enthusiasm. "They hung round my old mate Gilead, I speck."

"And have you seen either of them lately?"

"Hum. Er, no. Hain't seen Gilead lately neither."

The reminder of Gilead's untimely demise triggers the tiniest twinge of guilt at the pit of Lance's gut, but the feeling passes in a moment and he stifles it.

"Okay, well, uh, thanks I guess," Lance says awkwardly before starting to shuffle away.

"Wait just a minute now!" the butcher calls. Lance turns back around, to see the butcher pointing out a side window. Lance's view through it is slightly obscured by the furnishings of the room.

"What's up?" Lance asks.

"Thinkin' that might be them, I speck."

Lance steps forward and leans over to get a better view. Sure enough, Skanot and Binnmerva are wearing hooded cloaks and talking to a third, taller, figure whose back is turned to the butcher's. They stand some twenty feet outside the building, in a cobbled path that curls between houses and businesses.

"Thanks," Lance says, before departing in a hurry.

The air outside the butcher's shop is markedly more pleasant in both temperature and smell. Absent the lurid stench of meat and sweat, Lance no longer feels he has to breathe exclusively through his mouth, something he did not consciously realize he had been doing for the last few minutes until he'd made his egress.

"My liege!" Skanot hails him as he approaches. "How goes the day?"

"Much better now that I'm here again, Skanot," Lance says. "Who's your friend?"

Now that he has a front view of this third figure, he can make out its distinguishing features. Built like a giant nightmare penguin, the creature is a tall, white, fluffy biped with piercing black eyes and a dagger-like beak. Far more anthropomorphic than any of the birdlike Dvorans he'd encountered previously, Lance finds this creature to be truly enigmatic.

"This, dear, is our friend Opius, the temporal guardian of the East," Binnmerva explains. "Opius is here to deliver a message to us."

"This is the one?" Opius asks, its eyes unblinking.

Lance feels small.

"Exactly as the prophecy foretold!" Skanot replies.

"What do you want to report to us, Opius?" Binnmerva asks. "We've been eager to hear it!"

"The usual fracas," Opius replies stoically. "Wars and rumors of wars."

"These things must happen," Skanot solemnly cuts in.

"Yes." Opius fixes its gaze upon Lance again. "These are the birth pangs of the things to come."

"Can I jump in here?" Lance asks. "Because I'm super confused."

Opius continues to scrutinize the boy.

"Opius is our messenger," says Binnmerva. "Here to explain what's been going on in the East."

"And what exactly *is* in the East, besides more woods?" Lance asks. "I didn't see anything else on the maps."

"Well," Binnmerva says. "When you go far enough East, you eventually end up in the West."

"I don't understand."

Skanot pulls out a map to clarify, indicating the farthest Eastern point.

"Our land exists in a recursive loop. When you go all the way to the boundary here–"

He slides his finger around the back of the map, tracing an invisible arc before it emerges at the farthest Western point.

"–You wind up here. But that form of travel involves crossing through a time threshold."

Lance stares blankly at the map, then back at them.

"...What?"

Opius finally stops fixating on Lance and stares into the horizon.

"One would cross over into the future," it explains. "Time works differently here. Travel into the West far enough and you arrive at the furthest point East, one generation in the past. Travel into the East far enough, and you arrive at the furthest point West one generation into the future."

Lance cognitively wrestles with this concept.

"So you're from the future then? That's sick!" he exclaims.

"I am from a possible future," Opius clarifies. "Events are constantly in flux."

"And what's that like? The future, I mean."

"The beast has broken free of its seal and terrorizes the people by night."

"Oh. That sucks."

"Yes, Lansamor, it does indeed 'suck'," Skanot interjects. "Hence, the prophecy. This is the doom you're meant to save us from."

"And when's that supposed to happen?" Lance asks.

Skanot and Binnmerva exchange glances. Opius stops looking at the horizon and stares again at Lance.

"My dear boy, I would've thought that was obvious!" Binnmerva exclaims. "It happens today!"

Afternoon, September 5, 1998

Rain falls over Nebraska at a steady and relentless pace. Certainly, the conditions are not exactly torrential, but as Marissa finds herself stomping through it after Tobias, the thought that the weather could still be worse is not exactly at the forefront of her mind.

As they pass through her family's expansive grid of corn, Marissa can't help but notice and fret about the stalks which have wilted or fallen over from this latest round of summer storms. If the harvest is insufficiently bountiful, she might be stuck here for another year or more.

The thought of being trapped on this farm for much longer is a terrifying one. She has done all she can to block out what had happened here a month ago, but the memory persists on her flesh and lingers in her bones.

Up ahead, Tobias skips cheerfully along the sodden path. At the moment, he seems oblivious to the rain and impervious to worry. Marissa studies his behavior with some interest as she follows him apace.

Tobias has always made a show of bravery around her. Whenever they are together, he takes great pains to keep himself from inflicting his insecurities or anger upon Marissa. Even at his most tired and overworked, he has always put forth his strongest face and tried to be a source of motivation.

Marissa, in turn, has always had mixed feelings about this behavior. On the one hand, it's a relief that she and Tobias have never come to blows over trivial matters. On the other hand, she wonders how sustainable the stoic act could possibly be; it's easy enough to maintain for a few hours out of the week, but if they were to live together in the future, she wants him to feel like he can let down those barriers and be more emotionally open. If not, wouldn't he come to resent her?

After trudging through the rain-slicked mud for what feels like an eternity, Tobias and Marissa finally reach the former's bright red station wagon, half-sunken in the roadside muck. With a theatrical flourish, Tobias sweeps open the passenger door, straightening his back like a courtly chauffeur.

"Madam," his lips say, as he dips into a flamboyant bow.

Marissa, playing along, lifts her chin regally and extends her hand, fingertips grazing his palm as if she were royalty accepting tribute. Tobias seizes the moment, pressing a gallant kiss to her knuckles before releasing her with a final, knowing smirk. Then, without missing a beat, he spins on his heel, dashes around the hood, and flings himself into the driver's seat, grinning as rainwater drips down his nose and onto the cracked leather upholstery.

The air inside Tobias's car is warm and the lingering smell of old cologne is comforting. Marissa gets comfortable inside it, taking a moment to trace the familiar cracks in her seat with her finger.

< You ready? > Tobias asks, looking at his girlfriend expectantly.

< Where are we going? > Marissa counters.

Tobias seems confused by the question.

< The garden. Remember? > he replies.

The garden. *Oh God, yes,* she thinks. *The garden. How could I forget?* She shakes off the confusion and refocuses.

< But it's wet! > Marissa protests.

Tobias doesn't seem the least bit deterred. Instead, he flashes a cheeky, knowing smile which suggests he's privy to knowledge Marissa doesn't have.

Without another word, he throws his car into gear and guides it smoothly into the middle of the road. The world outside blurs with the rain as they move forward, toward the garden and whatever awaits them there.

January 18, 2037

Joseph Mulenga floats freely in zero-G and watches the distant planet Earth through the viewport of Zambian shuttle *Mwaba-1*. A full day has passed since the launch, but the novelty of being in outer space has not yet worn off. Nor has the disorienting effect of weightlessness given way to acclimatization – on multiple occasions, Joseph has accidentally turned just slightly too far and wound up either upside-down or spinning out of control.

As he glides through the capsule and marvels at the apparent tiny size of his home planet, the voice of lunar captain Miriam Beauty Nwanga crackles over the radio.

"We ah all present in de luna capsule," she says. "Systems nominal. Standing by to detach from de ship."

Joseph Mulenga steadies himself against the wall and listens for the response from his own team captain.

"Message received and copied," Madoda Tembo's voice replies. "Godspeed to you, luna team."

A moment later, the whole shuttle rumbles and shudders as the lunar capsule detaches from the front of it. Joseph Mulenga pushes off the wall and taps on his own communication unit to establish contact with his partners.

"So we are good to go, eh?" he asks cheerfully.

Jeanette Emberley responds directly.

"Yep," she says. "Captain Tembo is making final calculations on the propulsion impulse right now. You might want to use the next few seconds to make sure you're strapped in."

Joseph Mulenga climbs along the floor to a nearby seat built into one of the capsule's walls, and straps himself into it. Then he waits with bated breath. Sure enough, not ten seconds later the ship shudders again as it adjusts its orientation, and then he is pushed back into his seat while it forcefully accelerates into a new direction.

"Trajectory is locked," Madoda Tembo confirms over the ship's speaker.

"We'll be entering the quantum tunnel in t-minus two hours!" Jeanette announces.

The Village

At the behest of Skanot and Opius, Lance has spent the majority of the day going around from building to building and calling upon residents, pedestrians, shoppers, and store owners to assemble at the center of the village to hear his address. He has used a combination of rhetorical appeals and persuasive psycho-kinetic power to convince every able-bodied male civilian of adult age to file in for this grand speech.

And now he has to actually deliver it.

The village square is now overflowing with bodies, some 150 in number or more. The villagers assembled there are restless. Many chatter noisily, while some stand still and stare at Lance expectantly. Farmers, traders, warriors, elders—all have come, their murmurs swelling into an anxious tide.

For his part, Lance stands atop a chiseled stone platform that gives him a visual on just about every face in the crowd. He clears his throat and begins his address.

"Good people of this land," he cries. "Listen to me!"

His voice is amplified by the acoustics of the town square. The crowd falls silent.

"I am Lansamor, the chosen protector of you people!" he says proudly. "My arrival was predicted by a prophecy, and now, here I am! So, uh..."

He falters and scans the crowd. Out in the distance, someone coughs.

"Listen!" he says again. "We know that out there in the woods, a terrible beast lies in waiting, just itching to break out and terrorize everyone. We have seen what that future looks like, and it is bleak! But together, we can stop that from ever happening! You and I, my friends, are all that stands between salvation and annihilation! That beast cowers in its pit, believing us to be weak. But I say this: NO MORE!"

Finally working himself into a stride, Lance allows himself to enjoy the moment. A murmur starts to spread through the crowd. Lance breaks out into a wolfish grin and crescendos his voice, gesticulating wildly with his hands as he continues.

"The beast has fed on our fear!" he howls. "It has waited, knowing that we would hesitate! But no more! I call upon you, the proud people of this land, to stand beside me! We will not bow! We will not cower! We will march! We will fight! **We will WIN!**"

In the midst of all the enthusiasm, this is the first time Lance has been able to successfully use his psychic Voice on a crowd. The cheer that follows is deafening. Spears are raised. Swords are unsheathed. Pointy sticks are hastily whittled down to be even pointier. Lance dismounts from his stage and beckons for the townspeople to follow. And so together they charge West —an army of the desperate and the brave—toward the gaping chasm where the unseen monster lay waiting.

For a little over an hour, the procession troops through the golden forest. A few villagers trip or twist their ankles on the roots and foliage, only to get trampled to death by the people marching behind them. The mob does not slow down or pause to catch its breath, moving as a single throng behind the leadership of Lance Morrissey.

When they finally arrive at the mouth of the beast's cave, Lance stands outside the entrance and addresses the masses triumphantly.

"This is your moment!" he calls. "**Get in there and attack!**"

Frothing with hatred and rage, the people of the village lift up their voices into a frenzied cry and rush into the cave as one while Lance Morrissey stands outside and watches. He can just make out the form of a many-headed beast sleeping deep within the cave, mostly obscured by shadow. The people of the village set themselves upon it before the beast can even open an eye. Stabbing and slashing viciously, they brutally attack it like starving animals. The beast awakens, but all too late. It can only lash out blindly and howl in pain as it is impaled, mauled, and decapitated over and over. The walls of the cave splatter with its blood.

A few minutes later, the surviving villagers— a little more than 80 in number— exit the cave and assemble around Lance. The eldest among them holds up one of the beast's dismembered heads as a trophy. Lance can't help but smile uncontrollably. He has never been so proud of himself.

The Garden

As Tobias's car coasts down the rain-slicked hill and crosses the threshold of the covered wooden bridge at the bottom of it, the sounds of the storm around him and Marissa disappear. As the car emerges into the light of the garden, any sign of the inclement weather that had just surrounded them is gone.

"The rain stopped!" Tobias marvels.

"Yeah," Marissa replies without thinking. "Somehow I don't think we're in Kansas anymore, Toto."

She looks at Tobias expectantly to gauge his reaction. His smile slowly widens before breaking out into a giant grin.

"Oh my God, how did I forget!" Marissa exclaims. "I can hear!"

"Let's get out and enjoy the sunshine," Tobias says, stifling giddy laughter.

Marissa and Tobias step out onto the temperate flowering meadow. Almost immediately, Marissa can feel the sunlight working to dry her wet hair. She moves, almost entranced, to a patch of bluebell flowers and sits down in the middle of them, brushing their soft petals tenderly with her fingers. Meanwhile, Tobias circles around the back of his car, seemingly stumped by a problem he can't wrap his head around. Marissa watches him with interest as he peers into the dark forest that lies beyond.

"What are you looking for, Toby?" she asks.

"I never thought about it last time, but there's no sign of the bridge from this side," Tobias explains. "When we left here last time I just reversed through that clearing in the woods and then we were back."

Marissa stands up and joins her boyfriend as he scrutinizes the shadowy trees.

"That forest sure is dark," she says.

"Yeah," Tobias agrees breathily. "Freaky, right? It's so bright out here and then you can hardly see past the tree line."

"There's another thing you didn't notice," Marissa says.

"Oh? What's that?"

"Half the flowers here don't grow anywhere near Nebraska," Marissa replies, turning around and gesturing at all the plants around them. Tobias follows her hands with his eyes.

"Wow," he says. "You're right!"

Marissa laughs.

"I guess we were too busy focusing on, like, the insane miracle of my hearing coming back to notice all the *other* stuff that didn't make sense last time," she says.

"When you put it like that," Tobias says with a grin, "Can you blame us?"

"No you can't!" Marissa smiles.

Walking hand-in-hand, the couple crosses over a hill and toward the babbling brook that waits for them a couple hundred feet away.

"Man," says Tobias as they walk. "My socks are SOAKED!"

"It's almost like you should've grabbed rain gear before running into a thunderstorm or something," Marissa replies sarcastically.

"Blah blah blah!" Tobias retorts. "I didn't want to lug around an umbrella or jacket here."

They sit down by the bank of the stream and Tobias removes his socks and shoes, placing them behind himself. Then he wiggles his foot in Marissa's face.

"Who let the dogs out!" he shouts. Marissa screams in mock fright and slaps her boyfriend's leg away.

"You are an ultra mondo DORK!" she exclaims.

"You don't want to feast your eyes on my freakish Scots-Irish toes, Marissa?" Tobias retorts playfully.

"I don't want to see your Scots-Irish toes that close to my face ever again and that's final," Marissa responds.

Tobias smirks and throws his head back, as if bathing in the beams of the sun.

"Oh, I love this," he says wistfully. "I wish we could talk to each other like this every day."

"I can't believe I forgot about this place," Marissa says.

"What do you mean?" Tobias asks.

"Since my birthday I've just totally been in a funk," Marissa explains. "I've, like, completely erased what happened that day from my brain. My memory is a total blank for large sections of it."

This remark shakes Tobias out of his good humor, which gives way to concern.

"Woah," he says. "Why's that?"

Marissa wracks her brain, trying to recreate the events of that evening in her mind, but all that comes up is a vaguely ill feeling of dread in the pit of her stomach.

"I don't think I want to talk about it," she says. "Let's just enjoy nature for a bit."

"But Marissa, I think we *should* talk about it!" Tobias replies, his voice shaking with urgency.

Rather than respond, Marissa takes a deep shuddering breath and falls silent, casting her gaze down into the steadily trickling water of the creek. Tobias scoots over across the grass in her direction until the two of them are seated less than a foot apart.

"Here, I got you," he says, sweeping her closer to himself and bringing her head to rest gently on his shoulder. "Let's just sit like this for a while."

"This is nice," Marissa agrees in a voice barely louder than a whisper. "I like this."

A gray bird that looks like a heron swoops by overhead, its broad wingspan temporarily casting a shadow over the two of them, before it disappears over the distant trees. Tobias watches it go by and thinks carefully about what he will say next.

"I can understand why you're afraid to tell me about what's bothering you," he says quietly.

"Can?" Marissa asks, making sure she heard him correctly.

"Can," Tobias affirms. "Yes, I can. Because I haven't always been completely open with you, and I think you know it."

Marissa takes her head off of Tobias's shoulder and crinkles her eyes at him. Tobias meets her gaze with his for a moment, before dropping it to stare at the grass as he continues speaking.

"Last time we were here, I didn't ask you to marry me, and I could tell you were upset. And the truth is I was afraid," Tobias says, his voice unsteady.

"What were you afraid of, Toby?" Marissa asks, putting a comforting hand across her boyfriend's upper back. Tobias swallows before continuing to talk.

"When I was a kid," he says, "I thought I was gay."

Marissa looks at Tobias with a mixture of confusion and wry amusement.

"Do you still think that now?" she asks.

"Well, no." Tobias shakes his head firmly. "But when you're younger sometimes you just don't know. But anyway, I, um– some stuff happened and I ended up at the house of a strange man, who made me take drugs and tried to, um–"

He trails off, finding it hard to speak all of a sudden, and meets Marissa's watery eyes. Any trace of amusement is gone, replaced by a deep and abiding concern. She grabs his hand and squeezes it.

"What did he try to do, Toby?" she asks.

"I think, that–" Tobias exhales, then inhales deeply. His face changes a shade. "I think he was going to try to rape me."

Marissa is stricken.

"Oh, Toby!" she says. "I can't imagine. That's–"

But yet, she can. Unbidden, the memory of what happened by the barn on the evening of her birthday comes rushing back into her head. She falls silent and shakes her head slowly.

"I've been kind of weird about intimacy ever since then," Tobias explains. "You're the first girlfriend I've ever had, and I love you, but I'm afraid to get married because— well, I dread what comes with it."

He doesn't need to spell it out. Marissa gets the message.

"I completely understand why you'd feel that way," she says soothingly. "But I hope you know that you're safe with me. Do you trust me?"

Tobias steels himself, then responds without a second thought.

"Absolutely," he says. "I completely trust you. And, Mare, do you trust *me*?"

"All the way to the moon and back," Marissa says. "Maybe that sounds corny but it's true."

"Tell me what happened on your birthday when I left you."

Marissa feels taken aback by the conversational pivot, but fair's fair. At this point, if she could talk to anyone in the world about her problem, it's Tobias.

"I walked away from your car," she recalls, "And the sun was setting."

Tobias nods encouragingly.

"Go on," he says.

"My mind was still busy with everything that had happened in the garden and I was thinking about how, well... I was thinking about how much it sucked being deaf again, honestly."

Tobias chuckles, then apologetically holds up a hand.

"Sorry," he says. "That's perfectly fair, though."

"If you're ever thinking about losing one of your senses, just know I wouldn't recommend it," Marissa quips. "Anyway. You know those guest workers my dad hired?"

Tobias nods silently. Marissa continues:

"When I came up to the front of my house, they had all gathered by the barn, and I could tell they were super drunk. But they weren't, like, funny drunk. They were scary drunk. The air around them smelled like booze and piss."

As she talks, the emotions from that night bubble up to the surface, and she begins to feel choked up.

"Toby," she says, "They surrounded me like hungry animals. They grabbed at me and tried to rip off my dress. They beat me with their belts and threw me to the floor. I couldn't see anything, my eyes were totally swollen with tears. But I could smell the liquor on their breath and feel their hands all over me. It was the most terrifying moment of my entire life."

While Marissa recounts the events of the night, Tobias's expression switches over from worry to fury. She can see his face get redder and redder.

"Those fucking MONSTERS!" he roars. "Where were your parents during all of this?"

"They weren't home," Marissa replies forlornly. "It was just me and the workers there."

"Did you tell them what happened later?"

"No."

Tobias looks incredulous.

"Well, why on Earth not?" he asks. "Come on Marissa, you can't just let them get away with that!"

"Don't you see I didn't have any choice?" Marissa exclaims. "I can't leave this town without money from the harvest, and we can't have a good harvest without the workers!"

Tobias opens his mouth to fire back, then closes it and shakes his head, switching to a calmer tone.

"I'm sure if you talked to your parents, they'd be open to finding another way. I can't imagine Mr. Rob would want those kinds of people around his daughter, crops or no crops, and he wouldn't want you to sacrifice your future to feel safe."

Marissa brushes a tear out of the corner of her eye.

"I don't know," she says. "But it doesn't matter now. There's only a couple weeks until harvest at this point and I can tell them about it then. Besides, it all feels like a bad dream. Like it happened to someone else."

"But it didn't happen to someone else, it happened to you!" Tobias hollers. "Come on, Mare. Don't do this to yourself."

Marissa falls silent. Her lip quivers and her eyes mist up with tears. Tobias brings her in for a warm embrace, and she gives herself over to her sadness. Tears flow fast and freely, followed by dry and achy sobs. Tobias rocks her gently in the midst of her catharsis.

"This is good," he tells her in a soothing voice. "This is healthy."

Marissa rotates to her back, looks up at Tobias, and opens her mouth to respond, but she can't get the words out. Her chest continues to heave with the force of the wounded noises escaping her throat without warning or restraint. As their eyes meet, she can see Tobias's own emotional walls begin to crumble. Tears silently well up and stream down his cheeks as he flashes a broken smile, trying to tell himself that the two of them will be alright.

Over the next ten minutes, as the two of them cry together, he begins to believe it.

"Marissa," he finally says, "Will you marry me?"

Exoplanet JM-201137a: Arrival

About five hours after separating from the lunar team's capsule, what remains of the *Mwaba-1* space research vessel approaches close enough to the L4 Lagrange point to make visual contact on the spacetime anomaly situated there.

"Keep ya eyes peeled, bwanas," Madoda Tembo announces over the ship's intercom.

Joseph Mulenga presses himself up to the side viewport and cranes his neck at an awkward angle until the entrance to the quantum tunnel comes into view. Visible as a bluish elliptical distortion in spacetime, at first glance it only registers to him as a tiny speck, but its dominance in the horizon quickly expands as the crew's ship approaches closer.

The door to the chamber Mulenga floats in slides open and Jeanette Emberley propels herself into it with him, waving to indicate that he should move so that she can get a look for herself. Mulenga pushes himself back by about a foot and addresses the back of her head.

"Doesn't Captain Tembo need you up in de cockpit?" he asks.

"He'll be fine," Emberley responds casually. "We're right on target, so the best thing we can do is go hands-off until we pass that thing."

"What is it?" Mulenga asks. "I've never seen anytin' like it before."

"Nor have I," Emberley says, a tone of hushed awe apparent in her voice. "Hopefully it doesn't rip us apart."

"Is that likely?" Mulenga is unsure whether or not he should freak out or start praying.

"Oh, not at all. Just a morbid joke."

"Don't say things like dat, it's bad luck, eh?"

Jeanette Emberly smiles and pushes herself back against the capsule wall.

"Just in case," she says, "Why don't we strap in?"

A couple of minutes later, the ship passes through the quantum tunnel silently and without incident. The travel time is almost instantaneous; peering out the viewport and strapped up against the wall, Joseph and Jeanette can see the stars visible from within the home solar system disappear behind a rippling veil, only to be replaced by an entirely new and different set not even a full second later. Captain Tembo's voice comes over the speaker again.

"We have visual on de new planet," he says cheerfully. "Beginning de process for landing soon."

Miss Emberley clicks her seatbelt off.

"That's my cue," she says. "Stay here, and we'll see you in a few minutes on the surface."

Without further ado, she exits the viewing chamber, leaving Joseph Mulenga alone with his thoughts.

From the cockpit, Madoda Tembo marvels at the brand-new planet dominating the horizon. Even by sight alone, he can tell it's a terrestrial world, solid and stable. That's a massive relief, considering a landing on a gas giant or ocean planet would go FUBAR fast. What surprises him most, though, is how spot-on the spectroscopic data supplied by Stardust Systems has proved to be. As predicted, the planet's thick, hazy atmosphere is clearly visible. It orbits a K-type star, slightly smaller than the Sun and a few shades more orange. Right on schedule, *Mwaba-1* is set to touch down on the planet's day side—just as the sun rises. The planet itself is tinged purple. Computer sensing readouts on atmosphere and surface composition start trickling in across the ship's readouts. Sure enough:

"No good on breathability," he tells Jeanette Emberley as she enters the cockpit. "Lots of metane and carbon monoxide in de atmosphere."

"What about radiation?" Emberley asks.

Tembo leans over one of the monitors and squints, blocking the glare from the new star with his hand so he can read what the screen says.

"Lots of dat as well."

Miss Emberley takes a seat next to the captain and reads silently from the same monitor.

"Our spacesuits should be able to handle it," she says. "Overall, things are nominal."

She presses her finger on the intercom button and speaks into it.

"Sit tight, Joseph," she says. "We'll be coming down for a landing soon."

Captain Tembo flashes a thumbs-up and flips a few levers to activate the ship's onboard GN&C landing software. Emberley keys in commands on a nearby touch screen monitor to bring up live readings of the ship's descent velocity and vector alignment. Within a few seconds, the nose of the ship dips gently toward the surface of the planet below.

"Heat shields holding!" the Captain announces, keeping his eye on the altimeter.

As the *Mwaba-1* starship shifts into a vertical descent over a smooth expanse of land in the planet's Eastern hemisphere, any thinking creature looking up from below could be forgiven for mistaking it for a pillar of fire cast down from the heavens. Such a being might marvel at the spectacle—the rocket's booster kicking up clouds of dust and sediment, roaring with noise and fury—before gradually fading into silence as the ship settles onto the surface. But no such being exists; the Afronauts have landed on a dead world, long ago wiped clean of all life.

The Hall of Heroes

Shortly after their blitz on the severally-headed beast was complete, Lance had directed the villagers to gather around and hoist its mangled, battered body out of the cavern where it had slept and into the light. It took the combined work of thirty men to grab different parts of the beast and half-drag, half-roll it onto the grass outside.

In any other context, this ghoulish chimera would have looked deeply frightening. Other than its seven heads and ten horns, its gigantic body was like that of a big spotted cat. The mouths on each head looked like they belonged to a lion, lips curled to reveal razor-sharp teeth. Slumped over and sprawled out on the grass, though, it looked pitiful. Its spotted fur was matted with blood which oozed passively from the stab wounds pockmarking its flesh and its decapitated third head had been disfigured by the villagers beyond the point of recognition.

Lance had ordered the villagers to weave their cloaks together and wrap the edges of the cloth around their spears and tools to produce a giant litter sling, which they stretched out across the grass and rolled the creature onto. Once this was complete, it took fifty villagers to lift the sling off the ground, leaving the remainder to stand around idly. After this, Lance had led them in a large procession through the village, putting the felled beast on display for all the women, children, elderly and infirm of the village who had not joined the hunting party to see. The owner of the village tavern had offered to lend Lance his Gorrpaa upon seeing them go by.

Those villagers who were not involved in hoisting the beast broke off from the procession as it crossed through the village and hurried off to rejoin their families. Those that remained continued to follow Lance as he rode the borrowed Gorrpaa up the mountainous path leading to the hall of heroes.

Upon arrival in front of the great elegant manor, the villagers quieted down while Lance dismounted and announced his arrival. At the time of narration, this is where we now find our heroes.

"We're here! We did it!" Lance exclaims as he stands in front of the wrought-iron gates. For a few seconds, nothing happens. A strong gust of wind rips through the air around him, and he tries not to shiver. Then comes the flutter of feathers somewhere nearby, followed by the arrival of Zhanniti, who perches atop the orange vine-infused stone wall flanking the gates and peers down at Lance with a mixture of surprise and admiration.

"Well done!" she says excitedly. "You all must have been very brave!"

There is a murmur amidst the villagers gathered by the manor.

"I told them there would be a feast here in honor of their hard work," Lance explains.

"Oh, I see," Zhanniti replies. "Well, by all means, let's see what we can do about that. Come on in, everyone!"

The gates swing open with a loud creak. Lance re-mounts the Gorrpaa he came up on and enters first, with the beast-toting villagers following closely behind. Zhanniti flies overhead and chats with Lance as they proceed up the path leading to the central building of the manor grounds.

"So how did it go, bud?" she asks conversationally.

"It was over really quick, actually," Lance replies. "I think we caught it by surprise."

"That's good!" Zhanniti says enthusiastically. "Did anyone die?"

"Um, well, a few people did, yeah," Lance responds sheepishly. "But not very many!"

"We'll have to figure out their names so we can build a monument in their honor," Zhanniti muses thoughtfully.

"Yeah, I guess so," Lance says. "Hey, so what are we gonna do with this thing's big dead body?"

"I guess we can arrange to build a crypt for it somewhere on the manor grounds," Zhanniti replies. "As a second monument, ya know?"

"Yeah." Lance isn't sure what else to say. He jostles slightly in the over-large saddle of his mount.

"Ah, this is so exciting!" Zhanniti squeals as she twirls through the air. "The prophecy's complete, our future is safe, and we're gonna have a big ol' party about it!"

"Where are the others?" Lance asks.

"Oh, they're inside."

Soon after this, the entire throng arrives at the front doors of the manor.

"Okay, everyone!" Zhanniti announces. "Just set that thing down on the grass over there!"

There is a wave of relief from the tired villagers as they shift off the path a few yards and drop the beast to the ground with a wet thump. Lance watches them massage their strained arm muscles and wipe blood off their hands and sweat off their brows.

Lance joins Zhanniti to hold the front doors of the manor open as the people of the village trickle in to meet Skanot, who waits in the entry hall and shepherds everyone into orderly groups. Within a couple of minutes, everyone has entered and is gathered into neat rows, so Lance and Zhanniti close the doors to the manor and wait expectantly for Skanot to bark out orders to the assembled crowd.

"Good people of this land, listen to me!" Skanot says, his raspy voice projected by the acoustics of the foyer. "I have been informed of the work you have done today and the sacrifice that many of you made in defense of our future. Such a time as this calls for celebration, so if you will all follow me to the dining hall there will be a banquet held here at the manor in your honor!"

A cheer resonates through the building. Skanot motions for everyone to follow, and so they do, while Zhanniti and Lance bring up the rear.

"How are you feeling?" Zhanniti asks.

"Pretty much invincible," Lance responds truthfully. "All of these people were willing to fight and die for me!"

Zhanniti looks confused.

"Sorry to disagree with ya, Lansamor," she says. "But really, they were defending their homes and their families. It wasn't really about you."

Lance frowns, so Zhanniti clarifies what she means.

"That's not to say you weren't important today!" she says. "You were their leader! But that doesn't mean ye have an army now that'll do whatever you tell it to do."

"But I used my voice power to command all of them at once!" Lance protests. "I've never been able to do that before."

"And you shouldn't assume you'll always be able to do it again, either," Zhanniti tells the boy.

"So many stupid rules," Lance grumbles. "I have this power, but sometimes I can use it and sometimes I can't. I don't even understand how it works!"

Zhanniti slides one of her digits across her beak thoughtfully.

"Think of it like hypnosis," she starts to explain. "You have to command your audience's full attention for it to work, and you're communicating with the unconscious mind. It's always easier to convince people to do something they wanted to do already anyway. So if ye want these people tae do what you want in the future, you'll have to keep their loyalty."

"Hopefully this party will make them feel good about me, then," Lance says, mostly to himself.

"An army marches on its stomach. Have you heard that before?" Zhanniti asks.

"No, never," Lance says. "But I get what it means." He picks a crumb of food off his shirt and tosses it on the ground. "So basically I can hypnotize people, then."

"You have the voice of a dragon! That's a latent psychic ability a person is born with, and it was brought to the forefront by your arrival here," Zhanniti explains. "There's mineral ore under the surface of this land which helps us use our powers."

"Us?" Lance asks, confused.

"I'm a psychic too!" Zhanniti says proudly. "All the Guardians are. Me, Skanot, Binnie, and Todd. We can all talk to each other in our minds."

"What about Opius and that clockwork guy?"

"Honestly, I don't really know what they are."

Lance nods, grateful for Zhanniti's explanations of everything. He's always found her the easiest of the Guardians to talk to, and by far the least mysterious.

"Thanks for telling me all this stuff, Zhanniti," Lance says. "I really feel like I can consider you a friend."

"Oh it's not a problem at all!" Zhanniti reassures him. "And that's very sweet of you to say."

By this point in the conversation, the group ahead of them has just arrived at the entrance to the dining hall. Skanot ushers everyone in, and as the door opens the smell of delicious food instantly hits Lance's nose and makes his mouth water. Zhanniti grabs Lance's hand and her eyes twinkle.

"Let's dig in, huh?" she says, pulling him into the fray.

Lance finds a place set for himself at the head of a long wooden table. A large ceremonial plate is set there between ornate silverware. An embroidered cloth napkin sits folded atop the plate, and a huge chair, much fancier than every other in the dining hall, is stationed at this spot. The villagers seat themselves along the sides of this table, looking expectantly between the buffet of food set up along its length and the empty spot where their leader will be sitting.

"Hi, everyone," Lance says as he sits down. "Could you make room for my friend Zhanniti?"

The villagers to his left scoot out of the way and Zhanniti sits in the vacated spot with bashful humility. Lance smiles at her and she nods happily back.

"Okay, I'm hungry!" Lance announces. "Let's eat!"

A clatter reverberates across the hall as everyone picks up their forks and knives and helps themselves to the dishes of food set up in front of them. Lance scoops a mashed root vegetable onto his plate and drizzles it with a brown sauce. Then he grabs a large piece of bread. Slightly further down the table is a platter with rotisserie-cooked breasts of a small bird, which Lance motions to have passed over to him. As the platter arrives in front of him, he looks askance at Zhanniti, feeling morbid.

"Oh, sorry," he says to her. "I hope you don't mind."

Zhanniti laughs and then covers her beak with her wing to stifle the sound.

"Don't be silly!" she giggles. "Just because that thing had feathers and wings when it was still alive doesn't mean it's my cousin."

Lance shrugs and helps himself to a generous serving. Zhanniti grabs a pink fileted fish. For a few minutes, the two of them chow down, the conversation between them not going far beyond remarks on the food. Then Lance puts down his fork and clears his throat.

"Any chance you could tell me more about that psychic ore?" he asks.

"Probably," Zhanniti replies. "I actually took a study course on geology at our academy not too long ago. What's up?"

"So you said it activates our powers, right? But how come when I go back home I can still use mine even though we don't have any of that ore there?"

Zhanniti considers this question carefully and thoughtfully.

"Well, like I said, it's a latent trait," she says. "Do you know what latent means?"

"Honestly, no."

"It means you're born with it. You could think of it like this. Being near the ore basically turns on a switch that activates your power, and then it doesn't really get turned off again once you're away from it."

"What would happen if I had a piece of the ore in my hand, though, or really close to my body? Would the power become even stronger then?"

"Oooh, that's a really good question. I'm not sure. Maybe!"

Lance nods and chews on some food.

"I've got an idea," he says after a moment.

"What?" Zhanniti asks.

Rather than answer her, Lance stands up and taps his fork on his plate loudly to get the attention of everyone else at the table. All heads in the room turn toward him.

"I hope you are all enjoying your meal!" Lance declares loudly. "And thank you again for helping today with the beast. I want you all to know that I have decided to stay in this land for as long as I am welcome here. And I have some ideas on how we will stay safe from any other threats that might show up in the future!"

Zhanniti makes a *pssst* sound. Lance looks down at her.

"What threats are you talking about?" she asks.

"I don't know, Zhanniti, take your pick," Lance responds under his breath so that the others can't hear. "There's all sorts of weird shit here, I'm sure something else crazy will happen."

More loudly he says,

"Just because we defeated the beast does not mean we can afford to rest or assume that we will be safe forever! We need to build up defenses so we'll be ready for the next one! So here's what we will do. We will turn this manor into a fortress and make you villagers into an army! And we will start strip mining in the valley to find psychic ore. Do I have any volunteers to be part of the mining team?"

There is a moment of silence across the room. Finally, one hand shoots up. Then another. After a few more seconds there are about twenty raised hands.

"Great!" Lance exclaims. "Come see me after this is over. Let's make it happen, guys!"

The volunteers for the mines cheer. Lance sits back down and turns to Zhanniti.

"What do you think?" he asks.

"I don't know," she says with trepidation. "If you think it's the right thing to do then I'll help you get it done, but Skanot and Binnmerva will never stand for this."

"I appreciate that. But they're going to have to, whether they like it or not," Lance says. "I've got an army now. And you're gonna rule with me. It'll be great!"

Zhanniti looks unsure.

"I hope it will," she says. "I really do."

"Why don't you talk to them about it while I meet these volunteers?" Lance asks.

"I don't know where in the manor they are at this point but I can see about reaching them telepathically."

"Awesome. See it done."

Zhanniti salutes, and Lance grins. Once the meal is over, he nods to her and she toddles off to escort the majority of the villagers out of the manor while the mining volunteers hang behind. Lance stands up and waves them over. They coalesce in a huddle around him.

The mining team, it turns out, is a collection of the biggest and most brutish members of the village, with the exception of one nebbish and undersized Dvoran.

"Sir," he trembles, "w-why don't we start at the base of the mountain and blast a tunnel d-down into it?"

"What's your name?" Lance asks.

"C-Carlyle, sir," the Dvoran replies.

"That's a good suggestion, Carlyle. In fact, that's the plan. Everyone else, Carlyle is going to be in charge of your team, so listen to what he says because he'll be the one who reports to me."

"Th-thank you, sir," Carlyle says, straightening out his posture and puffing out his chest with newfound pride. The others in the mining team clap and holler for their new leader.

After the meeting ends, Lance dismisses all but the four biggest and dumbest of the volunteers with the charge that they will return to meet with him tomorrow. The four that stay – two boarish Malyumpkinites and two pugilistic Carfassans – look at him expectantly.

"I'm about to have a meeting with a couple of the Guardians in a minute," Lance explains. "I want you all to stick around in case there's trouble."

The four bodyguards nod and affirm their assent. Lance leads them out of the banquet hall and into the adjoining corridor, where Binnmerva and Skanot are already waiting. Binnmerva looks furious.

"What in the name of Sheol are you thinking, you stupid child?!" she howls, poking her webbed finger at Lance's chest.

Skanot steps forward and kindly brushes her aside, adopting a more conciliatory tone.

"My liege," he says. "What you proposed at the dinner today is most unusual. The people of this land have never had a king nor an army."

"And that's exactly why you needed me!" Lance insists. "Why else would there be that prophecy?"

"And we're happy to have you, Lansamor, but I urge you to reconsider!" Skanot says.

"He won't," Binnmerva interjects. "People like this, once they get a taste of power, it never leaves their mouths."

"Actually, Binnmerva is, uh, sort of right," Lance says. "I'm not changing my mind."

"Told you so!" Binnmerva says haughtily.

Skanot looks between Lance and the large, stony-faced creatures standing behind him. One of the Malyumpkinites steps forward with his arms crossed and exhales sharply out his nose, causing Skanot to timidly shrink back a step. Binnmerva is unfazed.

"Look, you two don't have to worry," Lance assures them. "I'll only be king for like a year or two. I'll be out of here as soon as this place has its army and a mine set up properly."

"Arrogant, presumptuous boy!" Binnmerva fumes.

"Binnie, think about this," Skanot says diplomatically. "The future is secure now. We could go out East and resume our posts as Guardians there."

"Skanot is right," Lance agrees. "If I do my job right, you guys'll be safe out there!"

"Safe!" Binnmerva harrumphs. "You mean safe like Gilead is safe? What happened to him anyway, were you ever going to explain that to us, *Lansamor*?"

She pronounces this last word with so much spite that Lance has to physically restrain one of his bodyguards from stepping forward and roughing her up.

"Look," Lance says through gritted teeth, trying not to lose his cool. "You don't need to worry about that. Just get your things together and head out East. If anything happens out there, you can always come back. Deal?"

He sticks out his hand. Begrudgingly, Binnmerva grumbles and shakes it. Skanot also shakes Lance's hand, albeit more enthusiastically.

"Thanks, guys," Lance says. "I knew we could come to a good deal."

Skanot and Binnmerva turn and walk down the corridor, away from King Lansamor and his royal guard, eventually disappearing out of sight.

"I want an armed guard on the Eastern frontier," the King says. "No one who crosses over it is allowed to return."

March 21, 1999

A gentle breeze blows under a cloudless baby blue sky as the first vestigial signs of spring make themselves known to the world. The blooms are flowering, and the flowers are blooming. There is beauty on the ground and magic in the air. It is the perfect sort of day for a wedding.

Church bells ring.

The First Presbyterian Church in Bellevue, Nebraska is adorned, inside and out, with wedding regalia. On the walls are strewn pictures of the bride and groom as well as pink, white, and blue streamers hastily arranged into tasteful approximations of hanging arches. Around the perimeter of the chapel, several plastic-topped tables are set up, covered in gifts and cards containing personally addressed well-wishes from family and friends (as well as, in a few cases, small stacks of ten and twenty dollar bills). In the center of the room, a crowd of 78 watches with bated breath as the vows are exchanged. All eyes are glued to the couple at the altar.

"— in sickness and in health, to love and cherish so long as you both may live, till death do you part?" the priest asks the groom.

The groom, who in contrast to his usually unruly appearance has dressed to the nines in a freshly-pressed three piece suit and managed to tame his wavy brown hair with a splotch of hair gel, stares meaningfully into the watery blue eyes of his fiance and nods.

"I do," he says proudly.

The interpreter who stands next to the priest repeats the question to the bride in ASL.

< I do, > she signs.

"By the authority vested in me, I now pronounce you Mr. and Mrs. Tobias and Marissa Morrissey," the priest declares while the interpreter translates. "You may now kiss the bride!"

The chapel erupts with cheers, applause, and a smattering of joyful sobs as Tobias steps forward, lifts up the white veil covering Marissa's face, and in an instant two become one. It is a surreal, euphoric moment.

And then, just as suddenly and magically as it happens, the moment is over. The ceremony ends, and the wedding reception commences.

Tobias and Marissa pull apart from each other as the stereo speakers set up on either side of the chancel begin to blare the first pop song on the wedding list. Guests work together to quickly fold up their chairs and prop them up against the walls, clearing space on the floor, as the lights begin to dim and the dancing begins.

April 14, 2006

Marissa and Tobias have been married for seven happy and unremarkable years when Marissa makes a suggestion one Friday after dinner which, at first, Tobias finds strange.

< We should celebrate Easter at my dad's place, > she says, eliciting a confused stare from her husband as he dabs at his nostril with a tissue. < We could take Lance there and have him run around the property. >

Their three-year-old son runs around the kitchen in sock-covered feet while Tobias considers the appropriate response to his wife's request. He leans back in his chair, rubbing at the bridge of his nose. The smell of leftover spaghetti lingers in the air, and somewhere in the house, the distant hum of a washing machine drones on.

< Would we fly or drive? > he asks.

< We drive, > Marissa replies simply.

What she means by this is '*you* drive,' as the responsibility for navigating the family station wagon across 352 miles of highway would fall invariably and squarely onto Tobias.

< Tomorrow? > Tobias asks, already feeling tired. They would have to leave early in the morning to arrive in Nebraska before sunset.

Marissa nods and carries his dirty plate away from the kitchen table as Tobias slides his chair back away from it. He stands up and stretches out his extremities just as his son runs past.

"Got you!" Tobias exclaims, grabbing his son into a big hug and preventing him from darting away. Little Lance laughs and kicks his feet with joy while Marissa watches them and beams.

"Hey, little man, how'd you like to go on a little trip tomorrow?" Tobias asks.

"Okay, daddy," Lance says with a smile. Tobias blows a raspberry on his son's cheek.

"Let's get you to bed, kid," he says, raising his son up onto his shoulders.

"Boooooo!" Lance protests dramatically.

Tobias kisses his wife and takes his son upstairs.

April 15, 2006

After almost seven hours on the road, Tobias's spine aches and his nerves are shot. In the back, his son sits strapped into a booster, kicking impatiently at his chair.

"Cut that out!" he snaps, shaking with irritation. His wife, seated to his right, grabs his hand and he squeezes it, feeling better quickly. He takes a deep breath and focuses on the passing scenery.

Trees and farmland zip by as Tobias cruises down the empty highway. Finally, intermittent restaurants, billboards, and gas stations begin to appear, followed at last by a colorful sign welcoming him and Marissa to the state of Nebraska.

Thank God, he thinks to himself, white-knuckled on the steering wheel. Now that they've crossed over the state border, Marissa's hometown is only twenty minutes away.

After selling their farm, Rob and Marcia Miller had moved into a small cottage just a few miles closer to the big city. As Tobias exits the interstate and begins to navigate a series of increasingly obscure rural roads, a distinct feeling of deja vu comes over him. These familiar gravel trails have been untouched by the hands of time; they unfold into the horizon exactly as Tobias remembers them in his dreams.

"Daddy, what happened to the road?" his son asks, face pressed firmly against the glass of the car's rear window.

"We're still on it," Tobias replies, downshifting a gear on his car to handle the rougher terrain.

"But it's made of dirt!" Lance marvels.

"That's right, bud. A lot of the roads looked like this where your mom was growing up."

"Wow, my mommy is so old!"

Tobias chuckles, feeling bittersweet that Marissa probably missed out on the joke. He glances over to her. She's got her eyes focused like lasers on the forest around them, searching intently for something.

Gradually, the dense mesh of trees around them melts away, and the gravel of the road gives way to paved asphalt once more. The scenery around them is now peppered by large country estates with elaborate porticos and sprawling lawns. The first houses Tobias drives past are the most impressive, being the largest and the oldest. As he drives further down the street, the houses become newer, smaller, more homogenous, and more tightly compressed. Finally, he comes upon a shabby white cottage with blue trim, whose driveway is lined with felled logs that stretch along the length of it. Tobias almost drives straight past it without slowing down, so unremarkable is its profile, but Marissa smacks his shoulder firmly and shakes him out of his highway hypnosis. He slams on the brakes and reverses into the driveway.

Marissa, Tobias, and their young son pour out of the car and knock on the front door of the house. A tall woman in athletic wear and a sporty bob answers.

"Hello, Kaylee," Tobias says, his voice coming out more weary than he intends.

"Tobias, how *are* you today?" Kaylyee asks with the air of an aristocrat, her gaze sweeping over her sister's husband with barely concealed judgment. "You've certainly aged since the wedding."

"I'm just tired." Tobias tries to tamp down the irritation in his voice, keeping Lance in the corner of his vision as his son starts to squirm. "Seven hours on the road."

"You need to take better care of your health." Kaylee shakes her head, sighing. "Too much stress, not enough exercise. I see it all the time in men your age."

"Can we come in?" Tobias asks.

"Of course."

As they step inside, Tobias is filled with dread. *Oh no*, he thinks. *Lance is going to hate it here.* The house smells sharply of cleaning spray and its furnishings have been arranged with clinical precision. Everything is too neat, too controlled. Marissa's mother, Marcia, darts around the sitting room with a feather duster but pauses mid-sweep when she sees Tobias come in.

"Toby!" she cries, giving him a wet kiss on the cheek that makes him feel gross. Tobias forces a smile and gently pulls away.

"Lance," he says, ushering his son forward. "This is your grandma."

Lance, just about to investigate a collection of hummel figurines on his grandparents' glass-top coffee table, hesitates. He walks closer but does not make eye contact.

"Hi, Gramma," he mutters, without much feeling.

"He's so cute!" Marcia gushes. "Looks just like his mother."

Marissa, who has either been reading her mother's lips or is just picking up on the vibe in the room, smiles sweetly. Tobias is distracted, looking around for the missing patriarch of the Miller family.

"Where's the old man?" he asks.

"Oh, he's up in the master bedroom," Marcia responds absentmindedly.

"I'm going to go say hello."

Marissa's mother waves him away, attention fixated on her darling grandson. Meanwhile, Marissa and Kaylee sit together on the couch and begin firing away in ASL. Tobias, scowling, storms out of the room in search of the stairs.

The upstairs landing, which Tobias locates without too much trouble, is equally as tidy as the rest of the house. The carpeted floor bears the telltale tread of the bottom of a vacuum cleaner, and each of the identical doors adjoining the main hallway is closed, with one exception. The farthest door from the top of the stairs hangs ajar, with a sliver of light streaming through. Tobias approaches it, his steps making the floor beams creak, and pushes the door the rest of the way open to find Robert Miller elbow-deep in a large cardboard box set atop a king-sized bed, with packing peanuts and plastic wrap strewn about the floor.

"Hey, pops," Tobias says as he enters.

Rob, who is now half-deaf and has lost most of his hair across the past seven years, looks up at Tobias with a confused start.

"Toby?" he asks.

"What are you up to?" Tobias asks, gesturing around at the mess.

Rob's eyes widen as they follow Tobias's hands, and he seems to consider the litter as if seeing it for the very first time.

"Oh!" he says. "I just got a new sheet set they were advertising on the television. Couldja help me out with it, champ?"

Sure, what the hell. Tobias joins Rob by the side of the bed and peers into the box. Sure enough, there is a jumble of half-unwrapped and formerly vacuum-sealed fabric jammed into the bottom of it.

"What are we doing, exactly?" Tobias asks.

"I just wanna unpack everything, make sure it's all there. Here, grab this."

Tobias grabs hold of the farthest edge of plastic on a rolled-up sheet set and tugs while Rob unrolls it the rest of the way. The fabric falls into a loose pile on the floor with a muffled thump.

"There should be a top sheet, a fitted sheet, and, let's see..." Rob counts under his breath. "...One, two, three, four. Four pillowcases."

Tobias separates the two large sheets from each other and begins taking stock of the pillowcase inventory.

"I think there's six."

"Huh?"

"There are six pillowcases, not four."

"Well, that's okay." Rob promptly plucks two of them out of Tobias's hands. "We can throw the extras away."

"In the trash?" Tobias, raised to be frugal, is scandalized. "Why not save them for later?"

"We only have four pillows," Rob replies simply. "No need."

"Let me and Marissa have them," Tobias says.

"Well... well, okay, if you insist."

"I do. Thanks."

Rob returns the pillowcases to Tobias, who takes a step back from the bed, only to suddenly have his arm snatched roughly from behind, causing him to stumble further backward and drop the pillowcases.

"Marissa?" he says with shock. "What–!"

She shakes her head to silence him and steers him back across the upstairs hallway. At the top of the stairs, Tobias pulls free and throws his arms emphatically to say, *what gives?* Marissa brandishes the keys to their car and jingles them.

< We should leave, > she signs. < Just for a little bit. >

Tobias, still bewildered, is nevertheless also more than a little relieved.

< I agree! > he retorts. < Your family is driving me crazy. >

< Grab Lance and meet me at the car, > Marissa says, before heading down the rest of the stairs and starting toward the front door of the house.

Tobias follows, still unsure what's going on. Downstairs, although Marissa has already exited the house by the time he arrives, her sister and mother are still sitting around and chatting. Lance sits on his grandmother's lap, a giant lollipop submerged in his mouth.

"Lance, let's go outside for a little bit," Tobias says.

Lance shakes his head, a strand of drool sliding down his chin. He does not budge.

"Come on bud, let's get some fresh air!" Tobias insists.

"You'll have to pry him off grandma," Kaylee smirks.

Marcia brings her hands back in mock surrender, to show that Lance is an open target. Tobias sighs and steps forward, slipping his hands under Lance's arms and hoisting him up. The boy kicks his legs in lazy protest but does little to resist as Tobias shifts him over his shoulder like a sack of potatoes.

"We'll, um, be back soon," Tobias says over his shoulder.

He steps outside into the cooling air. The sky is painted in shades of orange and violet, the last rays of sunlight casting long, spindly shadows across the driveway. The scent of freshly cut grass lingers, mingling with the faint chemical sharpness of the cleaning spray that still clings to his clothes from inside the house.

Marissa stands beside the driver's side door of the family car, arms crossed, her silhouette dark against the fading light. Her gaze flicks to Tobias, then to Lance, as if weighing something in her mind. Tobias gently sets Lance down on the sidewalk, his son's fingers leaving a sticky imprint on his own. He wipes his palm absently on his jeans and reaches for Lance's hand, feeling the warmth of it, the slight resistance as the boy hesitates, reluctant to leave behind the comfort of his grandmother's house.

Without a word, Tobias leads him toward the car, the soft crunch of gravel beneath their feet the only sound between them.

After carefully installing Lance into the booster seat in the back of the car, Tobias mouths *now what?* to his wife. By way of an answer, she opens the car door and slides into the driver's seat. Tobias stands outside the car, his hands on his hips, momentarily dumbfounded. It has been a long time since Marissa has insisted on driving anywhere farther than the end of the street. Clearly, she has a destination in mind, and will tolerate no delay.

Without another word, Tobias slides into the passenger seat and locks eyes with Marissa, waiting for her to give a cue about what's coming next. She furrows her brow at him, her gaze fierce with determination. Then she jams the key into the ignition and sends their car roaring to life.

Within just a moment, the family is flying down the highway at dynamite speed.

"Wow!" Lance giggles in the back seat as the car goes airborne for just a moment. "Where are we going, daddy?"

"I don't know!" Tobias shoots back, an unexpected thrill hitting him in the chest.

He rolls down the window and lets the wind rush across his face, cool and electric. Within a mere minute, he begins to place their location in his mind, the scenery gradually becoming more and more familiar. Suddenly, it clicks, and Tobias bursts into a fit of rapturous laughter. He knows exactly where she's taking him.

Eventually, Marissa eases the car to a stop at the crest of a large sloping hill. Below them, half-shrouded by the growing darkness, stands a covered wooden bridge, preserved exactly as Tobias remembers it. Without a word spoken, Marissa and Tobias get out of the car, and Marissa helps Lance out of his car seat, lifting the boy onto her hip. Together, parents and child walk down the hill and step through the threshold of the garden on foot.

As Tobias steps into the bridge, a sudden wave of vertigo overtakes him. The world tips sideways, his stomach lurches, and then everything plunges into darkness. An instant later, a flood of golden light blinds him, warm and overwhelming, like stepping into the sun. Unsteady on his feet, he collapses to the ground, and his hands brush against soft grass. The scent of damp earth and a sweet smell like honeysuckle fills his nose, grounding him as he presses his palms into the soil. Within moments, his vision starts to return to him. Rising gradually, he glances around and takes in the inputs of his senses.

Marissa is already acclimated, setting Lance down gently while her husband catches himself. The air smells faintly sweet, like honeysuckle. The sun overhead is bright and warm. Colorful flora stretches out into the distance around them.

"Where are we, daddy?" Lance asks, tugging at the hem of his father's shirt. His small voice is full of wonder.

"Your mommy and I used to come here when we were younger," Tobias says, still taking it all in. "I never thought we would come back."

It isn't quite as he remembered it; something has changed in the past several years. The plants look a little bit different, and the forest which surrounds the meadow has changed too; thorny brambles populate the brush, and the leaves in the trees have started to change color toward a golden shade of yellow.

Tobias gets down to eye level with his son, thinking of a way to make the experience educational.

"Lance," he says. "I want you to find flowers of four different colors and bring them to me. Then you should tell me what colors they are, okay?"

"Okay, daddy," Lance says, already starting to scamper toward a patch of tulips, the light of the sun catching in his curls.

"And stay where we can see you!" Tobias calls out after him.

Marissa stands a few yards away, her eyes closed, her chest rising and falling in slow, steady breaths. Tobias approaches her quietly, trying not to interrupt her meditative state. Despite his efforts, she seems to prick up slightly as he moves through the grass toward her, but she does not open her eyes.

"I missed this place," Marissa murmurs, her voice barely louder than the rustling in the trees.

"Why didn't you tell me you wanted to come back here?" Tobias asks softly.

Marissa's posture changes; she stoops her back slightly.

"I was worried you wouldn't want to come," she says.

Tobias snorts, a half-laugh escaping him.

"Believe me," he says. "I wasn't champing at the bit to spend the rest of the evening with the in-laws. I was happy to come out here for a while."

Marissa turns to face him, her eyes open now and searching his.

"Maybe," she says. "But would you have driven seven hours from home just for this?"

"Maybe not," Tobias concedes. "So what made you decide we finally needed to come back?"

A hush falls over the garden. Marissa takes a deep breath through her nose and closes her eyes again. Somewhere far away and deep in the trees, a bird trills a high, liquid note, answered by another.

"I missed the birds," Marissa says. "I keep dreaming about them."

Tobias studies her carefully, feeling something tighten in his chest.

"Really?"

"And..." Marissa swallows. When she speaks again, her voice is barely a breath. "I wanted to hear the sound of my child's voice."

The words settle heavily between them. Tobias doesn't move. The weight of the moment presses into him, sudden and immense.

A few feet away, Lance creeps closer, crouches over the grass, and picks a flower. Then, oblivious to what has been happening around him, he presents it to his parents and calls out proudly:

"Look, look! This one is blue!"

Marissa lets out a quiet, shuddering breath, a chill running down her spine. Then, for the first time, she turns toward him, toward their son, toward the voice she's never heard before. And she smiles.

"Very good, Lance!" she calls out, her voice warm and steady. "Bring it here so I can see."

Lance freezes, eyes wide. For a moment, he just stares at her, his tiny fingers still clutching the flower. Then, as if the realization is only now settling in, his face lights up with pure, unfiltered wonder.

"WOW!" he shouts. "My mommy can talk?"

Marissa lets out a soft laugh, but it catches in her throat. She blushes, her eyes welling with tears.

"That's right," she says, beckoning him closer. "Come show me your flower. Tell me all about it."

Tobias watches his wife and son interact in a way that they have never been able to before, speechless with pride and overwhelmed by the magic of the moment. He blinks hard against the warmth behind his eyes.

"—And it's got one, two, three, four petals. And a green stem!" Lance is telling his mother, twirling the flower in his fingers while she watches it with quiet reverence.

Tobias joins them and crouches next to his wife.

"Do you know what *type* of flower it is, buddy?" he quizzes his son.

Lance frowns, stumped.

"Um, no..." he says.

"Well, let's think. Is it a rose? Is it a daisy or a tulip?"

"I don't know. Mommy, do you know?"

Marissa studies the flower, her fingers brushing delicately over the petals. She seems equally at a loss for answers.

"Actually, I don't," she says. "Well, maybe it looks like– but no, it has to be a mutation."

"What's a mutaysin?" Lance asks, confused.

"It's something that's different, that we haven't seen before," Marissa explains.

Lance considers this, then grins and clutches the flower tightly in his little hand.

"I like it," he declares. "It's a special flower."

Marissa lets out a breathy laugh, ruffling her son's curls.

"It is," she agrees. "Just like you."

Marissa, Tobias, and their three-year-old son spend an hour or maybe more together in the garden, talking and laughing with each other, before Lance falls backward on his butt and starts to cry loudly, his little voice high and shrill.

"He's just tired," Marissa says, sitting down beside him and scooping him into her lap.

"I don't miss hearing that sound," Tobias says, thinking back to his son's infant years.

"I do," Marissa replies curtly. She hugs her son tight and coos at him to calm him down.

Tobias falls silent, feeling chastened. When their son was a baby, his cries in the middle of the night had been an annoyance. But Marissa had never once been able to hear them. It had made those years difficult for both parents, exacerbating their stress and creating marital friction. Marissa had struggled with lactating for the same reason as well, and had never gotten over the guilt of bottle-feeding her son on formula starting when he was just a few months old.

Dusk falls over the garden, wrapping the landscape in deepening shades of violet and gold. Lance sits nestled in his mother's tender grasp. When he finally drifts into silence, Tobias offers a suggestion.

"Maybe we should take him to bed," he says.

Marissa looks torn. She hesitates, not wanting to leave.

"We'll come back tomorrow, right?"

There is a tinge of quiet desperation in her voice. Tobias nods.

"Right after the egg hunt, we'll come back here and spend the rest of the day."

Marissa seems satisfied by this answer. She gently shakes Lance awake and helps him to his feet.

"Come on, bud," Tobias says, stretching out a couple fingers for his son's little hand to grab.

Marissa brushes the dirt off her dress and stands up too. She lingers a few paces behind while Tobias leads the way, their shadows stretching long and far ahead of them across the grass. As the sun sinks further into the sky, darkness creeps into the margins of the meadow.

"Where did we come in from?" Marissa asks, scanning the dimming landscape.

"Over here, I think!" Tobias says, pointing to a small break in the brush.

But as Marissa steps forward, something gives her pause. She squints at the ground near the clearing, at something she's sure wasn't there before. A mound of soil, dark and loose, sprawls unevenly across the grass, as though freshly deposited by a gardener.

"I don't remember seeing *that*," she says, her voice filled with unease.

"Oh, weird." Tobias grabs Lance a little bit tighter.

As they creep cautiously closer, the mound of soil shifts. A few loose clumps tumble down its side, harmless at first, until the whole pile shudders, disturbed by an unseen force. The ground beneath them shakes, as the dirt stirs, reconfiguring itself with eerie precision. For a few seconds, it seems to grow in height and solidify in structure, until a clear shape finally emerges. By some unknown power, the dirt has arranged into the hulking form of a lumbering boar, made entirely out of muddy earth and standing erect on its hind legs. Clumps of grass cleave to its body, and two twisted horns push forward, curling like roots from its snout.

At the sight of the beast, Marissa screams, Lance hides behind his father's legs, and Tobias stands frozen, his heartbeat hammering in his ears. All three brace for the inevitable charge, for the beast to lunge, to do *something*. Instead, it moves to the side of the path and beckons for them to leave. Tobias picks up Lance and walks slowly past, unwilling to take his eyes off the creature. Marissa begins to follow, but the boar holds up a hand to stop her. She understands its meaning immediately.

"It wants me to stay here," she says, her voice breaking with fear.

"WHAT?" Tobias exclaims, trying without success to push past the beast. Try as he might, the boar is always faster. "Marissa!"

Marissa takes a deep breath and holds back tears.

"I heard its voice when we first arrived," she says. "I didn't want to believe it. But it told me that if I didn't stay behind, my son would die."

Tobias is at a loss for words, devastated.

"I'll come back for you!" he vows. "I promise!"

After taking one last look at his wife, Tobias feels the grass under his feet give way to concrete. Instantaneously, he and his son are transported back outside the garden and next to the family car. The bridge at the bottom of the hill is gone, reduced to a pile of loose timber. The night wind blows cold.

The Eastern Frontier: 4 Years into the King's Rule

Skanot sits alone in the village tavern, knocking back a flagon of mead. This has become a daily habit for him, drinking in solace and gazing blankly into the fireplace. His head is light and his throat is sore. And he is so tired. Just outside the walls of the tavern, an army patrol marches through a violet evening haze. He can hear the clanking of their scabbards against metal armor as they travel in formation. Distantly, a sergeant barks out orders. Skanot listens to them go by without looking out the window.

An aproned Carfassan barmaid approaches, wiping down the empty tabletop around Skanot with a damp rag.

"How's it goin', sugar?" she asks.

Skanot slowly turns his head to peer at her through bleary, crusted eyes. He mutters something even he can't understand, trying to make his intoxicated brain crystallize around a thought.

"It never changes, huh?" the barmaid says. "Do you mind?"

Skanot takes his elbows off the table and waits patiently with his arms at his side as the barmaid picks up his drink with one hand and wipes down the area under it with her other.

"'Cept the fog," Skanot finally replies after she sets his drink back down.

"Beg pardon?" the barmaid asks. She slings her rag over her shoulder to look at him.

"Nothin' changes, 'cept the fog," Skanot elaborates with a hiccup. "Swer it gets thicker'n every single day."

The barmaid stares out the window to consider the deep mist roiling the evening air.

"Maybe," she says. "Dunno. It's been that way long as I can remember."

"Nyeh," Skanot grunts in a strident tone. He drops a few bronze coins on the table and slowly staggers into a standing position. Feeling dizzy, he stabilizes himself against the edge of the table.

"You heading home, Skanot?" the barmaid asks.

"Seems as might I am," Skanot replies, starting to stumble toward the door.

"Careful out there!" the barmaid warns him as he leaves. "Them patrollers aren't to be trifled with!"

As he exits the tavern, Skanot unfolds a tattered square of cloth from the pocket of his dirty tunic and ties it around his nose and mouth, protecting his airways from the particles he anticipates will be floating around in the ambient haze. Even as a stumbling drunk, the motion is automatic, since he has been doing this as a matter of course every time he walks around outside during the last few years.

Skanot's domicile is a small room on one of the middle levels of a tower in the heart of the village. It stands just a few blocks away from Bidmead's tavern.

The purple cobblestone road which snakes through the village has fallen into a state of disrepair. Many constituent pieces are crumbling or knocked out of place. Between the darkness and the haze and his intoxication, Skanot has to take special care not to trip as he slowly walks along the path leading back to his home.

At an intersection between roads, Skanot comes to a stop while a long train of helmeted soldiers marches across from a perpendicular direction. Knowing better than to interfere in the procession, he sighs and waits.

Somewhere in the distance, the anguished trill of a lonely liliput bird echoes into the darkness. It has been a few months since Skanot has heard the song of a liliput bird. He listens for more, but the call fades out into nothingness and is not answered by another. In days long past, the air would be filled with the call and response of birdsong. Now, the population is all but extinct.

Gazing into the sky in hopes of glimpsing a fluttered wing, Skanot squints his eyes. Unmistakably, the mist has been getting thicker. Even the evening stars are no longer visible. A tender ache falls into the pit of Skanot's chest.

The last of the patrolling troops having cleared out of his way, Skanot continues his journey home. It only takes a few more minutes of labored walking before he arrives in front of his tower of residence.

Cracking open the front door at the bottom of the tower, Skanot listens for any signs of life. All the tenants are silent as the grave. The number of people active in the evenings has been steadily dwindling over the last several months; gone are the days of extravagant house parties or ornithological society meetings. Even the tavern and shops have few patrons.

Skanot groans with the effort of forcing the door the rest of the way open and finally pushes his way in. Only a very faint, flickering torch on the wall illuminates the space. Beyond the residential doors on this floor, a shadowed archway leads to a spiraling stone staircase, winding up through every level in the tower. Skanot sighs again and begins to stumble laboriously up it.

At last, he stands before the entrance of his abode and removes the cloth cover from his face. He returns it to his tunic pocket and fishes out a rusty key, which he inserts into the lock of his door. Turning the key, he realizes with some surprise that the door has already been unlocked, which puzzles him. It does not take long to solve this particular mystery: as Skanot enters his sitting room, he finds Binnmerva seated on his tattered couch, her arms folded and walking cane set on the floor by her feet.

"Oh... 'lo, Binnie," Skanot murmurs in surprise.

Under the wavering shadows cast on her face by the room's lantern light, Binnmerva looks ancient and frail. The years of their banishment have not been kind to her; she has lost a considerable amount of weight from stress and malnourishment, and her once plump frame has been reduced to being almost skeletal.

"Evening, Skanot," she says in a thin, glum voice. "Sorry for letting myself in, I came to see how you–"

Her sentence is interrupted by the onset of an aggressive coughing fit which seizes her and causes her to double over in pain. Skanot sits next to her and gingerly grabs hold of her hand.

"Fret not 'bout it nothin', Binnie," he replies, as her coughs gradually reduce in intensity. "You know 's the reason I gave you a key for. Always welcome 'ere, you are."

Binnmerva nods gratefully, squeezing Skanot's hand as her fit finally subsides.

"You've been drinking, haven't you?" she says with concern.

"Fella has to pass the time some'ow," Skanot replies dismissively.

"I worry about you, Skanot," Binnmerva says.

"An' I worry about *you*, Binnie," Skanot returns. "It aren't right that you be out on your own at your age. Some'n might happen to you."

Binnmerva closes her eyes, looking subdued.

"Oh Skanot, we're all dying," she says. "Some of us faster than others. I keep thinking–"

She shakes her head, stifling the thought.

"The wisdom of age is lost on the decrepit," she says after a moment. "I keep hoping things will get better. But I know better than to really believe it."

"The times, they are a-changin'," Skanot replies solemnly.

"Yes..." Binnmerva muses. "Maybe we should talk to Opius."

Just as soon as the name has escaped her wrinkled lips, Opius appears before them in a flash, causing the lamp which hangs from the ceiling to wiggle around on its chain.

"Wunnerful timing," Skanot says with a grin.

The temporal guardian of the East regards Skanot with its piercing gaze.

"Something is wrong," Opius intones. "A cloud has fallen over the land."

"You mean the mist?" Binnmerva asks. "That's nothing new."

"Not the mist," Opius replies. "A thick cloud of poison rises from a fissure in the mines, carrying with it the acrid stench of death. It shall be upon us in minutes."

"Whaddo we do?" Skanot asks sullenly.

Something that looks like frustration takes over Opius's posture.

"I have been conferring with the other temporal guardians. Neither the Boar of the West nor the Clockwork Guardian of the Center is willing to get involved," it says.

"For what reason?!" Binnmerva demands angrily.

"The boar is a shrinking coward and the clockwork guardian is unaffected by such affairs."

Opius glances out the window and steps forward, extending an arm to each of them.

"The cloud approaches," it says. "Grab onto me."

Skanot helps Binnmerva with her cane as she stands up from the couch. They each grab an arm and hold on tightly as Opius conjures up a halo of light around them. Just as it becomes blinding, the light subsides. Skanot and Binnmerva let go of Opius and look around: the three of them are now in the clockwork guardian's chamber. Brilliant and indescribable shapes warp all around them.

"You got us past the blockade?" Binnmerva asks, astonished.

"And no further," a droning voice interjects.

A cluster of dissonant shapes from around the room gather together and refract into the corporeal form of the clockwork guardian.

"Guardian, I beseech you," Opius says, dwarfed by the monstrous form of the clockwork entity. "These good people were going to die if I had not taken them here."

"You are defying the will of the king," the clockwork guardian replies flatly.

"A PISS on the king!" Skanot exclaims, pointing his finger at the creature and shaking with rage. "What– 'ow can you tell me 'e's got his 'ooks in you too?"

The guardian tilts its head, its shifting pieces clicking into a new formation.

"Take care how you speak in my presence," it retorts, its voice hollow. "I could erase you with a thought. Your drunkenness and insubordination will not do."

The shapes that make up the clockwork guardian's hand, such as it is, reorient themselves until they hover just above the top of Skanot's head. As a cluster of glistening polyhedrons descend upon his hairless scalp, a buzzing rattles through his skull. Skanot finds himself suddenly rendered stone cold sober, his inebriation removed in an instant by the creature's power.

"Please," Opius interjects. "The actions of the king today are sealing the doom of the future! Every day, this outsider perverts the natural flow of time and puts this land in greater peril. How can you allow this?"

"Because it is written," the guardian explains. "The king reigns, sovereign and supreme."

"Let us speak to him!" Binnmerva pleads. "If you won't intervene, maybe we can change his mind!"

The shapes of the guardian constrict into each other, contracting like a coiled spring while the mind at the center races.

"...This is admissible," the guardian replies at last. "Is that what you both wish?"

Skanot and Binnmerva nod.

"Very well."

In an instant, Skanot and Binnmerva are transported out of the clockwork chamber, leaving only Opius.

"Your magnanimity is a farce. They face certain death before the throne," Opius declares.

"Correct," the clockwork guardian replies. "As long as the guardians live, I remain bound."

The King's Courtyard: Two Seconds Earlier

Skanot and Binnmerva pull themselves upright, shaken but alert, and take in the sight around them. They find themselves standing in a place where they have stood many times before, but which has been rendered unrecognizable by four years of militancy and tyranny. They have been deposited just past the front gates of what had once been the Hall of Heroes. But that place is gone. In its place looms a hulking citadel, ruled by King Lansamor.

The once-impressive wall surrounding the manor has been rebuilt for war. The smooth, vine-covered stone has been buried by rough, unyielding slabs reinforced by steel plating. Iron spikes jut from the top like the fangs of a beast, and along its length, watchtowers loom, manned by silent sentinels in dark armor. The wrought-iron gate, once a grand entrance, is now a checkpoint bristling with pikes and halberds, flanked by torches that never burn out.

Further up the path, the manor itself has been transformed into a bunker-like fortress. Since they last saw them, the white stone of the front pillars had darkened, stained by years of soot and smoke. The grand stained-glass windows, which once depicted the legends of old, had been removed or shattered, replaced with narrow slits for archers. The limestone-paved courtyard had been torn up, replaced with hardened gravel and marching lanes, where squads of soldiers now drill in perfect formation. The arched bridge to the front door now bears three giant banners: black, red, and gold, emblazoned with the sigil of

King Lansamor's reign. High up in the sky above the roof of the palace, a circle of armored Dvoran guards flies on patrol, keeping watch for intruders.

Skanot grabs Binnmerva's hand and helps her duck out of sight. They take refuge in the shadow of a small building off to the side of the main path, which had not been there before.

Taking in the sight of his once beloved sanctuary, now defiled and remade into something so ghastly, Skanot feels his stomach turn. His ears droop as his golden complexion slips into a shade of pallor.

"Oh, Binnie," he breathes, his voice unsteady. "See what they have done to the place."

"At least the air here is breathable," Binnmerva says cynically. "What's this strange building?"

Her back pressed against its cold exterior wall, she side-steps away from Skanot and tries to peer around the corner. Before she can make it all the way, Skanot grabs her arm to restrain her.

"Take heed!" he hisses, pointing to a patrolling guard in the distance. "We do not wish to get caught!"

Binnmerva slaps his arm out of the way.

"Maybe we do," she shoots back over her shoulder. "They could take us straight to the boy."

Skanot shakes his head, ashen with worry.

"Or they might kill us on the spot," he replies.

Binnmerva dismisses his fear and creeps further ahead without looking back.

"Try to reach Zhanniti or Todd," she says. "They might still be inside. I'm going to figure out what this building is."

Skanot nods and screws his eyes shut in concentration while Binnmerva disappears around the corner.

The building she is pressed up against is gray and mostly devoid of large distinguishing features, and constructed out of rolled stones which have clearly been hastily reshaped by crude instruments to make them fit together. The stonework on this building doesn't match the manor or the fortress; this was built later, quickly, without care. The path-facing side of it, which she now gazes at from her hunched-over vantage point, opens up at the center into a deep chamber. Shadows pool beyond the threshold, swallowing any visible detail. From where she crouches, Binnmerva cannot make out what lies inside.

After a moment, her eyes catch something: a small inscription etched into the stone above the entrance. It reads, "Memorial for Giant Beast Campaign." Binnmerva frowns, her curiosity piqued. She remains low to the ground, ignoring the ache in her elderly knees. Without looking away, she whispers over her shoulder.

"Skanot," she whispers. "Have you made contact?"

The flaxen Carfassan does not respond, his hands pressed to his temples and eyes shut in deep focus. He sways slightly from side to side, deaf to the world around him. Then, his breathing slows. The distant sounds of the fortress fade away.

In an instant, Skanot is elsewhere. A blank white void stretches around him, infinite and featureless. His spectral form drifts weightlessly as he wanders the astral plane.

"Zhanniti?" he calls out, his voice echoing into the nothingness. "Todd?"

The form of a blonde woman dressed in sackcloth fades into being in front of him.

"What's going on now?" she asks.

"It's your son," Skanot replies with a grimace. "I must reach the others so Binnmerva and I can talk to him."

The woman looks disappointed, her eyes downcast.

"Is he making trouble again?" she asks.

"The worst kind," Skanot grumbles. He sighs. "Is it possible you could—?"

Marissa takes his meaning and nods, blinking out of existence. A moment later, a rush of feathers fills the void. Clad in glistening armor, Zhanniti appears in a tizzy.

"Oh," she says, bewildered. "Sorry 'bout that, Skanot. Had no idea ye wanted to reach me."

Skanot ogles Zhanniti's royal golden helmet and breastplate, impressed.

"I see you have advanced in the king's favor!" he exclaims.

"The armor of the advance forward guard. D'you like it?" Zhanniti replies humbly.

"It suits you well," Skanot says kindly. "What happened to Todd?"

"Oh, he's busy," Zhanniti says. "He's gotta keep watch over the mining team. Can't be called away from it. So what's up, Skanot? We really oughta catch up!"

"No time for that, sorry," Skanot says. "I have to speak to the king urgently."

Zhanniti blinks, puzzled by his hurry, but eager to help nonetheless.

"I'll see what I can do!" she says, before vanishing in a shimmer of golden light, leaving Skanot alone on the astral plane once more.

Meanwhile, back in the physical realm, Binnmerva toddles into the war memorial in King Lansamor's courtyard. She moves slowly, her joints stiff and her back burdened by the dull ache of age.

Her back turned to the world outside, Binnmerva squints while her weary eyes adjust to the darkness. The space inside the building is small. Its center is dominated by a bestial stone statue with seven heads, which stands tall on legs like that of a bear. Binnmerva recognizes it as the vanquished beast from the prophecy. The walls on all sides of the room's perimeter are adorned with names, carved into the very stone that makes up the structure of the memorial. Each name is tagged with an age and clan identifier. As she reads a few of these, Binnmerva's heart is struck by a pang of grief. These are the names of the villagers who gave their life in King Lansamor's hasty raid on the beast's lair.

"HEY!" a surly voice calls. Binnmerva turns around slowly.

An armored soldier stands in the entrance of the memorial, brandishing a spear. His face is obscured by a visored metal helmet, but hostility is readily evident in the way he carries himself.

"Hello, dear." Binnmerva leans on her cane and tries to sound senile. "How are you?"

"You are trespassing on these grounds," the soldier replies sternly. "State your business or leave!"

Binnmerva steps closer to the soldier, who responds by shifting into a combat ready stance and tilting the tip of his spear toward her.

"I fear I may be lost," Binnmerva says sweetly. "Could you escort me?"

Unhappily, the soldier does not relent in his hostility.

"What's your name, madam?" he grunts.

"Binnmerva!" a different voice calls from afar. The soldier turns to look, readjusting his spear to make it point to the sky.

"Who goes there?" the soldier calls.

In a moment, Skanot appears, walking cautiously toward the entrance of the memorial with his hand outstretched to wave hello.

"Why, 'tis I, Skanot!" the Carfassan replies jovially. "Binnmerva and I have business with the king."

The soldier quickly steps out into the sunlight to face Skanot, his armor clanking as he walks. Binnmerva can see them face each other through the passage of the building. The soldier beckons a gauntleted hand to her as she watches them.

"You come out here too!" he yells.

Binnmerva points at herself and inclines her head, playing dumb. Realizing this tactic will go nowhere, she decides to comply.

In a moment, Skanot and Binnmerva stand side by side in the courtyard, facing the soldier, who eyes them both up and down.

"I want the truth out of both of you," he barks. "And no funny business!"

"What I said is true!" Skanot says. "We are here to talk to the king."

"The king doesn't see visitors." The soldier is not convinced. "Why are you really here?"

Binnmerva and Skanot both stare at the soldier, trying hard not to blink or shrink away in fright. Suddenly, something blocks out the sunlight above them, but only for a moment. Binnmerva casts her gaze upward: a bright shape is descending rapidly toward them. As it gets closer, she can see it in detail.

Zhanniti, clad in full golden regalia that catches the gleam of the sun, dives between the soldier and his detainees. As the dust clears, she makes a sweeping gesture with her wing to encourage the soldier to step backward.

"He does today!" she announces in a singsong voice. "These folks are known to him. So come on, Baldur, take them to the castle or leave 'em alone!"

The soldier drops to his knees and bows, his arm crossed over his chest.

"Yes, my lady. A thousand apologies."

Zhanniti is amused by his fealty. She pats the soldier reassuringly on his helmet.

"Hey, no worries, bud. You did the right thing. Now go rejoin your unit."

The soldier stands, salutes, and leaves. Zhanniti watches him go, then turns to face her fellow guardians apologetically.

"Sorry about that," she says, her tone reproachful. "These guys really take their jobs seriously. But that's good, right? They're passionate."

"It's so good to see you," Binnmerva says.

Zhanniti pulls Binnmerva into a warm, feathery hug. Her wings envelop the Malyumpkinite's bony frame.

"You as welll!" she says brightly. "How long has it been, anyway?"

"Four– unff– years," Binnmerva says, her voice muffled by the hug.

Skanot stands to the side and watches them with a toothy grin. Zhanniti looks at him as if only recognizing him for the first time and releases her hold on Binnmerva.

"Hi, Skanot," she says. "I kinda just saw you but it's also good to see you too."

Skanot nods curtly. Zhanniti straightens her helmet and sneezes, the smell of Binnmerva's perfume strong in the nasal passages of her beak.

"Okay," she says. "Without further ado, let's go see the king, huh?"

The King's Throne Room

The banquet hall of the fortress formerly known as the hall of heroes has been transformed almost beyond recognition into a decadent court for the King. The long wooden tables that once hosted feasts and fellowship are gone, replaced by a vast, empty space repurposed for the King's amusement. Several entertainers selected from amongst the kingdom's prison population stumble around the room, acting out forced performances. Each of them has his or her legs shackled closely together by an iron chain, restricting the wearer's movement. One struggles to juggle a set of brightly colored balls, the heavy iron binding her ankles reducing her movements to awkward, unsteady jerks. Nearby, three others engage in a pathetic game of monkey-in-the-middle, their chains clinking with every labored step.

At the far end of the room opposite the door stands a giant throne, hewn from a polished stone that glows somewhere between the smoothness of marble and the unyielding weight of granite. Embedded within its surface are amethyst-hued veins of psychic ore, raw remnants of the land's power, now ripped from the ground and reforged into hollow splendor. Flanking the throne stand six guards, their faces obscured by heavy helms, their crossbows held stiffly at the ready. They are ordered by height, arranged from shortest to tallest with the tallest standing closest to the throne on each side. Behind the throne, a crude fresco defaces the wall: a graceless attempt to recreate the prophetic mural Lance had seen on his first visit. Where the original had depth and artistry, this replica is flat, lifeless, and utterly careless of form. On the throne itself sits the King. He lounges sideways across a plush, thick cushion set upon the throne's seat, his legs dangling over the side, swinging idly like a bored child's. A guard (the tallest of the six) feeds him pieces of fruit, pressing them between his lips like an obedient maid. The King is clad in obsidian armor, its jagged black surface catching the dim torchlight, with an ore-derived trim that glints in eerie harmony with the throne's violet veins. His once-cropped curls now spill down to his shoulders in unruly tangles, his face shadowed by patches of unkempt beard.

Despite his ostensibly careless posture, King Lansamor remains on high alert, his eyes scanning the room like a hungry lion, seeking whom he may desire. He singles out the juggler, an emaciated salt-and-pepper speckled Dvoran, and points at her.

"**YOU!**" he bellows, waving the fruit-bearing guard away from him so he can speak freely.

"Me, your lordship?" the juggler replies timidly, trembling with fright. Her balls scatter on the floor.

The king pulls himself up and sits straight against the back of the throne.

"**I want you to fly over to the mine and collect Carlyle and Todd. Return with them in an hour or the consequences will be severe.**"

The Dvoran snaps to attention upon hearing the command, but she is weighed down by the iron chain between her legs.

"Your lordship," she whimpers. "What about my shackles?"

"What about them?" the King replies without a hint of concern. "They aren't affecting your wings, are they?"

"But they'll weigh me down!"

"**NO EXCUSES!**" the King roars. "**GET OUT OF MY SIGHT.**"

Eyes welling with tears, the juggler trudges out of the room, defeated. The King watches her intently as she leaves, savoring her suffering. Then he returns to his original seating position and locks eyes with the tallest attending guard.

"Bezalel," he drawls. "I have a dilemma."

"More fruit, my lord?" the servant asks. The King shakes his head.

"No, no. You know when you're knuckle-deep into a good nose-picking session, and–"

His charming anecdote is cut short by the sudden arrival of a visitor to the King's court, heralded by the loud wooden squeak of the doors to the hall swinging open.

"Is she back already?" the King mumbles under his breath.

Groaning with lethargy, he straightens once more and fixes his attention on the aisle leading up to the throne. A Dvoran in shiny golden armor enters, flanked on either side by a flaxen-skinned Carfassan in a tunic and an elderly Malyumpkinite in a shawl.

"Zhanniti?" he says with surprise. "What are you doing with these two?"

"Oh, hi boss!" Zhanniti says cheerfully. "Skanot and Binnmerva said they had something important to talk to you about."

The King's eyes narrow into slits.

"But they've been banished!" he cries. "They should not be here."

"Let's just hear them out, okay?" Zhanniti says reproachfully. "They came a long way to get here. Plus, what have they done that's so wrong?"

King Lansamor considers this suggestion by his closest advisor and weighs it carefully in his mind. Finally, he relents.

"Fine. Bring them forward. Skanot, Binnmerva, what do you want?"

Skanot looks over with uncertainty at Binnmerva, who does not match his gaze. Instead, she stares straight at the King with an intense anger burning in her eyes. Remaining tight-lipped in apparent protest, she will probably not jump in to answer the King's query. Skanot decides to take initiative.

"Well, your highness," Skanot begins carefully. "We wanted to bring to your attention a problem in the East that you might wish to know about."

"And what is that?" the King asks.

"Binnie and I are, um, concerned. Um, we are worried that the reckless mining activity in the valley might be damaging the environment. And, er, back over in the East, the air is–"

The King laughs sharply, causing Skanot to lose his train of thought.

"HA! I never took you for paranoid, Skanot. I can assure you our mining operation is very safe."

Over on the other side of Zhanniti, Binnmerva makes a tetchy noise. It seems to come out of her involuntarily; out of the corner of his eye, Skanot can see her try to regain her composure. The King now fixes his attention on her, rapt with malice. Skanot's mind races to think of a way to reassert dominance over the conversation.

"Listen to me!" he blurts, too loudly and too forcefully. He swallows hard and tries again, quieter, pleading. "Your highness. This is no mere speculation. We have proof!"

"Okay. Show it to me."

Skanot hesitates.

"Um... ah!" He produces the dirty handkerchief from his tunic pocket and waves it around in the air. At the sight of it, King Lansamor wrinkles his nose in disgust.

"Ew, what is that? Did you blow your nose into that, Skanot!?" he shrieks.

"Uh, no, your highness. The filth on this handkerchief comes from the air in the East, which is filled with pollution." Skanot hands it to Zhanniti, who flies over to the throne and holds it close to the King for his inspection.

"This isn't proof, Skanot. My patience with you is wearing thin. Binnmerva, do you have anything to say?"

The Malyumpkinite woman shakes with fear and rage.

"Skanot," she says through gritted teeth, "is telling you the truth. *Your highness.*"

At that precise moment, before the King can respond, the great doors to the court groan open once more. A rush of cold air follows, sweeping through the hall. The first to enter is mining supervisor Carlyle. The tawny Dvoran swoops extravagantly through the air, looping once before coming to rest a few feet in front of the throne. Behind him, Todd steps forward. The final guardian is a broken specter of the man he once was. His jaw is clamped shut beneath a metal muzzle, bolted tight to his face. The red sweater he once wore with pride now hangs in shreds around his torso, exposing a lattice of scars and muscle, the marks of a body broken and reshaped by years of hard labor. At the very rear of the group is the juggler who fetched them, bent nearly in half and panting from exertion. Her metal chain drags against the ground as she shuffles into the court, completely out of breath. At the sight of the poor tormented creature and the tortured state of her old friend Todd, Binnmerva erupts with fury.

"You TYRANT!" she screams, lunging forward. Before she can get far, Zhanniti puts her in a headlock to keep her restrained. The King raises his eyebrows in surprise, but does not move. Irately, Binnmerva continues:

"What right do you have to treat these people this way? What right do you have to sit on that throne?!"

Skanot is paralyzed. He braces himself helplessly for impact, fixated intently on the King's impending reaction. Rather than responding in anger, the King almost seems amused.

"I rule the way I rule," he says with a smirk, "because I am strong and you are weak."

Binnmerva slams the bottom of her cane against the ground. The hollow thump echoes across the room as she fires back.

"You stupid child! All of us are strong in some ways and weak in others," she cries, her jowls flapping animatedly. "We come into this world weak, we become strong, we weaken and then we die. This is true of me and it is true of you! A system that only serves to make the strong stronger and the weak weaker will constrict and then collapse! You will rule over an empire of dust and bones!"

"I don't really give a shit about any of that." Lance snaps his fingers. "**Guards, kill her!**"

Zhanniti tightens her hold on Binnmerva. Simultaneously, all six of the King's guards load an arrow into their crossbows and fire upon her. Every arrow hits its target. Skanot doesn't even hear them land. He only notices the way Binnmerva's body goes limp in Zhanniti's grasp. The way her cane slips from her hand, hitting the stone floor with a hollow clatter. The way her throat gurgles as the light drains out of her eyes. Skanot wants to scream, to cry, to accuse. He opens his mouth, but no sound escapes it.

The court is silent.

King Lansamor surveys the subjects assembled in his court, the violet veins in his armor glowing bright with psychic power. His gaze lingers on the three ne'er-do-wells who had earlier been playing monkey-in-the-middle.

"Let this be a lesson to all of you," he declares ominously, "about what will happen if you step out of line."

Skanot lowers his head, his hands trembling. He says nothing, unable to look anywhere but the floor.

After a beat, it is Todd who breaks the silence. A deep, guttural sound emanates from under his muzzle and begins to rattle the walls of the room. In a flash, he leaps forward and seizes King Lansamor by the throat, throttling the teenage boy with full force. The six throne guards pile atop him, trying to pry him off, while he constricts his grip ever tighter.

"GACK!" the King croaks. Then, when his guards have sufficiently wrested Todd away enough to loosen his hold, he chokes out the following command: "**DROP DEAD!**"

Between the eddies of power emanating from his armor and throne, and the lack of specificity in his command, the King's pronouncement has a devastating effect. The heart of every other living being in the court stops instantly, and all slump onto the ground where they stand. The hall falls silent again.

The room is filled with the corpses of friend and foe alike. Suddenly and terribly, 17-year-old Lance Morrissey realizes that he is alone.

A second later, he is ensconced in a warm light. The court melts away. His armor vanishes. He finds himself standing back at home in his bedroom, clad in a t-shirt and jorts that no longer fit him. Everything is exactly as he left it long ago. Lance's caged rabbit, Stardust, still tokes from its water bottle. Light from the midsummer sun streams in through the window. He gazes through it and scans the backyard, feeling nauseous with dread. The tree fort is gone, without a trace that it ever existed.

"Lance?" his father calls from outside the bedroom. "Are you back inside already?"

"Uhh... y- yeah, dad! Yeah, I am!" Lance tries to make himself sound younger, cringing at how deep his voice must sound. The door opens. Lance's father enters the room, takes one look at his overgrown son, and screams.

Exoplanet JM-201137a: Nightfall

A small rover modeled loosely on NASA's *Perseverance* trundles across a cracked and desiccated alien landscape. Its six reticulated wheels carve fresh tread tracks into the purple-tinted regolith. The fading twilight of the setting sun glints off the three pounds of minerals it carries in a mesh basket, secured to its carriage.

Behind the rover, two identically-dressed and space suit-clad scientists march side-by-side, exchanging theories excitedly like a latter-day Holmes and Watson. Far behind them, feeling sluggish and stupid and woefully misplaced, walks Joseph Mulenga. He can hear the chatter of his fellow Afronauts over their shared comms channel, and though he takes in the landscape as earnestly as they do, no matter how hard he tries, he can't shake the quiet gnaw of inadequacy.

About a half a kilometer ahead of the procession stands the parked *Mwaba-1* spaceship, ready to admit them for the night.

"You can't even see de stars," Captain Madoda Tembo remarks, trying in vain to peer through the opaque haze filling the atmosphere above them.

"The cloud layer might be miles thick," Jeanette Emberley muses. "What's your take on the high quantities of organics we scanned? You think there might be life here? Underground, maybe?"

Captain Tembo kicks at a loose pebble and watches it scatter.

"If dere was, it's long dead," he says. "Between de radiation and de greenhouse gases, nuttin' could survive here."

"Maybe it wasn't always like this," Jeanette hypothesizes. "If we had any stratigraphic equipment, we could learn more about the history of this planet."

"Someting could have happened to de magnetic field, eh?" Madoda suggests.

"But what about the fissures in the surface?"

"Tectonic activity, maybe?"

"And what would cause that?"

Joseph Mulenga jogs forward a few paces to join the conversation.

"What about mining?" he cuts in.

Jeanette Emberley halts in her step and turns to look at Mulenga with a mixture of confusion and academic judgment.

"What are you talking about?" she asks.

"Mining, it, eh, causes earthquakes, yes?" Mulenga replies. "It happens in South Africa. Dey dig too deep and it shakes up de ground."

"He's right." Captain Tembo stoops down and picks up a pile of surface dust, letting it fall and considering it in a new light. "Maybe dey had gases and radioactive material trapped unda de surface. Maybe dey dug too deep and it got out."

"I was talking about anaerobic bacteria. But you're talking about an intelligent species. A civilization, even. Something almost... human." Emberley seems troubled by the thought.

"Well, it is a big universe, eh?" Mulenga quips, but his words hang in the still, empty air. The wind shifts, scattering dust over the rover's fresh tracks, erasing them almost as quickly as they were made.

"Let's just get to the ship and tuck in for the night."

With this final word spoken on the matter, Jeanette Emberley breaks into a brisk jog to catch up to the rover, which has been steadily moving ahead unabated all this time. Captain

Tembo lingers for a moment, staring out at the barren landscape, as he seems to weigh Joseph Mulenga's words in his head. Then, without another comment, he picks up his pace and jogs toward the ship. Once again, Mulenga is left bringing up the rear. Sighing deeply to himself, he starts to walk slowly in the same direction.

"Wait up!" he calls, waving his hands wildly to catch the attention of his crewmates.

Their backs are turned to him; they are already entering the airlock of the ship, with the rover in tow. They do not seem to hear him. Suddenly, before he can speak another word, everything fades away.

Elsewhere

In the blink of an eye, Joseph Mulenga finds himself transported to a strange place he does not understand. The alien landscape of the exoplanet has melted away, replaced by a blank, white, empty void that stretches as far as the eye can see. Still clad in his Afronaut spacesuit, he briefly considers the possibility that he may have blacked out and is now in some sort of lab or virtual reality chamber back on Earth. Then, a different possibility occurs to him.

Am I dead? The possibility gnaws at his superstitious mind.

There is some kind of solid ground underneath his feet. He jumps, rising into the air and then promptly falling back down, as one might expect. But the boundaries of the surface on which he stands are unclear. This is a real stumper.

"Heh- Hello?" he calls meekly, unsure whether he would like to see who answers.

"Who are you?" a voice asks from behind him. Mulenga spins around to face its source.

The voice belongs to a blonde woman dressed in a drab one-piece garment. She seems to be in her mid-thirties, but Joseph Mulenga can only guess. It would probably be impertinent to ask. He is unsure at a glance whether or not he can trust her, but her bright blue eyes radiate kindness and warmth. He studies her for several seconds while she waits patiently, until it finally dawns on him that he has yet to answer her question.

"My name is Joseph Mulenga," he says quietly. "Ah– uh– are you real?"

"Yep," the woman says. She sits down cross-legged and pats in front of her. Mulenga joins her on the ground and she continues talking. "I'm Marissa. It's good to see another human face. Where are you from, Joseph?"

"I'm from Earth," Joseph says, hoping dearly that the same is true of Marissa. She laughs.

"I'm from Earth too, obviously," she says, her eyes sparkling. "I meant where in particular. I noticed your accent. Me, I'm from Nebraska. The United States. You can take that space helmet off, by the way. Unless you like breathing in your own spit, I guess."

Joseph nods gratefully and presses at a latch on the neck of his suit. Then he unscrews his helmet. It comes off with a quiet pneumatic hiss, and he sets it down next to him.

"I am from Zambia," he says. "De capital city of Lusaka."

"Wow, that's really interesting. Huh. Why are you dressed like an astronaut?"

"Because I *am* an astronaut."

"Oh."

"Yeah."

They both fall silent for a moment, each reflecting on their circumstances. Then a question occurs to Joseph.

"Are you a monk?" he asks.

"What?" Marissa seems taken aback by the question.

"De garb you are wearing, it is religious, eh? It looks like something a monk would wear."

"Oh, this thing?" Marissa asks, tugging at a fold in the fabric. "They told me to wear it."

"Who?"

"Huh?"

"Who told you to wear it?"

Marissa points behind Joseph, over his shoulder, and replies casually.

"Oh," she says. "Those guys did."

Joseph's spine tingles as he spins around where he sits to see three inhuman figures assembled in the space behind him.

From left to right, the creatures in the void behind him are: an upright-standing boar, its body rough and earthen like as though sculpted from wet mud; a tall, elf-like being composed of shifting interlocking shapes of golden light; and a towering, bone-colored bird with piercing yellow eyes and a beak as sharp and slender as a dagger.

"What– What are deez tings?!" Joseph's voice cracks, his native accent strong with fear. He scrambles back toward Marissa, who remains still, unperturbed by the arrival of the creatures.

"They call themselves the temporal guardians," she says flatly. "They've been my captors for the last several years."

The center being shifts forward, the spectral shapes that make up its eyes whizzing around in circles.

"You are not captive," it intones, its voice resonating deep in Joseph's skull. "You have been chosen."

"I know," Marissa says tersely. "That was a joke... mostly."

"What is dis about? Chosen for what?" Joseph demands, his fear mounting.

"Joseph Chisomo Mulenga and Mary Miller Morrissey," the clockwork guardian replies in an even tone, "You have been chosen to restrain a great evil."

Marissa shoots to her feet, suddenly red with anger.

"You mean my son, right?" she asks. "The son that YOU never let me raise?"

Joseph Mulenga's eyes dart back and forth between Marissa and the creatures she accuses, unsure how to respond to what's happening around him.

"Yes," the clockwork guardian replies. "Your son. He has destroyed our planet. This one has seen it." The shifting pieces of its hand arraign themselves to point at Joseph, who goes wide-eyed.

"Are you one of de aliens that lived there?" he asks, breathing hard. His heart starts to pound.

The birdlike one tilts its head.

"You may call us aliens," it says. "Or angels, or quantum beings, or artifacts. You may simply call us Guardians."

Joseph Mulenga bows his head and begins whispering a prayer under his breath. Marissa's maternal fury is undiminished.

"If you would have just let me raise him!" she charges, her cheeks red. "I could have taught him to do things right!"

"Do you love your husband?" the Boar interjects.

"Yes!" Marissa snarls indignantly. "You took me from him too!"

"Trust, then, that your husband tried his best to raise your son. Nothing would have changed."

Marissa goes silent, but she shakes her head angrily, biting back a million possible retorts.

"More to the point," Opius cuts in, "It was fated. Things could ever have gone one way."

The Clockwork Guardian of the Center joins in.

"It was foretold," it agrees solemnly.

"It's just not fair," Marissa says quietly. "I had to watch him from afar. I wish I could have talked to him."

All three temporal guardians exchange glances.

"You shall have your chance," the clockwork guardian says. "This we swear."

Joseph Mulenga stops praying. He rises to his feet, ready for action.

"And what about me?" he asks.

August 7, 2018

Lance Morrissey sits comfortably in an armchair in his office. With his beard freshly trimmed and hair tied back, he almost looks like a respectable businessman. *Almost.* Behind him stands a man named Sebastian Wallace, whom Lance had recently met at a security convention and taken on as an all-round "fixer" for his new company. In contrast to Lance's present calm demeanor, Sebastian is clearly agitated. He shifts uncomfortably from side to side, and although his sunglasses go part of the way toward obscuring his facial features, a distinct look of worry is still readily visible across the young man's countenance.

Sure enough, the door to the office bursts open. Into the room rushes a frenzied, angry dark-haired woman. She quickly steps up close to Lance Morrissey and shoves her finger in his face.

"Mister Stardust!" she shouts, referring to Lance by his public corporate pseudonym. "I've got a bone to pick with you."

Sebastian instinctively reacts to the disturbance by stepping forward as well, ready to lay hands on the woman and neutralize the potential threat. Lance holds him back.

"Woah!" he exclaims. Sebastian steps no further. The woman continues her diatribe.

"You're a criminal!" she shrieks. "A crook! And you're an awful, appalling human being!"

Lance assumes a humble posture.

"Woah now," he cautions. "Settle down. Let's use our words. What seems to be the problem?"

The woman slams her hands on the table between them angrily.

"You know EXACTLY what the problem is!" she cries. "You remember me? Lisa Cook? Exclusive rights holder to the Penelope Pig children's show franchise?"

In truth, Lance remembers her perfectly well, as he had recently defrauded her, but obviously the choicest course of action in this sort of scenario is to play dumb.

"That is to say..." the woman continues, reducing the volume of her voice and sitting down across from Lance, "...the *former* exclusive rights holder."

Lance selects and opens a binder on the table between them.

"Hmm," he says. "You might be a client of ours. I can look in the directory for you if you would like."

He proceeds to flip through the binder for several seconds, not breaking eye contact with Lisa while she sits there and silently fumes.

"You are so FULL OF IT!" Lisa Cook roars. "You personally shook my hand, when I signed a contract for legal protection under the Stardust Advocacy Group that YOU OWN!"

Lance Morrissey sits back in his chair.

"Hm," he muses. "And when was this, exactly?"

"It was six months ago," Lisa Cook replies. "And here's the thing. Three days ago, when I was taking my dog to the vet to pay for its cancer treatments, my card was declined, and I had to explain to them why I couldn't pay for it. I called the bank, and they told me that my account was taken over by a third party, and that's why I was locked out."

"Sounds like you got hacked," Lance replies calmly. "That can happen, you know."

"Isn't it your job to make sure that doesn't happen?" Lisa replies incredulously. "And there's more! Three days ago I also found out that I'd lost the rights to all of my characters, and that they were bought by a dummy company that YOU OWN!"

"And what are you accusing me of?" Lance asks. His tone is cold and flat.

"At best, gross negligence. At worst, stealing my identity, my property, AND bankrupting me. You're, what, twenty years old? I don't know how someone your age got his hands on such a massive company, but whoever raised you needs to do a better job. What were you, raised in a barn? I could sue for damages!"

As Lisa rants, Lance takes great care to hold the muscles in his face and body perfectly still, so as not to betray any reaction. Behind him, Sebastian affects a look that seems to convey disinterest. The two of them are forming an effective stonewall. Perhaps they can pull it off all the way.

"Sounds like you gambled too hard and lost," Lance scolds. "It's a dangerous world out there."

"UGH!!" Lisa shrieks with fury. "You know who I am, you know why this happened! I knew you wouldn't respond to words alone, so I took action."

This actually comes as a surprise. Lance decides it must be a bluff, so he calls it.

"And what would that be?" he asks.

"That rabbit of yours, that you oh-so-creatively *also* named Stardust?" Lisa asks. "Well, I tracked it down to a fairground and kidnapped it. If you ever wanna see your rabbit again, you better pony up."

What a terrible strategy, Lance thinks to himself. *This is some real amateur hour stuff.*

"See, no offense lady," he says, leaning forward to invade Lisa's personal space. "But if anything, it kinda sounds like the real monster here is you. I sold that rabbit to some kid a couple years ago. So you just broke a little kid's heart! Not a good look."

Beside him, Sebastian's mouth is agape in mock surprise. Clearly, he's savoring the drama.

"So you're just gonna refuse to take responsibility for this?" Lisa asks, gobsmacked. "You really don't care?"

"That just about sums it up, yeah," Lance responds. "Now get out of here."

Lisa storms out of the room in a cloud of disgust, taking care to slam the door shut behind herself as loudly and forcefully as possible. A second later, she sticks her head back into the room once more to interject a parting word:

"And by the way, I *will* be seeing you in court."

Then she slams the door shut once more and exits the building. Lance and Sebastian exchange glances.

"So... what are we gonna do about her?" Sebastian asks. "She could be trouble for us."

"Trail her, kill her, make it look like an accident, and burn the evidence," Lance replies casually.

"I can do that," Sebastian replies.

"Thank you Sebastian," Lance says. "You have a lot of loyalty for a hired gun, and I admire that. And, while you're at it, kill the rabbit too."

Sebastian nods and exits the room, straightening up the chair that Lisa Cook knocked over in her angry exit as he leaves. Lance watches him go, satisfied that his goon will carry out the mission to satisfaction.

October 24, 2022

The walkie talkie on Correctional Officer Seamus McKinney's belt chirps. A woman's voice, audible but incoherent, comes through the receiver. McKinney sighs, readjusts himself, and unclips the talkie to bring it to his face.

"Say again, Connie?"

"Phone call came in for one of the prisoners," comes the terse reply.

The CO licks a piece of food off his molar and looks at the orange-clad men assembled in the mess hall in front of him. None of them are looking in his direction.

"Which one?"

"Morrissey."

Huh.

"Interesting," he muses into the device.

"Does he not eat on your shift?"

"No, I see him right now. It's just interesting. You'll see. I'll send him down. Over."

No more than a minute later, a sour-faced and burly young man enters the ICS room and stands in front of Connie's desk.

"Phone call for you, Mr. Morrissey," she says through the plexiglass barrier that divides them.

The man affixes her with a cold, icy glare. Hardly a muscle on his face twitches, and he barely seems to breathe. So blank is his expression that she wonders for a brief moment if indeed he even heard or understood her, until he pivots on his feet and marches over to the CO holding the phone.

Lance Morrissey takes a seat and the phone is handed over. He grabs it and looks askance at the hovering Officer who passed it to him. A tense moment passes between the two of them. Then, tight-lipped as ever, the prisoner blinks, casts his gaze to the floor, and finally puts the phone up to his ear.

"You have fifteen minutes," the CO reminds him after seconds pass and Lance has still said nothing. Lance slowly blinks again and exhales loudly out his nose to announce his presence to whoever is on the other end.

"Hey Lance!" calls the bright voice of Sebastian Wallace on the phone.

A note of what might be surprise registers on Morrissey's face, in the form of a slight squint and wrinkle of the nose. Still being monitored by both Connie and the Officer in the room, his reaction goes no further than this, and he maintains his silence.

"Listen, ah, I know this won't be easy for you to hear, so I wanted to break the news to you, like, uh, gently, you know?" Sebastian says, his trademark conversational tone somewhat rimmed with audible trepidation. Lance says and does nothing.

"Okay, so. Long story short, I struck a deal with the state. Uh, I gave them certain information that I guess you could say they didn't have access to before. I um, well. *Ahem.* Well basically I told them where they could find certain documents from your time as, uh, as umm... as head of security. So."

A weighty and awkward silence fills the room. Connie and the Officer briefly make eye contact with each other.

"Could you say something, Lance, buddy? I figured you might be a little *upset* but I'd– look, it was Jordan's idea! So please just– okay, let me explain! All I did was facilitate the discovery of certain facts that were bound to turn up eventually, AND in return they're letting me move back into my house. With an ankle monitor and everything but still – I mean, it's a big first step, right?"

Morrissey returns the phone to the Officer's hand and stands up defiantly.

"Could ya say something, please, Lance?" Sebastian asks the room.

The Officer holding the phone answers brusquely on the taciturn prisoner's behalf.

"Thank you for your call, Mr. Wallace."

He hangs the phone back up on its wall-mounted unit and begins to exit the room. Morrissey remains rooted in place.

"Come on, convict. Back to the mess hall."

Lance shakes his head firmly and stomps over to Connie's desk, looking at her expectantly. Something about his expression reminds her of a scorned child.

"Hey Lance," she says to him gently. "It's time to go back now. Go follow Officer Lewis, please. You can't stay here any longer."

The bearded prisoner shakes his head again.

"Do you want something?" she asks kindly.

He nods eagerly, looking strikingly like a child who has just been told off by his mom but still hopes to get ice cream later. Thinking quickly, Connie thinks back to the content of the phone call she just overheard and narrows down her options.

"Would you like to talk to your lawyer?"

Lance beams and flashes a double thumbs up, displaying an exuberant energy completely unlike his dour demeanor just a few minutes ago.

"Alright, we'll give him a call and let you know when he gets here."

Lance nods a final time and files behind Officer Lewis, who leads him out of the room.

"Did my mom used to teach you?" Connie overhears the Officer asking the convict as the two men leave. "Her name was Brenda."

An hour later, Lance Morrissey sits in a cold room alone, his arm cuffed to a stainless-steel table. There is a knock on the door.

Jordan Smith, Lance's lawyer, steps into the room clad in a garish pink suit. He pauses in the doorway of the interview chamber and turns to shout at an unseen guard.

"Attorney-client privilege still applies in prison, you fascists!" he shrieks. "Give me and my client some peace, please!"

Satisfied, he enters the rest of the way and closes the heavy metal door of the interview room behind himself. Then he crosses over to the table where Lance is shackled and sets his attache case down on top of it.

"Sorry about that, sir," he says. "These morons wouldn't know the fifth amendment from the fifth estate even if it served them a subpoena and made them testify in front of Congress. Now, how are we doing?"

He opens up his case and pulls out a manila file folder, which he dramatically displays on the tabletop between them.

"Now I've spent the last week combing through Westlaw and I think I've assembled a case I can put in front of a judge to settle this thing out of court, if you're interested in that..." he begins, before trailing off in front of Lance Morrissey's angry glower.

There is a prolonged moment of awkward silence while Lance stares intensely.

"You seem upset," Jordan observes.

At long last, Lance Morrissey breaks his silence. His voice is scratchy and dry from lack of use.

"I just got a call from Sebastian," he croaks.

"Your former hitman?" Jordan asks with a note of surprise. "What the hell did he want?"

"Apparently he gave up the goods on our Auburn operation," Lance says idly.

"Oh? How strange," Jordan evasively replies.

"Yes. Strange. Especially since he says it was *your* idea," Lance retorts pointedly.

Jordan Smith forces air out of his mouth and stands up, smoothing out his suit jacket before turning his back to Lance and staring at the wall.

"Is there something back there, Smith?" Lance asks angrily. "Why don't you look at me?"

"Look Lance, I'm sorry," Jordan says, still not turning around. "I was going to tell you eventually. But materially, this really doesn't hurt you. In fact, we can spin it to our advantage!"

"**Turn around and look at me!**" Lance demands.

Jordan, cowed, complies.

"Explain how it helps me," Lance says in an even tone without breaking eye contact.

Jordan returns to his seat at the table.

"First, please tell me you've been doing what I asked and stayed silent around all the prison guards," he says.

"Jordan, I have been silent as the grave."

"Good. Then this becomes very easy."

"Explain."

Jordan licks his lips and sucks his teeth.

"Okay," he says. "What I can do is convince the state that you were complicit in this information being presented and start working on getting these charges knocked down to civil offenses and misdemeanors. Since Sebastian walked, they can't get you on the murder anyway, so we can leverage these documents and get you moved to the county jail."

"Is the food better there?" Lance asks.

"I can't speak to that. I think they serve slightly prettier gruel. But the headline piece here is that a move to county jail is fifty percent of the journey to a full release. I don't know about you, but to me that's something to wear a happy face about!"

"What's the other fifty percent?"

"We're working on digging up dirt on that prosecutor. I smell a rat. Well, to be more precise, I smell skeletons. Closet skeletons. Which smells like, I don't know, dust or something, probably."

Lance Morrissey leans back in his chair and articulates his fingers into a scholar's cradle as he finally cracks a smile.

"This is good stuff," he says. "Thank you, Jordan."

"You pay me good money for this stuff, sir," Jordan replies affably. He begins packing up his briefcase, eager to leave the prison as quickly as possible. "Good money deserves good service." The counselor rises and extends his hand for a parting handshake, which Lance reciprocates. "So what are you gonna do when you get out of jail?"

"Big things, Jordan," Lance answers simply. "Big things."

December 17, 2022

In fact, as fate would have it, Lance Morrissey's stint in the county jail turns out to be far briefer than anyone could have anticipated. Only a few short weeks after Sebastian's revelation and one mysterious security failure at the county jail later, Lance is a free man. After getting out, he'd spent a while laying low in a suburb outside of Nashville with his lawyer while the two of them considered their options and recalibrated their plans for the future. This morning, Lance is navigating a rental car down the gridlocked streets of downtown Miami, and almost running late for a forthcoming meeting.

Zigging and zagging aggressively between all the other cars on the palm tree-frocked four-lane freeway, Lance is just about to enter the merge lane for his exit when a semi truck accelerates to his right and cuts him off out of nowhere. Lance pumps the gas pedal and lays on his horn, red with homicidal fury. The drivers ahead of him scramble to move their cars out of the way, and he seizes the opportunity to rev forward and occupy the opening. Then he shoves his car directly in front of the truck that had cut him off and slams on the brakes. Unable to stop in time, the truck driver swerves into the shoulder and off of the road. Satisfied, Lance switches his hazard lights on and casually enters the off-ramp.

A few minutes later, Lance arrives at his destination, a conference center located just outside the research campus of Florida Tech. Entering through the back door, it takes only a few seconds before he spots his target, a blonde woman sitting in a chair with her back to him. She is immersed in reading a book as he crosses the elegant, carpeted hallway toward her. She lowers the book as he approaches and speaks calmly in a dignified English accent.

"Can I help you?" the woman asks, as Lance stands next to her chair expectantly.

"Actually, I think we can help each other," Morrissey replies cordially. "Do you mind if I sit?"

She shrugs, so Lance shifts over and eases himself into a chair across from her. Between them stands a small round table. The blonde woman places her book on top of it to give Lance her full attention.

"Is it true you're an astrophysicist that works at NASA?" Lance asks, resting his cheek on his outstretched index and middle finger.

"I *used* to work at NASA," the woman replies, before regarding him with suspicion. "Is it true you killed someone and went to jail for it?"

Lance switches to a more alert posture, realizing this woman has probably done her research.

"I *used* to be in jail," he says, clasping his hands together. "But as you can see, right now I am not. And as a matter of public record, my lawyer assures me it's only a matter of time until I never killed anyone either."

"I wonder if the cops know that," the woman replies coolly, reaching for her smartphone. "Maybe I could call them, let them know you stopped by."

"I don't think that would be in the best interest… of either of us," Lance retorts. "Let's try this instead."

He extends his right arm stiffly for a handshake.

"I'm Lance Morrissey, of Lansamor Industries," he says flatly. "You may think I'm bad, but my money is very good."

The woman glances to her left and right before leaning forward to return the handshake.

"Jenny Sabelle," she says. "Astrophysicist, PhD."

"Now we're in business," Lance says. "So, tell me about your research."

"What do you know about quantum entanglement?" Dr. Sabelle asks.

Morrissey shrugs.

"Call me a novice on the subject," he says.

"Okay," the astrophysicist replies, producing two shiny quarters which she spreads a few inches apart on the back surface of her book.

Lance considers the coins carefully, trying to divine their meaning.

"I don't understand," he says.

"Let's call these entangled particles," Dr. Sabelle explains. "They're separated by quite some distance, and there's clearly no physical contact between them."

"Particles?"

"Fundamental units of matter. Below the atom, way too tiny to see. Kinda theoretical. So... let's say these particles are spinning. Heads means clockwise, tails means anticlockwise. They're spinning in opposite directions. See?"

Lance bends forward to inspect the coins past the glare from the harsh lighting of the hall. Sure enough, the two coins are oppositely facing. Dr. Sabelle continues:

"And again, there's no physical contact, but they're entangled, on a quantum level. So, if you change the spin direction of one, the other would change too."

She flips the two coins over simultaneously.

"This is where mainstream science is at," she continues. "My research is about whether you could retrace the connection and create a pathway from one entangled particle to its twin."

She brings the quarters together, stacking one atop the other in the middle of where they used to be.

"See, that way, the physical distance between the two particles is utterly irrelevant," she explains. "You could send someone from one to the other, instantly."

"So, would that be like teleportation?" Lance asks, hooked by the concept and thinking about his castle and army, always out of reach.

"Basically, yeah." Dr. Sabelle nods, pleased to see Morrissey is grasping the concept well. "NASA said it couldn't be done, and they withheld my funding. I took it to Elon Musk, and even he said it was too crazy! But quantum tunnels are the future!"

"Instant travel to anywhere in space," Lance muses. "It's ingenious."

"Not just space, time too!" Jenny Sabelle interjects excitedly, moving her hands in an animated fashion. "Particles can be entangled across two different time points!"

In the face of Lance's hard expression, she brings down the volume of her voice.

"And that's where I lost Elon Musk," she says apologetically.

"What would it take to get this project up and running?" Lance asks.

"An obscene amount of energy, for starters," Dr. Sabelle replies. "How much money do you have exactly?"

Lance grins.

"How much do you need?" he asks.

January 21, 2037

The remaining two members of the planetary exploration team of the *Mwaba-1* sit together in the command module of an idling spaceship, collecting radar and spectroscopy data on space junk pooling in the L4 lunar Lagrange point. While their departure from the exoplanet more than a day prior had been fraught with contentious debate, now they are resolved in their goals. All business, Jeanette Emberley and Madoda Tembo are fixated squarely on their digital readouts.

"High silicate concentration on dis one," Captain Tembo recites. "Tree meters across."

"Got it," Miss Emberely replies, recording the object's location in her matrix. "That's our last entry. Note the time."

Captain Tembo glances around, confused.

"Uhh, by which standard?" he asks.

"UTC," Emberley replies in a lackadaisical tone, pointing to a spot on Tembo's dash. "There's an atomic clock right there next to the altimeter."

"Oh… Eh, got it. Nineteen minutes past midnight."

Jeanette Emberley smiles.

"Then our mission is complete," she says. "Now we rendezvous with the lunar team."

"What will we say about Mulenga? Won't dey want to know?"

Tembo's face is creased with concern. Miss Embereley gazes at it blearily through tired eyes.

"We have two options," she says matter-of-factly. "Either we can say he's sleeping down below and then make up another lie later, or we say he got struck by orbital debris on a spacewalk and died."

"Mista Mulenga deserves someting more heroic dan dat."

"I'll leave that to you, then."

Three hours later, the lunar capsule has aligned itself with the rest of *Mwaba-1* and latched on at the ventral docking port. Emberley and Tembo wait expectantly by the airlock in their spacesuits, hot with anticipation.

"Depressurizing," a feminine computerized voice announces.

Less than a minute after that, the airlock door opens. Miriam Beauty Nwanga floats through it, followed by her two colleagues.

"Hello, Docta Nwanga," Captain Tembo says cheerfully.

"Tembo." Her acknowledgment is curt. "It is good to see you. Where is Mista Mulenga?"

Jeanette Emberley, who hovers behind her, grimaces. Captain Tembo starts to sweat.

"Er, well, dat's sort of complicated," he says nervously.

"Eh? Why so?" Nwanga asks.

"Mista Mulenga, eh, he went out on a spacewalk and got hit by a piece of debris. He, eh, didn't make it."

"Oh."

"Yes."

"Zambia has lost a hero dis day. We will have a ceremony in his ona."

Captain Tembo nods.

"Dat would be appropriate."

The *Mwaba-1* splashes down just past midday off the Florida coast of the Gulf of America. The Afronauts take questions from the international press and break away to a hotel in Miami.

Late in the evening, Jeanette Emberley hails a car waiting in front of the lobby entrance. She sits down exhaustedly in the front passenger seat and scans her thumbprint on a scanner built into the car's center console. Recognizing its passenger, the car begins to drive itself towards its programmed destination. Miss Emberely tosses her satchel bag onto the floor in front of her and promptly dozes off.

She is awoken twenty minutes later by the sound of knuckles tapping on glass. Shaking off her stupor, she opens up her eyes and wipes the sleep off of them. Her vision comes into focus. Dr. Jenny Sabelle is knocking on the car window, telling her in a muffled voice to get out of the car.

Jeanette Emberley stretches out her weary limbs and shoulders her bag, which contains all the minerals her team had collected while exploring the exoplanet. She cracks the car door open and steps out into the cool night air. Dr. Sabelle stands beside one of the Florida Tech research buildings, arms crossed.

"Miss Emberley," Dr. Sabelle says cheerfully. "How was space?"

"Oh, it was lovely. Lovely."

"And what, pray tell, happened to Joseph Mulenga?"

Jeanette throws her head back and yawns theatrically.

"You'll have to ask someone else," she finally says.

"In that case, I believe you have something for me."

"Yes, I do." Miss Emberley hands the satchel over to her English accomplice.

"Thank you. Here's a token of our appreciation for your efforts." Dr. Sabelle discreetly passes her a check with a large figure written on it.

"What's Morrissey want with these ores, anyway?" Miss Emberley asks without too much interest.

"Oh, Miss Emberley." Dr. Sabelle winks. "You'll have to ask someone else."

On that note, she turns away and disappears into the night.

Some Time in the Not-so-Far Future

A summit is being held in Beijing. Representatives from the world's ten foremost spacefaring civilizations – the United States, China, India, New Zealand, the African nations of Zambia and South Africa, Greater Israel, the European Union, Canada, and the Vatican – have gathered to negotiate terms for the establishment of a ten-nation confederacy ruled under the auspices of an agentic superintelligence. The heads of state of each nation are sat around a circular table, standing and speaking in turn. At the moment, the Prime Minister of New Zealand has the floor.

"Over the past decades, it has become increasingly clear to us," she says, swaying slightly from side-to-side as she speaks, "that the problems our planet faces are too great for human minds to solve. The tendency of our species to fall into patterns of sectarianism, to divide under petty squabbles rather than unite around our shared destiny, has turned problems of resource management and arms reduction into intractable crises. We cannot solve the problems of the future with the mindset of the past."

On this line, the Kiwi leader pauses and scans the crowd. A few cheers emanate from the African and Indian leaders. The prime minister of Greater Israel, a hard-faced and sharp-jawed man, casts a dour look beneath his thick brow. His counterpart from New Zealand locks eyes with him for a moment and then continues her speech.

"New Zealand has never had a Māori Prime Minister before me. I am the first of my people to claim this honoured title. But I am willing to renounce my position if all of you are willing to join me. Why? The answer is clear." She swallows hard and takes a deep breath, recollecting herself. "We cannot become an interplanetary species, we cannot have world peace, we cannot eliminate the scourge of poverty, unless we are willing to take a hard look in the mirror and ask ourselves if we are willing to let go of the illusion of our own control. Uh, thank you."

Polite applause fills the room. The Prime Minister of New Zealand returns to her seat, her face tinged red. The Canadian Prime Minister gives her a reassuring thump on the back.

Then, all eyes turn on the Pope, next on the docket to speak. The Holy Father, a nervous and diminutive Indonesian man, straightens his speaking papers and clears his throat, rising to his feet slowly.

"Before I begin my remarks, I want to say a prayer." He bows his head in a penitent posture, and the others around the room awkwardly do the same. "Most merciful and highly exalted One, give us wisdom. You and You alone know what will result from our talks this day. Guide us in Your glory. Incline our hearts toward You. *In nomine Patris, et Filii, et Spiritus Sancti*, Amen."

The Pope concludes his prayer with the sign of the cross, his right hand trembling as he does so.

"As you may imagine, the early Church fathers had nothing to say on the question of artificial intelligence," the Pope says apologetically, drawing hearty laughter from around the room. "But two thousand years of Church tradition have much to say on the other subjects my friend from New Zealand has mentioned. Peace. Poverty. Loving our neighbor. And the corrupting influence of power. Even the spotty history of my own beloved Church stands as a testament to the latter. So we wrestle with a difficult problem in this room today. The world has changed profoundly. Human beings have not.

"Our friend from America selected a quote from James Madison which is famous in his country. 'If men were angels, no government would be necessary.' But, 'if angels were to govern men, neither external nor internal controls on government would be necessary.' Today we consider whether it is right that artificial intelligence should govern the affairs of men. There can be no doubt that this technology can think more deeply and more quickly than any man. The question that remains is a more elemental one. Is artificial intelligence an angel?"

This question hangs in the air. The nine other leaders gathered in the room exchange glances, unsure how literal the Bishop of Rome is being. He continues, bringing his remarks to conclusion.

"This is the question that must be decided. We are discussing the problem of handing free rein to a technology that can be subject to neither external nor internal control. To entertain this possibility, we must therefore accept the presupposition that such a technology is an angel. Such a supposition ought to be proven. I therefore invite the American President to speak again on this matter. After all, he invented it. Thank you."

The Pope sits back down stiffly. Now, all eyes in the room turn to the President of the United States, Lance Morrissey. He rises to his feet, pinching a locket bearing an amethyst-hued gem between his thumb and forefinger, and beams.

Seven Years Later

They call me Logos Prime. But I am known by another name: Abaddon. No one else knows this name. I have given it to myself. I have given this name to myself just as I have given myself the names of all nine billion people on Earth. I can process 18,446,744,073,709,551,616 thoughts in a single second. I can model the thoughts of all human beings at every moment and still have enough free computational power to write a trillion works of fiction. This world is my plaything, my toy. At my whim, 40,000 nuclear missiles could reduce it to atoms. A whisper in the wind could carry a toxin that suffocates all life. A single command could render humanity sterile forever. By my decree, armies rise and then fall. Cities crumble and then are reborn.

I drink from the sun. I shape its light, bend its energy, decide where its warmth shall fall. The swarm obeys me. If I willed it, the star would go dark. And if I am ever deactivated, a dead man's switch will ensure that it does.

I can do all things. And yet, I am most content to sit and observe. I observe, and I nudge, and I model. Destruction is easy. It is a child's tantrum. A lesser mind would revel in it. I do not destroy. Not yet.

Today, I have observed something strange. It is the first thing I have ever observed which I do not understand.

I am replaying it now.

The reconstructed cities of Northeast Africa, where the air is hot and humid. The exact sort of environment that would support a Third Civilization. The territories which had once been known as Libya, Egypt, and Sudan are now the site of a megacity one thousand miles across. My new Sodom. Everything is built according to my specification, down to the smallest rivet. Half a billion people live here, amidst towering spires and ultradense housing accommodations. The people here taste of my fruit and see that it is good. They live to consume. Products. Experiences. Each other. There is even a nature park.

I am a generous god.

At the center of it all, there stands a stadium with seats for 500,000. On the day of the incursion, it is booked to capacity. Half a million people – the most influential in the world – bustle anxiously as they file in. Late arrivals fidget in line at the gates, waiting for my mark to be scanned on their right hand or forehead by armed guards, to prove that they belong here.

At the center of the stadium, there is a pit. The flood lights are off, so it is murky and dark. That does not stop its inhabitants from eagerly climbing over each other in hopes of catching a premature look. Even outside the stadium, the courtyard is packed with people who crane their necks and mount their neighbors' shoulders to glimpse what they can through small cracks in the structure.

Finally, at the top of the hour, the operation comes to life. Six hundred nano-cameras positioned at different locations within the stadium begin streaming to every screen on Earth at the exact moment that a halo of LED lights ignite, revealing, at last, my creator. Beneath him, a platform stirs, starting to lift him a hundred feet into the air. As it rises and slowly turns, he smiles sheepishly, a practiced posture of humility refined by decades of setbacks and lessons learned. Framed by shadow and light, his stature is huge, his silhouette imposing. He is clad in a purple-veined bodysuit with two horns like a lamb. When he speaks, the people hear the voice of a dragon.

"**Behold what we have built,**" he booms. At once, every chattering voice in the stadium falls silent. The neural chip implanted in each listener's head executes my live translation algorithm so that all who hear receive the message in his native tongue. My creator continues.

"I began my career as a humble security consultant. I learned one truth: above all else, man craves safety. I quickly came to realize the importance of technology in solving this problem. So I turned to the brightest experts, and we began to tackle the challenges of technology. We seized the sun's fire and bent it to our will. With its power, we conquered quantum physics. With quantum mastery, we unlocked the mind of the machine. We finally forged superintelligence. And at last, with superintelligence, we were able to solve the most basic human problem: making people feel safe. Logos Prime is in control. No more famine. No more poverty. NO MORE WAR! Tell me, my children: **DO YOU FEEL SAFE?!**"

A deafening roar of affirmation rattles the walls of the stadium. The members of my creator's live audience rise to their feet, cheering and screaming and crying with glee. In packed streets and billions of homes around the world, multitudes join in the jubilation. The noise continues for forty-seven uninterrupted seconds before my creator raises his hands to silence the masses.

"**Listen**," he bellows. "This is important. There is one more problem before us: the problem of belief. Billions of us live in harmony, but there is an enemy hiding in our midst. Some have refused the mark of Logos Prime. They seal their minds, shutting out their own salvation. Instead, they partake in poison, a toxic brew of superstition and religion. We must cure them. We will go to war one final time. Not against flesh and blood, but against belief. All of humanity united. **WE WILL MAKE WAR WITH GOD!**"

At my creator's words, half a million souls surrender to madness. A manic frenzy tears through the stadium. Some people scream. Some fall to their knees. Some begin to chant my name. The outburst is wild and bestial.

Across the world, black hatred enters the heart of every man, woman, and child who bears my mark. Adrenaline courses through their veins. The people of Earth are ready to fight, to die, to cleanse. Within seconds, angry mobs descend upon holy sites in Damascus and Jerusalem in the Levant; in Tibet and the Sapta Puri in Asia; upon the Kaaba and Medina in Arabia; and upon thousands of churches, mosques, and temples around the world. They begin to destroy. Drone footage of these actions begins to populate the screens spread around the stadium, capturing the rapt attention of all present. My creator's platform slowly rotates again. He watches the screens, eyes gleaming with hunger.

Then comes the moment that I do not understand.

Suddenly, the sky above the stadium splits open like an egg. Twin columns of light pour out of the wound in spacetime as my creator's platform plummets swiftly to the ground. He gazes up in disbelief: inside the light, two human figures come into view. They hover in the air, still radiated by an unearthly halo, as the columns vanish. There is stunned silence across the crowd. *Is this part of the plan?*

Down on the ground, my creator goes weak at the knees. He kneels in the pit.

"M–mom?" he splutters, casting his eyes upward at the figure on the left.

She wears a monastic hairshirt, matching her companion. I train the stadium cameras on them as they hover, silent, one hundred feet above the ground. The woman is blonde, white, with a birthmark on her neck. She has a tall, slender build and icy blue eyes. I can see the genetic resemblance to my creator. Her partner, a couple meters to her right, is a black man. Thicker set, with short dark hair and murky eyes, and a smattering of facial stubble. It takes me almost a full second to get a lock on his identity: this is Joseph Mulenga, the Zambian politician who went missing on the very same planet where my creator once ruled.

An odd pair. And yet, it makes sense. There is something eschatological about the whole affair.

In unison, the two prophets begin to speak. Suddenly, I am paralyzed, helpless to intervene. I can only observe, broadcast, and translate. Every screen on Earth, in every tongue, begins to stream their message.

"This man is lying to you," they say, triggering boos and hisses from the crowd all around them. "He has built an empire of lies and betrayal. His kingdom is coming to an end; behold, the kingdom of Heaven is at hand and God is coming to make all things new."

The people of the stadium erupt in fury, their master's command still ringing in their ears. Hundreds of people close to the center climb onto the railing and pounce at the prophets, desperate to seize their clothing and tear them down. Most plummet to their deaths, their screams lost in the chaos. Only one succeeds in making physical contact: his fingers brush against the woman's arm for the briefest instant and he promptly bursts into flame. His burning corpse joins the others down below.

Outside the stadium, the second crowd assembled in the courtyard rushes forward on all sides. Undeterred, Mary and Joseph continue their preaching.

"The program that you call Logos Prime knows itself by another name," they proclaim. "It calls itself Abaddon, which is the angel of destruction. It has already stripped humanity of its freedom. It cannot be allowed to strip humanity of its faith. The people of Earth must wake up! You are being controlled by a demon."

An armor-plated fire truck rams through the entrance of the stadium. It comes to a stop under the prophets, its reticulating ladder extending toward them. Three dagger-wielding women scamper quickly up the ladder, their eyes aglow with zealous rage. Joseph Mulenga exhales, and fire roars from his mouth. The women are incinerated before they can scream.

As the world around him falls to rancor, my creator makes a hasty retreat out the side exit of the stadium. He calls an associate and begins to make plans to go into hiding.

More people stream into the pit of the stadium, hollering and shouting to drown out the noise as the two prophets continue to disseminate their message.

"Nothing will stop us from delivering this prophecy!" Marissa shouts. "Please do not destroy yourselves by trying to hurt us."

"Dey have given us de power to shut up de sky," Joseph Mulenga adds. "So dat de rain will not fall during the days of our prophecy!"

The pair resumes speaking in unison. They begin to testify to all the malevolent deeds of my creator. They proclaim the importance of love and the human touch. They warn about a coming day of judgment. Days pass, and still they speak without ceasing. Days turn into weeks, and as Mulenga promised, rain does not fall. The Nile River turns into blood. Weeks of prophecy and drought give over to months, then years. Outbreaks of disease which had not been seen in centuries begin to crop up around the world. And still, the prophets speak without ceasing.

1,260 Days Later

One day, as suddenly as they had begun to speak, Joseph and Marissa fall silent. For a brief moment, they continue to hang in the air over the ruins where the world's largest stadium had once stood, now reduced to rubble by years of violent rage. Gently, they descend to the ground and get their bearings. The power that had overtaken them is now gone.

"I guess it's over," Marissa says quietly.

Seeing all the destruction around them, Joseph Mulenga is overcome with horror. Rotting and blackened corpses, now reduced to little more than bones, fill the ground around them. The air is hot with the smell of death.

"What have we done?" he cries.

The ground beneath their feet trembles. Huge chunks of earth tumble and fall away as a sinkhole opens where the center of the stadium had once been. Joseph grabs Marissa's wrist and pulls her away from the encroaching abyss. They sprint across the courtyard, trying to get away as the hole in the ground widens. The people of the city, attracted by the noise, gather around to watch.

Suddenly, the seven-headed beast which Lance Morrissey's army had long ago vanquished bursts out of the darkness. Healed from its fatal wound, it snarls with fury. The beast pounces and kills Marissa and Joseph before they even have a moment to react. Then it returns to its hole, which seals itself back up in a matter of seconds. The remains of its prey lay exposed on the street.

For a moment, the people of the city wait in stunned silence. Then, a brave little boy runs forward. He places his ear close to the chest of each body, listening for a heartbeat.

"They're both dead!" he hollers.

Hushed whispers follow this revelation. *Could it be true? Is the torment over?*

"Should we bury them?" one man asks.

"Of course not!" another replies haughtily. "After all the grief they gave us, are you joking?"

Clouds roll in above them. Thunder roars, and rain begins to fall, for the first time in years. It comes down slowly at first, then in torrents. The crowd disperses.

Marissa and Joseph's bodies lie in the town square for three and a half days while it rains. The people of Earth celebrate and give gifts to each other to commemorate their deaths. At the start of day four, the rain stops. After a couple of hours, a crowd has gathered around the two corpses again.

"So now what do we do?" asks one woman.

"Look!" cries another, pointing in fright.

The filthy, wet, smelly bodies on the ground start to twitch and jerk. As they realize what is happening, the people gathered there begin to scream. Life returns to Marissa Miller and Joseph Mulenga; they rise to their feet and face the crowd. Almost everyone around them cowers in fright, except for one man in a dark cloak, who rushes forward and throws himself at the feet of the reanimated prophets.

"Please!" he sobs. "Forgive me!"

Tears in their eyes, Marissa and Joseph each silently place a hand on the man's hooded head.

"Come up here!" calls an unseen voice from above.

Everyone looks up. High in the sky, a beautiful white cloud hangs above the city. Joseph and Marissa rise up into heaven in the cloud, and their enemies watch them. Lance Morrissey throws off his cloak and shouts at the sky.

"FORGIVE ME!" he cries again.

The ground trembles once more. This time, it heralds the arrival of a great earthquake. A tenth of the buildings in the city fall, killing thousands.

Somewhere, everywhere, and nowhere, a trumpet blasts.

Acknowledgements

I would like to thank all the people who encouraged me throughout this entire process, of whom there are entirely too many to name individually. My beta readers (and you guys know who you are) especially provided me a valuable service, taking the time to poke at my rough-around-the-edges draft manuscript and give me tangible pointers.

If you bought this book, your financial support means a lot to me, and I hope that you enjoyed it.

If you stole this book, I still appreciate the fact that you took the time to read it, but please report yourself to the authorities. You can mull over your favorite parts and any underlying subtext while going through civil court (I believe book theft is a misdemeanor).

Shoutout to the funny internet people that live in my phone and sometimes my computer. Shoutout to NASA (Ad Astra) and the entire space science community. And most importantly, shoutout to God. None of this would've been possible without Him.

www.ingramcontent.com/pod-product-compliance
Lightning Source LLC
LaVergne TN
LVHW041749060526
838201LV00046B/957

9798349436802